Paul De Lancey's *Do Lutheran Hunks Eat Mushrooms?* will put you into dimensions that exceed any you might find eating magic mushrooms!"

    – Matt Pallamary - author of *Phantastic Fiction* and *Land Without Evil*

"The fate of humanity has so often hinged on small things – a small fire, a car accident, a single spear thrown just right in one crucial battle. Paul DeLancey masterfully takes this concept all the way down to a solitary mushroom. Good. Evil. Fungi. Along with some of the best humor writing I have ever read. A masterpiece."

    – Stacey Roberts, author of Trailer Trash, With A Girl's Name

---

Do Lutheran *Hunks Eat Mushrooms* is chocked full of interesting historical details that add to the hilarious plot of good versus evil. I highly recommend it to anyone who enjoys a humorous read.

    – Candace C. Bowen

Add two cups quirkiness, a dash a drama, half-bake for an hour, and chuckle to taste.

    – Lisa K. Nelson, writer: "Ellen", "Everybody Loves Raymond", "Last Man Standing"

Do Lutheran Hunks

Eat Mushrooms?

Do Lutheran Hunks

Eat Mushrooms?

A Novel by

Paul R. De Lancey

Published 2015 by HumorOutcasts Press
Printed in the United States of America

ISBN 0-692-46105-1
EAN-13 978-069246105-1

Cover Design by Mark A. Clements.

DEDICATION

To all the people of the Southern California Writers' Conference, including Michael Steven Gregory, Wes Albers, Mark Clements, Matt Palamary, Judy Reeves, and many others, thank you for wonderful times and for teaching me so much.

ACKNOWLEDGMENTS

To Donna Cavanagh, the Empress of Comedy for encouraging me and for believing in this story... Paul's Flying Squirrel Squadron is forever at your command.

"A grocery store can't expect repeat business if its checkers unleash Armageddon."

- Debbie Devil

"Ja caramba."

- Pedro Erickson

CHAPTER 1-A LOAF OF BREAD

The universal triumph of Evil was only one bite away. Joe Thorvald's eyes never left the sports page as his fork headed toward the mushrooms on his Hopalong Cassidy dinner plate. Darned exciting writeup of Albondiga's twenty-two strikeout game. Go Padres!

Heavenly angels, Bambi and Helga, shivered outside Joe's open kitchen window. Would Joe Thorvald, eighty times great grandson of Saint Peter, eat those mushrooms?

"Don't eat those mushrooms," yelled Bambi and Helga. "They're evil. Eat them and you'll go straight to Hell." But Joe heard nothing. B & H had cheered themselves hoarse rooting for Juan Albondiga in the VIP seating at Petco Park.

Joe poked at the grayish buttons. Bambi put a downy wing over her face. Not so, Helga. She snapped her fingers. Pip! A prepared pea-shooter popped onto her perfect pinky. Phoot!

"Ow!" Joe put down the newspaper and rubbed the reddening sore on his neck. His eyes fell to his supper. The horror. The horror. "Jane, honey, you know how I feel about mushrooms."

"But Hungry Hank's had them on sale," said the good Jane.

"Sweetheart," said Joe, "this is the 900th time in a row you've served mushrooms."

"But Joe, they've been on sale for that long and you know I never have much grocery money."

"I know." Joe shook his head. "Still, I wonder about a store that runs a 'For Lutherans only' sale."

Jane smiled. "But Hungry Hank's gave me a cookbook. See? *To Serve Lutherans Mushrooms.* Give the mushrooms a try, Joe."

"Sweetheart, for the 900th time, no."

And with that the angels flew toward Heaven. They had watched well. Joe never did eat a mushroom on their 900-dinner shift. When replacements would come on duty, who they would be, they didn't know. But B & H could already taste that divine root beer awaiting them at Pedro Erickson's Smorgasbord *y* Cantina.

"Couldn't you serve something different?" asked Joe.

"Like what, dear?" asked Jane.

"Anything edible, anything. There must be something else on sale somewhere. Hmm." Joe, of the churning stomach, perused the ink-smeared pages of the *Po' Folks Gazette*--Serving the Slums of Rancho Santa Fe for 40 Years.

"Dang!" His left fist came down hard on the hated mushrooms. Grey bits flew in all directions, decorating the plaid, yellow-orange stucco walls. "No sales on beef, none on chicken, fish, peas, or even green peppers. Are there no other sales at all?"

Joe turned the page. "Thank God, Hungry Hank's Supermarket is having its first annual Mix-and-Match-Pig-Balls sale. Most underappreciated part of a pig. Tastes like rooster. Only six cents a pound."

Our hero wiped mushroom paste off his hand and his "God-fearing Lutheran" t-shirt. "Hungry Hank's delicacies cry out for sandwiches. Jane Thorvald, my dear, I'm going out to get some pig balls and a loaf of bread."

Joe tore out of the house and into his souped-up Geo Metro.

Soon, Jane heard the mighty pipping of the car engine, squeaking of tires, and the yipping of the neighbor's arthritic dachshund, Inerto, giving fair chase.

Jane Thorvald paled. Didn't all men say they were going for pig balls when they left their wives? Would he come back to their two-room house on Calle del Relleno? Would he find a better looking woman? She ran to her tiny pine closet that hid her only heirloom, a full-length mirror once belonging to Abigail Adams.

Jane looked inside at the gilt-edged mirror. Looked hard. What could a man not like? She possessed golden blonde hair with a face that outshone the one on the Venus de Milo. But her breasts, my gosh, each breast rivaled the Hindenburg before it exploded in flames over Lakehurst, New Jersey in 1938. Not that she'd inflated her breasts with hydrogen nor even the safer inert gas, helium, thank you very much.

If only he'd come back, she'd serve him something, maybe tacos, even lutefisk tacos if she could find some clothespins for her nose. She knelt before the silver cross on the wall and prayed for Joe's swift return from Hungry Hank's.

Joe Thorvald pushed his empty shopping cart through the supermarket. There had to be more to life than fetid mushrooms and his mind-numbing work.

Joe drove the ball-retrieving truck at the Shady Lie Golf Club. The truck's whirling blades picked up those golf balls at the driving range marvelously well. They also picked up from the golfers' mats and buckets. And, oh yes, they could knock down and shred three-legged Pekinese and Pomeranians.

Joe felt the woman golfer had been at fault for bringing her tiny, three-legged dogs to the driving range; four-legged ones surely could have gotten out of the way.

Thank goodness he was the only one living in Rancho Santa Fe willing to work for minimum wage. So, he continued to daydream and run things down.

Like now in Hungry Hank's.

"Ow, you unspeakable son of a bitch, low-life, pond scum."

The first rays of awareness dawned in Joe. His shopping cart wouldn't move. Damned, stupid wheels. Always getting stuck. He gave the cart a good shove.

"Ow, ow, ow. Stop it, you heathen. You, you Democrat!"

Joe's reverie gave way to its old foe, implacable reality. He looked down. A pair of fat, puffy albacore-white thighs blocked his cart's progress. He looked closely. Yep, those thighs were swelling already. Only one way to free his cart now; he'd have to reverse. He did so, but the lady--ha, not with that un-Lutheran ranting--declined to be grateful.

But being a gentleman, Joe apologized at length to the bloated mass of hate screaming on the floor. "Sorry."

Then he thought, if life gives you rotten lemons, make rotten lemonade. He asked the writhing, prone, veteran shopper where he could find bread. The woman summoned up great reserves of articulation, enunciation, and volume to tell Joe to find nature's bounty up his ass. Joe forgot immediately this common insult just as he did at work. Forgot to lift her up too.

He found no full-length mirrors in the supermarket, hadn't anywhere for years, so he appreciated the thoughtfulness of a passing woman in a white tennis outfit who said, "Hello, you look like a man who can't find a mirror."

Joe nodded. "Yes, what do I look like?"

"Well," said the intruding tennis lady, "you're six-feet tall and weigh 170 pounds. You sport lush, brown hair. Overall, your physique resembles that of a middle-aged Greek god, and you wear Buddy Holly glasses.

"You know, Greek statues don't wear Buddy Hollys. I've been all over Europe and haven't seen one wearing glasses, not even bifocals on some of the lesser gods. Don't even get me started on trifocals or blended lenses. And don't let the optometrist dilate your eyes."

Joe smiled. "Thanks, ma'am."

"You're welcome." The tennis lady gave Joe a long look, her lip licking insinuating a wild hour of addressing and stuffing envelopes. "You know you really should try out for the Lutheran Chippendales."

She waved goodbye, turned the corner, screamed, and was never seen again. Perhaps the bright reflections off the floor's gold tiles blinded her, perhaps she got lost in Hungry Hank's endless Lithuanian-food section, or perhaps she had talked too much and an enraged group of Ronald Reagan mimes got to her.

Joe brought his loaf of Roman Meal bread and pig balls to the Ten-Items-or-Fewer line. In front of him, a blood-splattered Young Republican, Hiram the Insignificant, unloaded the entire contents of aisle 6A onto the checkout counter. Joe thought about moving to the Eleven-Items-or-More lines, but he had only two items. And Lutheran discipline expressly forbade such chicanery. So for 2.9 minutes he dreamed of mushroom-free Thanksgiving dinners until his items moved up to the checkout lady, Deborah Devil.

The parchment skin of her face barely covered her skull. She sported a long bony nose that could double as a handy letter opener. Two golden horns emerged from the scraggly growth of her silver hair. The tip of a small tail swished just below the bottom of her dress. Hungry Hank's sure took its role as equal-opportunity employer seriously.

Deborah Devil, or as The Supreme Evil preferred to be called, Debbie, did not permit Joe to see any of these demonic warning signs. He saw her as Shania Twain. Why a beautiful, fabulously successful singer worked the Ten-Items-or-Fewer line at Hank's, he couldn't say. But his heart pounded. And pounded.

No, some of that pounding came from his fist hitting the conveyor. Part of his brain had revolted against a grave injustice. "The customer in front of me had way more than ten items."

Debbie sneered. "So?"

"It isn't right. You should have directed him to another line."

The evil checker pulled the plug to the cash register. "I don't like your attitude."

"That's outrageous."

She smiled and leaned forward. Damn, how come Hungry Hank's let Shania wear her blouse so unbuttoned?

"Sure, hon, I know that. I wanted to get your attention 'cuz Lutheran men make me so hot. And you're all Lutheran.

"Tell you what, I'll ring you up, Joe. All you have to do is be mine tonight, just tonight. C'mon, let Debbie make life fun for you."

Joe sighed and in just two attempts averted his Lutheran eyes from her heaving breasts. "No, I love my wife. She's the best. You're great, but you're not her."

Debbie grimaced and pointed a claw-like hand–which always counted against her in beauty contests--toward the display of George's Mushrooms. "Then buy those. Eat them. Then I'll ring up your bread."

"No way, mushrooms are the Devil's food. I learned that way back in Lutheran Sunday school."

Debbie's chest heaved as she drowned out the store's Lutheran love songs with laughter. "But that's how I'll make you leave your Episcopalian mushroom-cooking wife for me."

Joe shook his head.

Shania licked her lips.

Joe gripped the Roman Meal. "The answer is still no, and I demand to talk to the manager."

The horned lady rested her elbow on the platinum counter, her chin on her wart-encrusted hand. "Honey, no one manages me."

A quite distant relative of Achilles came up behind Joe and asked Debbie, "Gonna serve anyone this century?"

Her red eyes flashed and the customer turned into a short monotoned economist. The man scurried away to explain the notion of constant elasticities of substitution to slow fleeing grannies.

One at a time, Shania fixed her eyes on Joe. "I'll do the same to you if you don't eat those mushrooms and leave your wife."

"Mrs. Twain, you should be ashamed of yourself. Doesn't your husband object to your affairs?"

"Call me Debbie. And no, that limp loser is too busy fighting a forever feud with that holier-than-thou Big Guy to notice my doings and my NEEDS. Shoot, and the sausages on the men that come in here just aren't big enough, if you know what I mean."

Debbie leered at Joe's burgeoning crotch. "But man, ain't you history's best hung Lutheran." Joe blushed. She stared again at his groin. "Man, I've worked this job 900 days waiting for you to come along, ever since I met your wife at *Chez* Episcopalian Beauty Parlor." Debbie licked her lips. "But your wife didn't say you were such a hottie."

She panted and gestured for Joe to come hither. Joe thanked God for the Swedish heritage enabling him to stand firm against offers of fun. He placed his right hand over his heart. "I shall never eat enslaving mushrooms, no way. I shall never dally with you, nor shall I ever, ever leave my wife while I am in my right mind and blood flows through this body."

The evil temptress laughed. "Fine, then you'll continue to get new minds and new bodies until you give in." She looked up. "Oh Blackhand, I need you."

Debbie snapped her fingers and black clouds swirled around Joe's head. A tall thin British cook clad in a black chef's apron, velvet black gloves, and a black chef's hat as tall as twenty kippers stepped out from the fog and bowed toward Mrs. Devil.

"Madam, Bertram Blackhand at your service."

The horned lady pointed toward Joe. "There, Bertram, change him, change him. Change his memory, his body, his circumstances, his era, his life. Keep trying. Experiment. Keep changing everything about him until you get me a Joe Thorvald who loves mushrooms and me. Make him my dream lover."

Visions of Joe making hot monkey love to her atop a mountain of fresh mushrooms the size of basketballs filled Debbie's mind. Loud braying issued from her mouth as her body shook with the sort of orgasm only the wife of Dave Devil could have.

Her activity sort of got everybody's attention. Even the stiff fourteen-year-old skinhead by the magazine rack stopped drooling over the dog-eared pages of Pamela Anderson in *Architectural Review*.

The horned lady pointed to Joe and gasped, "Blackhand, change him until you make him my dream lover. I'll give you that gold ring you've always had your psychic eye on."

Bertram bowed again. "Thank you, dear Lady. I shall not rest until I get you a Mr. Thorvald who meets your requirements."

The chef jabbed into Joe's mind, taking with it Shania Twain's songs and leaving in its place the soothing sounds of Perry Como. Joe felt his brain flutter. He felt faint. He grabbed the sides of the checkout counter. The last thing he saw was the Roman Meal.

Bertram jabbed again. Gone was Joe's memory of seeing Madonna getting on his elevator, her saying "Five, please," Joe's left index finger pressing the five button, her saying "Thank you." The British chef filled that memory void with Bill Gates sitting with him in a sky box at the Super Bowl.

Bertram's black-gloved hands thrust into Joe's mind yet again. Gone were memories of eating McDonald's burgers while driving home to another mushroom dinner. Arriving were visions of eating Steak *au Poivre Vert* at Mille Fleurs.

Bertram robbed him of his Dad taking him to see the Padres on his eighth birthday. The hand gave him his Dad buying him the Dodgers for his sixteenth birthday.

Bertram altered our hero's body. He now resembled a Germanic god who had let himself go. The hand took away his beloved Jane, his wonderful Joe Junior, all memories, all feelings of joy, the best things in his life.

CHAPTER 1B-BAD GUYS

"Geezo, Debbie, it's colder than North Dakota in here. Why do we have to meet in the meat locker?"

"Because," said Debbie Devil, "this is the only meeting room I could afford. I don't see you offering to pay for a place." Her right eye bored into Mr. George, Chief Evil Officer, of George's Mushrooms. It found him a short, wiry man adorned with an orange Hawaiian shirt and green cargo pants.

Debbie stamped her fuchsia Red-Wing slingback and extended her arm. "Bless it all, George, give me my eye back."

George put the eye in Debbie's flour-white hand. "Geezo, Debbie, I didn't take it. You know you should take better care of yourself."

Debbie made a face, then completed it pushing the wandering orb back in its socket. "Last time I checked you didn't have all your parts either."

"Now see here, Mrs. Devil!"

Bertram Blackhand coughed. "Pardon me, Mrs. Devil, pardon me, Mr. George, we are here to discuss Joe Thorvald.

"Mrs. Devil here needs to get laid. Thorvald's a fine strapping Lutheran chap and as we all know, the powerful men in Hell are well, shall we say, equipped with wilted celery stalks." Bertie stared at Mr. George. "Oh, no offense meant."

Mr. George growled, "None taken. Get on with it. Tell us your plans for Joe Thorvald."

Bertram held up a pasty hand. "A moment, if you please. God might be listening. I think we should hold our little *tête à tête* under the Mushroom of Silence."

"Geezo, Bertram, the Mushroom of Silence isn't tall enough for us."

"Nevertheless, sir, I insist. I sincerely doubt God's mind shall want to penetrate a thick layer of an especially evil mushroom."

Mr. George eyed Debbie. Debbie shrugged. "Let him do it."

Bertram bowed toward Debbie. "Thank you." He straightened and pressed a flashing red button labeled, "In case of fire."

A great gray mushroom descended on them. It kept descending.

"Geezo, Bertram, our heads are sticking out. God can still hear us. I told you the Mushroom of Silence wasn't tall enough."

Bertram sniffed. "And if all the minions of Hell took such a defeatist attitude then we might as well not even show up for Armageddon."

"Whoa, whoa," said Debbie, "stop it you two. Bertram, just tell me your plans for Joe."

Bertram smiled at her. "Certainly, m'lady. As you might have sensed, I took Joe's soul away and put it in a heartless corporate raider. As we all know, those sort are particularly partial to mushrooms.

"And if we get him to eat even one of Mr. George's splendidly evil mushrooms"--He pointed to Mr. George, who bowed--"well, then we've got his soul and Debbie Devil has her Lutheran love toy."

"But," said Debbie, "don't you need some item, some memento from Joe's life to make sure his soul stays in place in his new incarnation?"

"Yes," said Mr. George, "every preschooler knows that even a spatially, temporally transplanted soul needs to see something familiar from its last moments, something it focused on, to survive the first new moments."

"Precisely," said Bertram, "Joe will awaken to see a loaf of Roman Meal bread."

"Roman Meal bread, geezo, Bertram, why?"

"Because Mr. George the Romans persecuted the early Christians. Fed them as lunch to the lions." Bertram looked at Debbie expectantly. No response. The evil chef sighed. "Roman meals, get it?"

Debbie arched an eyebrow at the damned punster. "But Roman Meal is good for you! And didn't the Romans give their support to

Christianity in the fourth century? So, isn't Roman Meal a double-edged sword for our purposes?"

"Well, m'lady," said Bertram, "it was either Roman Meal or pig balls."

Mr. George's teeth began to chatter. "Okay, okay, Roman Meal it is. May we go now?"

Debbie nodded.

"Cheerio then," said Bertram.

"I'd better be going back," said Debbie. "There's probably long lines at the other cashiers. They'll need me to open up my checkout stand."

And if I don't get Mr. Joe Thorvald for my Lutheran love toy in thirty, no, twenty-six tries there won't be any checkout stands. Descendant of Saint Peter or no descendant, there will be Mrs. Hell to pay.

CHAPTER 2-MULTIVERSE

1

Joe Thorvald, a 36-year-old man with thinning blond hair, sat atop his quilted bed. The quilt, well over a hundred years old, depicted important corporate takeovers and factory closures in the Thorvald family history. Joe shed one tear over the square showing enema factories surrounded by verdant, rolling hills and swift streams. Sure, that series of closures brought the Depression to Eastern Kentucky, but more importantly it enabled Grandpa Thorvald to make a killing in legal enema futures at a time when gangsters elsewhere were killing themselves over illegal booze.

Joe removed his robin's egg pajamas, carefully folded and put them in his chest of drawers fashioned from old-growth Swedish oak. My word, what were that Lutheran cross and loaf of Roman Meal bread doing on the dresser top?

The corporate raider opened his sock drawer and gazed at 36 pairs of neatly rolled socks. As always the immaculate order of his socks filled him with controlled pride. The pair on the left was labeled with black thread, "1,472 A," or Angstroms. The next pair lay behind an index card reading "1,397 A," telling Joe that the wavelength of the second pair was 75/1,000,000 of an inch less than the first. This information told Joe the second pair had a slightly brighter color than the first; he didn't need to trust his eyes.

The offending, intruding loaf marred all his blessed order. He'd talk to the baritone doorman about that.

Joe finished dressing a scant hour later. He looked at his clothes in a mirror and at a chart on the wall. Yes, his clothes matched. His Lou Dobbs line of underpants represented his one hidden concession to wildness.

He strode into the hallway starting with his left foot as always. He looked at his detailed and perfectly cut Persian rug, made by artisans from the Persian coastal city of Abadan in 1782. Joe admired the world of 1782. He wished he could inhabit it. But hey, Rancho Santa Fe in 2007 wasn't a bad second.

Joe picked up his leather briefcase, valued at over $2,000, and turned the pearl doorknob with the identical clockwise motion he always used. He flung open the door to the street. He inhaled deeply. He'd close a mushroom-canning factory today, putting 13,000 more people out of work. Life was good and so was okra. Yes, he hungered for a good okra sandwich.

But not for long. On the other side of Okra Street, clad in a happy-face ski mask, crouched an assassin for Mushroom Canners Local 2272. His laser-sighted Bushnell .303 hunting rifle put a bullet through Joe's once orderly brain.

Bertram Blackhand appeared from nowhere and tapped the dead body. "Dash it." Maybe Joe would eat mushrooms in his next incarnation.

2

Joe Thorvald, a 36-year-old-man with thinning brown hair sat on the edge of a fold-up cot that came from the Salvation Army. The Millard Fillmore blanket likewise hailed from the same place. Heck, the clothes rack came from the Salvation Army, as did the two t-shirts, two pants, two pairs of socks, and two underpants that hung on it.

All the clothes were dirty. He sniffed each article to determine which stank the least. Stuck his nose deep into one pair of underpants, then the other. Smelled the same to his blocked-up nose.

Joe shuffled over to his prized poster of Abigail Adams. Provocatively posed in full-length blue chiffon she truly deserved the words at the bottom, "First Lady, First Babe." He sighed. She just wasn't possible; out of his league and some two-hundred years dead.

He picked up a bottle of Jack Daniel's lowest grade of Tennessee whiskey and poured it down his parched throat. Oh Abigail, Abigail!

Damn, the liquid felt good burning down his throat before scouring his ever-empty stomach. He did not sample the Roman Meal. Too much mold.

Fortified with whiskey intelligence, Joe felt up to making a decision. He picked up a quarter, which constituted 100% of his financial portfolio, and flipped it in the air. It came down heads. He put on the Hanes underwear. "Sorry, Bugle Boy, hope you're not jealous."

It was a balmy August day in Pleasant Valley, Kentucky. Joe wore his well-worn "Aaron Burr for President" t-shirt and his thinner, shinier pair of pants. He put on the pair of socks with smaller holes and slid his feet into a pair of faded, crumbling Converse high tops.

Joe turned the plastic handle. The door didn't budge. No problem. He punched the cardboard walls until a sufficiently large hole appeared and thrust his wiry body through. Mrs. Kleinschmidt, a boozy 42-year old Mrs. Adams substitute, adjusted a threadbare wig and hiccupped a hello.

"Hi there, Abigail, er, Squeeze," said Joe. He pointed to the new hole in the wall. "Step right in. Got the Daniel's for our party. Why don't you get a head start?"

Squeeze furrowed her brow. "Where are you goin'?"

"Gonna kill that man who closed my factory, took away my job."

"Good for you, Joe, you been talkin' about it for months. Look, I brought lunch." Squeeze waved a can of Abigail-Adams brand mushrooms and a fresh loaf of Roman Meal in his face.

"When I come back." Joe grinned. Food, woman, a just killing. What more could a man want? He waved good-bye and walked to the end of the hallway. Our hero tugged the door open and stepped outside.

Across the street and disdaining cover, a home-schooled assassin for the Okra Vigilantes used a laser-sighted Bushnell .303 hunting rifle to put a bullet through Joe's head.

"Oh dear, late again," said Bertram Blackhand.

3

"Smiling" Joe Thorvald woke up and got dressed. He walked to the front door and looked through the peep hole. Next to The Big Okra, an assassin stood in plain view, aiming at his front door.

"Oh, fuck this bullshit," said Joe. He ran upstairs and opened a window. He grabbed a hand grenade, pulled the pin, and tossed it at the assassin. Blew that scofflaw to bits.

"Thank goodness," said Joe as he bit into a slice of Roman Meal, "Now, for a cup of latte. I'm a bear until I get my first cup."

CHAPTER 2B-BAD GUYS

Mr. George was tapping his foot when Bertram entered the meat locker at Hungry Hank's.

"Well, you certainly botched things up," said Mr. George. "Imagining trying to get Joe to come over to our side by trying to kill him. How about something like, oh I don't know, *feeding* him mushrooms?"

Debbie's fangs bit into a small ketchup packet and squirted a vertical line of ketchup on the wall; she hated the sight of blood. "One," she whispered to herself.

"I'm learning on the job," said Bertram Blackhand.

"Learning on the job!" said Mr. George. "Three similar failures, you stupid kipper cooker." He turned to a shivering Mrs. Devil. "Debbie did you even look at his resume? Bless it, you hired a cook, that's what you did."

"But he's an evil cook," said Debbie Devil.

"Geezo, Debbie, all English cooks are evil. Hell is full of them. They even have their own sports complex on the fifth level. What we need is a competent soul crusher. I insist you find one."

Debbie's eyes turned red, her horns emitted static electricity, and her tail swished.

"Little man," she said, "if I say Bertram Blackhand is the right man for the job, he's the right man for the job. Or do you want me to restore you back to your previous existence? Hmm, let's see. What did you do before you died and I gave you George's Mushrooms. Oh yes, I remember, you drew the pictures for those *Where's Waldo?* books. Didn't you draw thousands and thousands of them when one adds in all those rejected pictures?"

"Yes," said Mr. George through clenched teeth.

"Then I suggest you let me pick the help if you want to stay away from Waldo."

"Yes, ma'am."

"Besides, Bertram is my husband's chef. It makes me laugh just picturing my Dave on level seven waiting and waiting on his throne in Hell for a mushroom and kipper omelette that will never come."

Debbie laughed. It sounded like a donkey braying.

A stock boy pounded on the meat locker's door. "Debbie, are you okay in there?"

"Crikes," said Bertram, "if that boy sees an English chef and a mushroom magnate in an American meat locker, he'll suspect the plotting of bad evil for sure."

"Settle down," said Debbie, "I have a plan. Bertram, just do your best."

"Righto."

The door opened from outside. Steve the stock boy came in and said, "Who the heck are they?"

"Oh," said Debbie, "they're telemarketers for an insurance company. Relentless, aren't they?"

"But don't those folks use the telephone?"

"Oh no, not since California passed a law against that. Now they have to make house calls. Well, I'd better hurry back to my checkout. Hungry Hank's doesn't like long lines. Our motto is 'In and Out in Less Than Three Minutes.'"

Mr. George sighed. "Geezo, Debbie, sometimes I think you care more about checking here than in stealing souls from Lutheran hunks and starting Armageddon."

"I'll never quit this job, Mr. George, never. Besides, you can't count on mass destruction. Sometimes the world is too blessed safe."

Steve's eyes grew big. "Gosh, ma'am, you're sure you're okay with these folks?"

Debbie put her hand on Steve's shoulder. Steve blushed. "I'm fine. Insurance men just talk about 'stealing souls' and 'starting Armageddon' to scare prospective customers. People buy more insurance when they're scared."

"And gosh, you're all standing in a giant mushroom. What's with that?"

Debbie put her other hand on Steve. "Don't worry about the mushroom, hon. It's just a promotional gift insurance people give customers to get their feet in the door. The bigger the mushroom the better their chances of a sale."

She stared at Steve's crotch. "Say, do you happen to be Lutheran?"

"No," said Steve, "I'm a Unitarian."

Debbie turned her gaze to the vertical stripe of ketchup. "Pity."

CHAPTER 2G-GOOD GUYS

General Robert E. Lee looked around the room. On the wall behind him rested the True Cross. To the right showed a map of the Earth where several amber lights flashed. The light by Rancho Santa Fe flashed red. He drummed his fingers briefly before regaining self control. Well, those people were up to something.

The wall to the left showed the Archangel Board.

GABRIEL: Surfing on Big Waves Planet near Orion

MICHAEL: Ditto

RAFAEL: Ditto

Lee wondered why God allowed his top three officers to go on vacation at the same time. He dismissed the thought as rebellious and prayed for the Lord's forgiveness. Perhaps their act built *ésprit de corps*.

Across from Lee hung a big blank, white board.

Suddenly, a shout rang out, "Attention, attention, extreme evil alert. Please read the incoming message on the big board.

The Finger of Fate wrote in gold on the big board:

ENDANGERED SOUL: Joseph Thorvald

RATING: Good soul

RELIGION: Lutheran

EVIL ONES: Debbie Devil, Mr. George, and Bertram Blackhand. Lee whistled softly. The Big Three of Evil. The Finger of Fate having written that moved on.

OBJECTIVE OF EVIL ONES: To enslave Joseph Thorvald for Debbie Devil's love toy.

IMPLICATION: Success over the direct descendant of St. Peter would prove to all the entities in the Universe the superiority of Debbie over God.

Lee felt his chest tighten. Didn't that damned woman ever give up? She had tried to enslave him that night in Texas. He shuddered.

Thank goodness that little unpleasantness with the North had broken out. It had given him an excuse that she could accept. Even the ever-horny Debbie had to respect men going away to kill each other by the hundreds of thousands.

The moving finger continued: PRIMARY WEAPON: Mushrooms.

Lee's heart raced. Just thirty more days until that seaside vacation on that peaceful planet near Alpha Centauri. His wife Mary was so looking forward to it. He sighed. This would surely be a long campaign. But duty called.

Even so, he needed help to deal with this gang. He reached for the red telephone.

"Good afternoon, Almighty Father."

"Hey dude, what's shaking?"

Lee winced. After more than 100 years here he still carried a stiff demeanor.

"God, Bambi and Helga left too early. Left us with an immense problem," said Lee.

"I know, dude. I know everything."

"Lord, I could use some help. Could you send me back one of the Archangels?"

"Look at the Archangel board. They're on a surfing safari."

"With all due respect, Almighty, can't their safari wait?"

"And miss those primo waves on planet Big Waves. Totally awesome. Like wow, those dudes had been under some gnarly stress fighting evil lately. Like they were totally tensed up, dude."

Lee sighed and closed his eyes for a spell. Another of the Eternal Father's phases. He'd seen so many and he'd see an infinite number more. And what would Jesus the Surfer have been like?

Lee took a deep breath. No matter the phase, God would always be all merciful and all powerful. Always. Lee said, "Heavenly Father, I really need some help with this crisis. If it pleases you, I need the best soul available. I need Colonel Winston Theodore Pugh."

"Sorry dude, already on assignment."

"Almighty God, then may I have Saint Francis?"

"Sorry dude."

"John the Baptist, gracious Father?"

"Sorry."

"How about Stuffy? As you know, God, Stuffy was Mr. Thorvald's childhood teddy bear."

Lee winced inside. His eyes even rolled. Of course, the omnipotent Lord knew.

God cut Lee some slack. Let it slide. "It's not that serious, dude. Yet. Besides, he's on special assignment in North Korea."

Lee sighed inwardly. "Then whom may I expect for help, Lord?"

"Hey dude, I'm sending you Pedro Erickson."

Lee's head slumped forward. He gripped his stomach and moaned softly. The Almighty's ways were truly inscrutable.

Major Erickson! Lee hadn't seen him since West Point. Erickson had been wilder than Lee. Lee could understand that, for who hadn't? He couldn't fathom, though, why a promising army engineer chose to graduate as an army chef. And his choice of entrees? Pain flashed in his gut.

But his heart counted the countless acts of friendship by little, clumsy Erickson. Pity that the Late Unpleasantness with the North had separated them. Lord, just let him arrive without his culinary creations.

A few moments later something thumped against the door. Lee heard, "*Ja caramba*," come from the other side.

Lee arose and opened the door. A cuddly golden-haired man clad in a chef's apron looked up at him. The chef pointed to a smashed jar on the floor.

"I was holding that jar of picante sauce with one hand and a plate of Swedish meatballs with another. Then I ran out of hands when I tried to knock on the door. The jar fell. Broke to bits. The bits mixed with the picante sauce. *Ja caramba*. I hate to waste good picante, don't you?"

Lee said, "Sir, you have my profound sympathies."

"Oh, don't fret, General. Heaven's great. Look!" Erickson snapped his fingers and the mess disappeared.

Lee stared at Erickson. "If you are quite ready, sir, I shall relate some quite disturbing news."

"Oh, I know, General." He walked over to the big board and pointed to the name, 'Bertram Blackhand.' "You see, that man is my twin brother."

Lee's jaw dropped one fiftieth of an inch. "You jest, sir. I knew you at West Point. You were the only child of Mexican and Swedish parents. Sir, what you say is not possible."

"It is possible, General."

"And you've gotten taller."

"I can explain that."

Lee sighed. "Please, do."

Erickson waved his hand. "Oh you know how it is. It's almost a cliche. Swedish Mexican gets accepted to West Point. West Point engineer changes to a major in culinary arts. Culinary artist gets appointed as chief chef to General Halleck in Washington. Chief chef serves jalapeno poppers to General Halleck. General Halleck gets a case of massive indigestion."

Lee smiled and nodded while Erickson continued, "Disgraced cook gets broken in rank to private and sent to Fredericksburg. Private gets slain charging the heights above Fredericksburg in 1862."

"I trust you did not suffer," said Lee.

"Oh don't worry," said Erickson. "Your Rebs didn't have anything on army hardtack. Let me tell you the Army of the Potomac really could have used some good old Swedish funnel cake.

"Anyway, God reincarnated me in 1967. He meant to have only me be born, but Debbie Devil got involved and I had a twin brother, Bertram Blackhand. Bertram followed the evil path and enrolled in the London School of Cooking.

"I recalled my culinary skills from my previous life to found a nationwide chain of Swedish-Mexican fast-food restaurants, called Taco Erickson's. But no doubt you've heard this story many times before."

"Well, sir," said Lee, "I have. Soldiers throughout history have always told such tales. I must admit, though, this is the first time I believed it."

Erickson bowed. "Perhaps you had one of my famous shredded-beef tacos?"

"I had not that honor," said Lee. "I died many years before that."

"I could order you up a couple," said Erickson.

Lee shook his head. "Thank you kindly, but I've already dined. And sir, I didn't know our Almighty Father was partial to reincarnation."

"Not as rule, no," said Erickson. "But God loves tacos and Swedish meatballs." The chef moved closer to Lee and lowered his voice, "Just as mushrooms are pure evil, tacos and Swedish meatballs that go in them are the secret, culinary weapons of the Lord, just like the ones in my hands."

Lee frowned. "Erickson, sir, your hands are empty."

The chef looked at each hand in turn. "Well, you'll just have to imagine a taco in my left hand and a Swedish meatball in the other."

Lee sighed. "My story varies somewhat from yours. After the Almighty saw fit to end the war with a Northern Victory I had the honor to run Washington University. Even taught an art course in Pre-French Impressionism. Not very well attended. Thank goodness, history forgot it.

"God's had me doing staff work ever since my soul came up here."

A heavenly alarm pip-pipped. The red light by Rancho Santa Fe disappeared. The time and date over the map vanished. So did the map.

The Eraser of Fate appeared to erase the Finger of Fate's writing. Fate shook itself at the eraser and wrote:

LOCATION OF THORVALD: unknown

TIME OF THORVALD: unknown

LOCATION OF BERTRAM BLACKHAND: unknown

TIME OF BERTRAM BLACKHAND: unknown

QUANTITY OF HELL'S MUSHROOMS: unknown

"Well, Mr. Erickson," said Lee, "the enemy has stolen a march on us."

"*Ja caramba*," said Erickson.

CHAPTER 3-WE'LL MEET AGAIN

Crack! Shazzam! Kabluie! No, that doesn't sound right. Maybe it doesn't matter. Does lightning striking a pond in pre-life Earth make a sound?

It did create life, a single-celled *paracimonium*, in fact. And a darn smart single-cell existence, too.

"Wow," said the paracimonium, "I'm a paracimonium. Look at me!" No one did. Nothing else existed, except that cup of piping hot Colombian coffee.

"Well, fudgies," said the world's only critter, "I'm lonely." The cell tried to shed a tear, couldn't. That ability would have to wait for millions of years of evolution.

A day later, another thought flashed through the nucleus. "Time to conquer the world." The cell kicked its cilia and swam through the pond for several hundredths of a second and met no resistance. Okay, it had conquered the world.

The paracimonium slapped its cilia against its membrane. "Stupid, stupid, stupid. Name yourself first, then conquer the world."

"No matter, I shall name myself now. I shall call myself Joe. No, that's not big enough for me. Look, how many cilia I have."

Joe couldn't look. That too, would have to wait for evolution. He didn't try to cry again, an astute paracimonium, you bet.

The ramblings of the intruding author millions of years in the future did not bother Joe. He continued his world-class cogitating. "I shall call myself, Joe Thorvald. Yes, that's a good name."

Pangs of hunger radiated from, from, well, Joe called it a stomach and now we're stuck with the term.

Joe's permeable cell wall drooled for a good, medium rare Quarter-billionth Pounder. He couldn't find one. He did bump into a cup of coffee. "Bah," said Joe, "it's cold."

Joe tried eating particles of sand. He expelled them. He swam and he swam all over the pond until he bumped into a thistlewort seed. Joe's famished stomach didn't even care that the seed came courtesy of the European Union's Intertemporal Subsidy Program of Agriculture.

Perhaps Joe ate too much. Perhaps he gained too much in size. His fluid innards roiled.

"Wow, I have a splitting nucleus ache." In fact, Joe experienced a splitting stomach and other dividing innards, as well.

Joe panted in the pool. "Whoa, what was that?"

Something crashed into his side. He didn't know sand could swim. Something tried to suck him into itself. Every cell in his body, one, convulsed in fear.

Life! Life had crashed into his side! "Ouch!"

"Hey, whatever you are, stop eating me. I've conquered the world."

"I'm so very sorry," said Joe's daughter/son/brother/sister, "have I committed a faux pas? I thought you were a Quarter-billionth Pounder."

Joe repaired the damage to his membrane and laughed. "Oh, that old mistake." Our hero extended hundreds of cilia, "The name's Thorvald, Joe Thorvald."

The new form extended its own cilia and shook Joe's. "Why, I declare," said the new paracimonium on the block, "you are a real gentle cell. I am right pleased to meet you."

Joe blushed. "Aw, shucks."

The new cell said, "Why, I think I'll name myself, Jane Thorvald. I'd be mighty honored to be known as a Thorvald."

The happy pair spent many glorious days together. They promenaded hundreds of arms in hundreds of arms, often to nowhere, dined at *Chez Pond*, discussed the meaning of life, and played their little paracimonium love games.

But even at the dawn of Existence, happiness remains vulnerable to life's little troubles such as a huge, exterminating meteor showers, or continental drift.

Continental drift did, in fact, separate life's first couple. Suddenly, over the course of ten years, a chasm, a canyon, okay, a tiny crack widened in the middle of the pond draining water until two smaller ponds came into being. Each new pool had a Thorvald in its deep end.

Joe cried, "Jane, Jane, forces of plate tectonics beyond our control have torn us asunder."

Jane, being a demure paracimonium, just cried.

The relentless forces swirling in the bowels of the Earth separated Joe's and Jane's pond another micron.

They felt it. Felt the awesome implications.

Joe shouted, "Jane, I love you. There will never be another paracimonium like you."

Jane covered her membrane with her hundreds of cilia and sobbed the sob of life's first separated sweetheart.

"Jane, Jane, do you love me? I need to know."

A weak voice came back, "I love you, Joe, I love you. You are my first and only love."

The Earth's shifting plates forced them even farther apart.

"Jane, Jane," shouted our hero, "we'll never bump into each other again." Jane's sobbing made Joe's membrane crawl.

"Jane, I'll write. I'll write you every day. My address will be South America. Yours will be Africa."

"Oh Joe, you know in your nucleus that communication will never be there for us. We're probably hundreds of years away from a functioning, global postal system."

Joe lost the desire to speak anymore. He waved goodbye and swam to the western edge of his pond.

He bumped into something new. Tried to eat it. Spat it out. The new thing tasted vile. Joe called it "mushroom." Joe shuddered. Evil had come to the paracimonium's brave new world.

CHAPTER 3B-BAD GUYS

Bertram Blackhand finished passing out the warm jackets. Each had a picture of a devil swiping at a hockey puck. Underneath the picture ran the red words, "New Jersey Devils."

"I got these on sale at WalMart," said Bertram. "Only $6.99 each. What do you think?"

"Very nice," said Debbie Devil, "red is my color. And I appreciate you keeping the costs down."

Bertram bowed.

"However," she continued, "I'm not wild about you getting these at Walmart."

"Why is that?" asked Bertram

She pouted. "Someday, WalMart might drive Hungry Hank's out of business. Then where would I be? Where would I get income? They don't pay much, but it's enough for a little apartment, a Geo Metro, and the occasional night on the town sending poorly hung agnostics to Hell.

"But more importantly, this job gives me an identity, a reason to get up in the morning, knowing that I can make Hungry Hank's shoppers' day a little better."

"That and your daily attempts to seduce Lutheran hotties and to dare Armageddon," said Bertram.

Debbie Devil shrugged. "Sure, I'm a Renaissance type gal with multiple interests."

"So, m'lady," said Bertram, "do you think seducing Joe Thorvald and claiming his soul with mushrooms will bring about Armageddon?"

"Oh yes." Her eyes flashed red. "If he's as pure of soul as I think he is, God will have no choice but to fight for him."

"Then," said Mr. George, "we'll certainly be up against God's best."

Bertram gasped. "Not Stuffy?!"

Mr. George shook his head. Bertram beamed. Mr. George did not.

Bertram's smile vanished. "Not my brother, Pedro Erickson."

"I'm afraid so," said Mr. George.

"Crikes! That blighter sent me to Hell just before I was to serve mushrooms and kippers to the World Peace Conference. Bless, bless, and double bless!"

Debbie put her hand on Bertram's shoulder. "Bertram, courage. You have friends, too. We'll just have to be more vigilant, that's all.

"We all make mistakes. Remember that time you served gourmet food to the American President at Buckingham Palace instead of English fare? Remember?"

Bertram managed a weak smile.

"Ah, there's my evil chef," said Debbie.

Mr. George coughed. "Excuse me, please. This is all very touching, but the fact remains Bertram failed in those three incarnations. He didn't do enough."

Bertram stiffened. So did his tall chef's hat. Chefs can do that to their hats, but they won't tell how. Code of the Culinary Artists.

"As WE should all know," said Bertram, "evil soul transporters are allowed one medium and one evil intruding object. My hands are tied in this matter. The medium comes from the previous incarnation; the coffee mug in this case. The evil object must be a mushroom. Nothing is more evil than a mushroom. If you wish I can bring you the manual for these sort of things next time we meet. It's quite clear on this matter."

Mr. George shook his head. "Don't bother. I still don't get why Bertram introduced the mushroom so late. That man should have put it in Joe's world much sooner." He fixed his eyes on Bertram's. "EVERYONE knows that new lovers are so full of joy that mushrooms couldn't possibly appeal to them, even if the lovers are paracimonia. You should have put the mushroom in Joe's pond before he divided and met Jane, you idiot!"

"I'm learning on the job," said Bertram.

Traces of a smile appeared on Mr. George's face. "I must admit, though, it was quite clever of you to put Joe's soul in a single-cell organism. Less intelligence, less resistance to mushrooms. Brilliant, really."

Bertram bowed to Mr. George. "Why thank you. I'm sure I will get better at execution."

Debbie beamed. "Great, great. This is the can-do spirit that started the Black Death and World War II. What's next for Joe?"

"Well," said Bertram, "I thought I'd rather enjoy seeing him become a dinosaur."

"Great," said Debbie.

Steve the stock boy knocked on the freezer door. "Mrs. Devil, you really should make up your mind about insurance one of these days, we need you to open up your checking stand."

"Coming," said Debbie as she squirted another stripe of ketchup on the wall. That made two.

CHAPTER 3G-GOOD GUYS

Lee and Erickson waited for the Golden Finger of Fate to finish writing its message.

"You'd think God would give this room an up-to-date display room," said Erickson.

"There is something in what you say, Mr. Erickson," said Lee, "but Microsoft makes those displays. They're prone to freezing."

Lee leaned close to Erickson and whispered, "Confidentially, the Almighty gave permission to Microsoft to install their system in every room in Hell. He's trying to make Hell freeze over."

Pedro Erickson returned the grin. "Why, General, you made a joke! Heaven certainly agrees with you."

Lee's smile vanished. He pointed to the golden words on the display.

LOCATION OF THORVALD: Pangaea
TIME OF THORVALD: Jurassic
LOCATION OF BERTRAM BLACKHAND: unknown
TIME OF BERTRAM BLACKHAND: unknown
QUANTITY OF HELL'S MUSHROOMS: increasing

"*Ja caramba*," said Erickson, "we still don't know about Bertram."

"I think we do, sir," said Lee. "I'm learning the methods of that man. He shall be somewhere with Joe Thorvald."

"But where? Pangaea is big. The Jurassic Period ran for millions of years. How can we possibly help Mr. Thorvald? And if we can't help him, he's doomed!"

Erickson gave himself up to crying. Lee thought of putting his hand on Pedro's shoulder, but stopped. He said, "Cheer up, Erickson, we can rely on the constant mistakes of evil's minions. Much like your Northern generals."

Erickson looked up and glared at Lee.

"My sincerest pardons, Mr. Erickson. Fredericksburg must still be fresh to you. But cheer up. We still can do our best. We'll arrange to air-drop beef tacos at random places and times all over Pangaea."

Erickson sniffled. "Think that will help?"

"Why surely, beef tacos contain a natural antidote to the evil properties of mushrooms. How I wish the Army of Northern Virginia's cook had known about tacos. It might have made all the difference. Ah well.

"And don't forget, Buddy Holly glasses shall give our man Thorvald an extra bracing of courage."

Pedro managed a small simile. "Just like Swedish meatballs do for me."

"Exactly my dear Mr. Erickson. Exactly."

CHAPTER 4-JURASSIC THEME PARK

Joe Thorvald reached into his to-go bag and withdrew 50 Quarter Pounders. He loved them, but then again what meat eater did not? Joe handed the bag to Sam, a fellow Allosaurus. Sam liked McDonald's too. The two liked many of the same things. In fact, the former Army Rangers were great friends, having saved each other's lives at least three times in the Great Gondwanan War ten years ago.

But all that lay behind them as they strolled through the picturesque, but nearly empty Walking Land on their way to the ever-popular Mammal World.

"Everyone says ROAD RAGE is one of the best car rides in Mammal World," said Sam.

"That's what I heard," said Joe.

Joe smiled. They walked past six obese meat eaters who lurched forward, looking down, and mumbling, "Gas foot, other foot."

Then there it was. ROAD RAGE. They saw the cars race around the track. They saw drivers giving the finger and firing wooden pellets at each other. Thank goodness the motorists' steel helmets and flak jackets stopped most of the pellets.

"It doesn't get any better than this," said Joe.

Sam grinned. "Sure doesn't."

They walked to the end of the line, only three dinosaurs in it. Joe gestured for Sam to go in front.

Two minutes later, the line moved up three spots. Joe got out his park pass, turned the corner around the green plastic fence and saw . . . The Line.

The line snaked back and forth until it filled an entire valley. So that the waiting meat eaters might keep an eye on their prize ROAD RAGE, free mounted binoculars dotted the line every mile–dinosaurs never did go metric. How do we know this? We just do.

"Oh mammals," said Joe, "this is one long line. How about we head to another ride?"

Sam wished for an eyebrow to raise. "What? And lose our place in line?" He pointed to the line behind them.

Joe sighed. Already a mile of dinosaurs had lined up behind them. The line lengthened 10 yards every second. "Alright, Sam, we'll stay. Maybe this ride will be worth it."

A little Hare Krishna, as usual a ceratosaurus, turned back to face them. "Everybody says it's a great ride. I only wish I had gotten a Quik Pass. I was due back at the airport months ago." The Krishna raised his face and claws to the sky. "Geez, how many times can one chant Hare Krishna? One more time, I guess. Hare Krishna, hare Krishna, Krishna Krishna . . ."

The surrounding dinosaurs took up the chant with practiced ease. Hours later, Joe and Sam and a few close-by dinosaurs ate the Hare Krishna.

"Well, that Krishna tasted okay," said Joe.

"Yeah," said Sam, "and we did make that airport a little more pleasant. Still, I'd rather have a hundred Quarter Pounders, but at least we didn't have to leave the line."

"Can you imagine how long the lines would be if we allowed herbivores in?" asked Joe.

An alluring female allosaurus finished munching her share of the Hare Krishna. She said to her boyfriend, "Maybe I shouldn't have eaten that ceratosaurus. Say, do you think I look fat?"

"No, dear," said the boyfriend.

Two hours later the sun went down and so did the temperature. The dinosaurs' blood cooled and they fell asleep. This caused ROAD RAGE's usual nocturnal accidents.

Rumbling stomachs greeted the dawn. Personnel carted away dead dinosaur drivers. Mechanics fixed or replaced the crashed cars.

"I sure could use a breakfast sandwich," said Joe.

"We would have to leave our place in line," said Sam, "and I'm not doing that, not with all those hours I waited yesterday."

Suddenly, a sexy compsognathus with curves in all the right places sprang out wearing nothing but the latest fern-green stockings from Victoria's Secret. She looked straight at Joe and Sam and winked. "Hey, you hotties want a McMushroom salad?"

Sam raised his claw. "Two salads, here."

"Coming right up, big boys."

Six salivating ceratosaurs jumped in front of the two friends. "Me, me, me," they all said. The comely compsognathus frowned.

"Oh, let the little babies go first," said Sam. He turned to Joe. "Did you see the haunches on that one?"

The compsognathus winked at Sam. "I'll be right with you, sweetheart." She continued to hand out salads.

Joe bit Sam on the neck, just hard enough to draw blood.

"Why'd you do that?" yelled Sam.

"Put down your danged claw," said Joe. "We'll be getting no McMushroom salads from that one."

"Why?"

"Something is wrong with that compsognathus."

"Like what?"

"Dang it," said Joe, "if you had a pea-sized brain like me instead of a dust-sized one you would have noticed that she's selling herbivore food. A salad is made up of plant food."

"So?"

"We're meat eaters, Sam. We don't eat plants."

"Doh." Sam hit his head so hard that it bled.

"And that's not all. She's putting mushrooms in the salad."

"So?"

"Don't you remember how mass mushroom poisoning killed off all the dinosaurs in the Triassic Period?"

"Aw, Joe, you don't really believe those myths."

"Yes, I do." Joe pointed a claw at the ceratosaurs. "Look at the scales on those guys. They're starting to turn light pink."

"Holy cetiosaurus," said Sam. "What made those guys so horny?"

"The mushrooms in her salads. The ancients knew well that mushrooms pump up the sex drive of dinosaurs to that of rutting mammals. The sexually enraged males viewed each other as competition to be killed. And so they did, wiping out nearly every dinosaur species. It's taken tens of millions of years for dinosaurs to come back."

"Look," said Sam. The scales on the ceratosaurs pulsed a deep red. "They're going to kill each other."

"What are we going to do?" asked Sam.

"When they're all dead, we'll eat them," said Joe.

"Sounds good."

And so Joe and Sam soon feasted. Other allosaurs joined in, so many that the killing and eating became general. The blood and gore settled a few hours later.

"Look," said Sam, "they killed that compsognathus."

Joe shrugged.

"And look at all the dead dinosaurs."

Sure enough, about a third of the waiting dinosaurs lay dead with the survivors taking great chomps out of their ripped-open bellies.

"Well, maybe some good came out of it," said Joe.

"Like what?"

"Well, Sam, the dead dinosaurs are no longer in line, are they?"

Sam smiled for the first since they got in line. The smile quickly faded.

"Joe?"

"Yes, friend."

"That compsognathus really wanted to give us the salads, didn't she?"

"Yes."

"Then it would have been just us two fighting to the death."

"Yes, I know."

"Then you would have won. You're the better fighter. You would have killed me."

"But it didn't happen, Sam."

"I know, Joe, because you were onto her." Tears formed in Sam's eyes. "I guess I just want to say thanks for not killing me and eating me."

"Aw shucks," said Joe, "you're too bony to eat. Besides, I didn't fancy being the love slave of a little compsognathus. Only one-thousandth my size. It wouldn't have lasted."

Sam put a hand on his friend's arm. "Joe, I have the feeling this is going to be the start of a beautiful, safe friendship. Let's promise that no matter how hungry we get we will never eat each other."

"I promise," said Joe.

It was a darn good thing the friends made that promise. Day after day, the carnivores waited to get on ROAD RAGE. None ever left the line to visit the park's overpriced restaurants. Day after day, the ravenous meat eaters ate each other.

Finally, the two friends got to the front on the line. They got into their shiny cars and strapped on their seat belts.

"No bumping the car in front," said the attending dilophosaur.

Sam said to the attendant, "I was getting tired of waiting. Sure lucky for us that all the dinosaurs in front of us got eaten."

"It wasn't luck at all," said the attendant. "It's all an herbivore plot. They let us ban them from all the theme parks. Then they bought the parks. Then the herbivores made the lines long with killer rides, lines so long that mass killings and eating in lines would be inevitable. They'll be taking over soon."

Joe squinted at the attendant. "If that's so, how come the herbivores are letting you tell us this? If you know so much I'd think they'd have to kill you."

The attendant said, "Oh, all the attendants know this. But you're wrong, they don't have to kill us. Sooner or later, the food will run out. And did you notice, all the gates are closed? There's no way out. Sooner or later, you'll have to eat me."

Joe looked in the attendant's eye. "It won't be anything dinosaural."

The attendant shrugged. Joe and Sam got into their shiny cars.

"Strap yourself in," said the attendant, "and don't bump the car in front of you. Safety first."

Joe gritted his sharp teeth and floored the accelerator. He'd certainly savor this ride.

Suddenly, a massive comet shot out of the clouds, plummeting onto Joe's car incinerating Joe, Sam, the attendant, and all other dinosaurs on South Gondwana. The comet also wiped out all evidence of their astounding achievements: automobiles, airplanes, the cure for cancer, skyscrapers, DVDs, Impressionist art, Willard Scott, and Quarter Pounders.

Well not quite all dinosaurs got killed. There were those dinosaurs on Laurasia and North Gondwana, loafers everyone of them. They never created anything, never used a single tool. But still they survived and reproduced.

Those ne'er do wells provided the only evidence of Jurassic life that paleontologists more than 100 million years later would find. One paleontologist, Bob Cumin, even asserted the discovery of thousands of fossilized beef tacos next to dinosaurs in dozens of sites. But most of his colleagues refuted his claim, saying, "Bah! What a stupid idiot."

CHAPTER 4B-BAD GUYS

Mrs. Devil squirted another red stripe on the meat locker wall. "Three," she said.

Bertram Blackhand came laughing into the meat locker.

"Well," said Mr. George, "we almost got Joe that time. Real close."

"Yeah." Bertram giggled in that irritating way that made generation after generation of Vikings ravage the British Isles. "And they didn't even get their taco-and-meatball antidotes sent anywhere near Joe Thorvald."

Debbie seized Bertram and Mr. George with her sharp, bony fingers and lifted them up. "Listen, you two. I want to get me some of that hot, Lutheran man flesh. Know what I got last night?"

The two minions shook their heads.

"Two solid hours of reality-dating shows."

She released them. "And just to piss me off even more, I'm sure God put the idea into all advertising execs' head to lace those shows with ads for Viagra."

"Well," said a red-necked Bertram, "why don't you give some Viagra to your husband?"

The little horns on Debbie's head glowed an ominous, purple hue. "Because, little English chef, everyone but you knows that Viagra doesn't work in Hell."

Mr. George whispered to Bertram, "It's something to do with a patent dispute."

"Bummer," said Bertram, "but we came close. We almost outfoxed Joe."

"Outfoxed him, outfoxed him," yelled Debbie. She clenched her fists—as usual this caused an internet virus to appear in Peoria. "You under-spicing idiot, Joe Thorvald was a dinosaur. He had a pea-sized brain. You couldn't even outfox a pea-sized brain!"

Bertram's chef hat drew itself up to its full height. "Well, at least I tried. I was readying myself for another attempt when someone, I won't mention names, hurled a comet and obliterated life on a whole half-continent.

"And my dear Debbie, not just innocents died in that comet, but a lot of evil-hearted dinosaurs as well."

Debbie shrugged. "I was cranky. I was having my period."

Bertram and Mr. George paled. They took a few, quick steps backwards. They darted a glance at each other. Neither would talk. They both knew Mrs. Devil couldn't have kids; the sulfuric fumes of Hell had seen to that.

They also knew Mrs. Devil yearned for an heir. A special little demon with dimples and golden curls to take over her checkout stand at Hungry Hank's, someone to say "mama," someone to grab her hand and help her send plagues, initiate global wars, fry people's souls, and freeze computers.

Then Joe Thorvald entered her life. A hunk. And a Lutheran hunk, no less, and of Swedish descent. Surely, he would have sperm powerful enough to give her a child. And if not . . .

CHAPTER 4G-GOOD GUYS

General Lee gazed at the screen as it replayed Debbie Devil's last attempt on Joe Thorvald. He almost sneered. Debbie's minions behaved just like U.S. General Joe Hooker at Chancellorsville in 1863. They had stolen a march on him and had shown up with Joe in an unexpected spot, just like Hooker had. They had left him unmolested too long, just like Hooker. They had used a small compsognathus as the vanguard of their attack, just like Hooker.

Lee shook his head. Would the other side never learn? He hoped not. He could always turn their missteps against them. Lee took out his gold watch, opened it, and looked. Pedro Erickson was late again.

Lee heard a knock. "Come in."

"Hey Lee," said the voice on the other side, "open the blessed door, I have my hands full. *Ja caramba.*"

The Southern gentleman walked with measured step to the oaken door and opened it. "My dear Mr. Erickson, have you every Tupperware container in Heaven in your arms?"

The struggling Erickson nodded vigorously. "*Sí, sí, ja, ja,* full of tasty lutefisk and Swedish meatballs."

Lee let slip a muted moan.

A Tupperware container fell to the floor and popped open to reveal lingonberry preserves.

The old Southern gentleman smiled. Couldn't help it. "My dear Erickson, you old rascal, you didn't tell me you had lingonberry preserves with you. Much obliged, I'm mighty partial to them."

Pedro Erickson smiled back. Wasn't Heaven great? "I know, and what would lingonberry preserves be without limpa bread?"

Lee leaned forward an eager sixteenth of an inch.

Erickson patted his chef's uniform. "Nope, not there. Now where could it be? Aha, I know!"

Erickson doffed his white chef's hat and a loaf of life-giving limpa bread fell into his arms. "Well, Lee, I do believe there's something in this feast for you after all."

Lee bowed, and waved his arm. "After you, my dear Erickson, after you."

As he followed Erickson to the great table he asked, "And my dear Erickson, how do you come to have so many wonderful dishes with you?"

"Oh that," said the chef, "I was catering a big shindig for the graduating class of Guardian Angels. It's their last chance before they hit the real spiritual world, so they really whoop it up."

And the two warriors of God feasted quietly on lingonberries and limpa bread. Erickson burped. Lee burped internally. Afterlife was good.

"Splendid, splendid repast," said the old general, "but I feel my duty to bring up some small points about our last operation."

"What points?" said Erickson. "We smoked the forces of Evil, we smoked them."

"Well, yes," said Lee, "but still I feel constrained to point out that our beef tacos fell nowhere near Joe Thorvald in his hour of need, Joe Thorvald bested the compsognathus on his own, and we let Debbie Devil destroy a thriving civilization—one that produced Quarter Pounders and Willard Scott—and one third of all life on Earth."

"*Ja caramba*, I did my best. I didn't know where Joe would be. His position wasn't on the screen. And just you try conjuring up a billion tons of shredded beef tacos on a moment's notice. That's hard, even in Heaven. Next thing, I suppose you'll be running to God to ask Stuffy to help you!"

Lee flinched inside. Am I so obvious? Have I been so unkind? "My dear Erickson, the fault is all mine. I did not provide you with enough warning nor sufficient coordinates.

"Next time, I will do better. Your God-sent antidotes to Debbie's evil mushrooms will be better placed next time, I promise you."

"Well, okay," said Erickson, "would you like a bowl of lutefisk soup?"

Lee's stomach whipped up tidal waves of acid. "I'd be much obliged."

CHAPTER 5-DINO 'ROBICS

Blip! Joe Thorvald blinked his eyes and yawned. His massive jaw snapped shut. These DinoPong games could go on for hours.

His beautiful wife, Jane, stirred, moved her trackball. Blip! Her virtual paddle darted to the right and sent the white square representing a ping-pong ball back across the console to Joe. She leaned across the screen and scratched his chest. "You sure were great last night. Roar!"

She scratched him again. Drew blood.

Joe laughed. "Careful with those claws, dear." Blip. The white square traveled back to his wife.

Jane laughed. "Anything you say, hero." She angled her neck toward his face. "My word, just look at this hickey you gave me." Blip.

Joe examined the circular array of bloody puncture wounds in her neck and flashed a sheepish grin. "Sorry about that, dear. Guess I went a bit wild last night." Blip.

After four hours the score stood zero to zero. Joe had everything he wanted. He stood at the top of the Cretacean food chain with a wife who could match him exactly in DinoPong.

"Why I do declare, the Earth must have shook something fierce last night," said Jane. Blip.

The lovers would have blushed, but they were Lutheran tyrannosaurus rexes from North Pangaea and had scales instead of skin.

"Say, Jane," he said, "would you care for some breakfast?" Blip.

"Breakfast would be right welcome." Blip.

"Well," said Joe as he nodded toward the Maytag meat locker, "Omaha Steaks mailed us some ornithomimus, some orodromeus, and muttaburrasaurus. What would be your pleasure?" Blip.

"Orodromeus would be heavenly." Blip.

Joe dipped his head, nudged open the meat locker, clamped his jaws around a particularly succulent orodromeus prime rib, flung it back to her, and closed the locker lid just in time to move his paddle in place. Blip.

"Thanks, hero." Blip.

"Let us give thanks for this bounty," said Joe. Blip.

"Thanks," said Jane. Blip.

"Thanks," said Joe. Blip.

Klaxon sounds issued from the console. "Please insert amber token to continue play." Joe inserted a token from his enormous stash by the console. Even in the Cretaceous Period, one could do well by skillful dabbling in thistlewort futures.

The love dinos spent the rest of the morning at the DinoPong consol, biting, champing, chewing, chomping, crunching, gnashing, munching, and tearing their lovely repast. Blip, blip.

Around noon the couple started belching for an hour. They took turns with Jane going first, for Joe was a gentleman. Blip, blip. Score, zero to zero.

Joe patted his massive paunch with his non-DinoPong hand. "Ah, a most satisfying repast."

Jane massaged Joe's belly with her free hand. "I just adore your love handles." She licked off the blood that flowed onto her claws.

"And I love your love handles," said the dashing, handsome Joe.

"I declare, life at the top of the food chain is sure good," said Jane.

"Sure is."

Joe and Jane spent the early afternoon Ponging away, snacking, uttering little tyrannosaurus endearments, and petting each other bloody.

But into every Cretaceous world an irascible carnotaur must come. The one who strode into the Thorvalds' clearing called himself Carl. Blip.

"Ho, ho," said Carl Carnotaur, "I see the so-called 'Kings of the Dinosaurs' are playing DinoPong again." He spat at Joe and Jane. "You two are so addicted, you are not even kings over the little compsognathus."

Jane sneered. "You carnotaurs. Y'all are so gauche."

Carl spat at Jane's feet.

Joe growled. "Apologize to her, now!"

Carl pretended to shake. "Ooh, ooh, you make me so scared. Ooh, ooh."

"I'll show you who's king."

Carl beckoned Joe with his own stubby arms. "Come and get me, *King*."

Jane stamped her petite clawed-right foot. "Mister Carnotaur, I expect you'll be learning better manners, right soon."

Joe tried to jump up but couldn't. Couldn't. Tried again. Just grunted. He pushed against DinoPong's glass top with his arms. "Err, err, oof." His ponderous belly lifted off the console.

Carl laughed and laughed. He clutched his sides; a minor mistake as his claws punctured his flesh. Bing! The white square edged past Joe's paddle.

Joe stared at the score on the screen. Jane 1, Joe 0. His cold blood ran tepid. The voices of generations of T-Rexian DinoPong players cried out in pain. Joe lowered his head and charged the ten steps between him and Carl. Well, charged the first six steps and plodded wheezing the last four.

At the sight of Joe's huge belly flopping up and down Carl guffawed so hard that he barely dodged Joe's snapping jaws.

"Stand and fight, coward," said Joe between gasps.

"Come and get me."

Jane shadow boxed encouragement. "You show him, Joe."

Joe charged again. This time, he managed only four quick steps before stopping. He wiped sweat from his forehead. Air rushed into his lungs in one painful blast after another.

"Na, na, na, na, can't catch me. You're too fat," said Carl.

"I'm not fat," said Joe before rushing for two steps.

Carl took a slow step to the side and spat in Joe's eye.

"Oh yes you are. Fat head, fat belly, fat thighs."

"Stop it."

"Fat thighs, fat thighs. The only thunder you'll make is with your thighs. I think I'll call you 'Thunder Thighs.'" Yes, all simple and cruel insults originated in the Cretaceous period.

Carl stomped on Joe's food locker, crushing it.

"Mr. Carnotaur," said Jane, "you ARE being dreadful. That Maytag had been in my family for nigh on eight-million years now. You, you beast."

Carl snarled at Joe and Jane, revealing a set of teeth riddled with mercury-amalgam fillings. He pointed at the flesh spilling out the holes of the crushed meat locker. "This sort of food is mine from now on. That's all meat. It's mine. Got it?" He pointed a claw at Joe. "But don't worry, maybe you'll find a compsognathus who'll share his mushrooms with you." Carl skipped away roaring with laughter.

Tears welled in Joe's eyes. Minutes passed before he could look into his wife's eyes.

"I'm so sorry," he sobbed, "it seems you married a mushroom-begging loser. I think I'll just head over to that tar pit beyond the hill and jump in."

Jane sashayed over to Joe and gently opened a small gash in his cheek.

"Oh nonsense, dear," said Jane. "I married the best T-Rex around. You're just as handsome and fierce as the day I met you.

"Remember it? You were feasting on a triceratops. Not many T-rexes can kill one of those. And there I came, hungry as a brontosaurus at a flea buffet.

"You took one look at little old me with my gaunt body and offered to share your kill. Why, I didn't even have to ask. I fell in love at once. And you know, hero, I'm still just as in love."

Joe permitted himself a smile. Thank Food, he was a tyrannosaurus. All the dinosaurs knew that tyrannosaurs from the South made the best wives. And he had the best of them. The best of the best.

Joe looked down at his puffy belly rippling onto the console and at his thunder thighs and imagined his buns of flab.

He looked up at the gentle smile on his wife's face. Resolution filled his heart. An idea filled his brain, crowding out the resident thought. He roared his vigor to the sky. A flock, a gaggle, an exultation, or just maybe it's a pretzel, of pteranodons took fright and flew away.

He gazed at his wife and grinned. His wife jumped from one foot to the other. "I must say, you have an idea. You have an idea," she squealed. "What is it? What is it?"

Joe roared. "Aerobics. Got to get my cardiovascular system moving. Got to shed these pounds. Going to join DinoPong Anonymous, too."

Joe began to sing. Verse one went, "Hmm, hmm, hmm." The chorus went, "Hmm, hmm, hmm." He launched into a lusty rendition of verse two which ran, "Hmm, hmm, hmm." Sure Joe had a simple song, but he had a simple brain, too.

Jane joined in. "Wee hee," she said, "this is fun!"

Joe and Jane danced and danced.

Their tyrannosaur neighbors, Sam and Sally, waddled over and stared.

"Hey, Joe," said Sam, "what are you doing?"

Joe waved to Sam. "We're doing aerobics. Going to shed a few pounds and look up that Carl Carnotaur. Going to show him he can't push me around anymore."

"Good for you, Joe," said Sam. "Mind if we join you? We've been having trouble with our own carnotaurs. Time we T-rexes showed those upstarts who's boss around here."

"Great."

More and more flabby tyrannosaurs joined the daily workouts. At first, they danced only when the sun's heat blazed warmth into their blood. Over the next several weeks, as their bodies became stronger, leaner, and firmer and as they became addicted to their daily endorphin rush, they started earlier and earlier.

Before long, they began to dance as soon as the sun rose. Soon, they were ready. Ready to annihilate the carnotaurs.

On July 12th, 65,000,001 B.C.--Yes, we do know the exact date-- the tyrannosaurs set out as one and attacked. They ran circles around the carnotaurs, killing everyone in the most aerobic way possible.

"A good carnotaur is a dead carnotaur," said Joe.
"No, a good carnotaur is an eaten one," said Sam.

They roared their good-natured laughs to the sky.

Joe dipped his head to take another bite out of Carl Carnotaur's stomach. "Yep, revenge sure tastes good."

Sam swallowed a chunk. "Yeah, but I prefer the dark meat."

They both chuckled at that 1.7-million-year old gem.

"Once again, we're the undisputed kings of the world," said Sam.

"Life doesn't get any better than this," said Joe.

Joe was right. Life didn't get any get better than that. But that huge Portobellium-235 laden comet Bertie Blackhand sent was streaking across their sky.

Which reminds me. Mass extinction has no bearing on copyright law. Your copyright will expire at the end of the specific term, say 100 years, whether your species get wiped out or not. Which is the other reason why the Cretacean inventors of DinoPong couldn't sue the makers of Pong.

CHAPTER 5B-BAD GUYS

La! La! La! La! How the two leprechauns frolicked in the meat locker of Hungry Hank's. Then the door to the locker opened. In strode Debbie Devil.

She put her hands on her hips and said, "Sean, Seamus, what are you leprechauns doing here?"

Sean, who towered over the other leprechauns at two-foot-six squeaked, "Top of the swing shift to you, darlin'. We're frolicking. Would you be joining us?"

"No," said Debbie. "Why here?"

Sean took out a pipe and a pouch. "Ah me darlin', Ireland hasn't been so pleasant for us Little People since it joined the European Union."

"That's right," said Seamus, a pixie and a leprechaun only by marriage, "and then there's that business with the Euro. Why, it . . ."

"Demonetized our Little-People currency," said Sean.

"Nay," said Seamus, "'twas a classic application of Gresham's Law; bad money drives good money out." Seamus stamped his tiny foot. Debbie tried not to smile at this unintentionally cute act.

"Oh aye," said Sean, "and this bit of economic wisdom from one who can't even name the three major components of Gross National Product." So went the second highest level of economic discourse ever witnessed in the Hungry Hank's meat locker.

"Then the Irish government confiscated our pots-o-gold," continued Seamus. "Said we owed several hundred years of back taxes. Now I'll be asking you, do leprechauns fill out tax forms?"

"And the bloody sods used the principle of eminent domain to seize our burrows," said Sean.

"And they kicked us out of the Emerald Isle for not getting our immunization injections," said Seamus.

"I already know all this," said Debbie.

Sean grinned. "Then you'll be letting us stay then?"

"No, I'm pure evil." She snapped her fingers, turning all of them into dust.

Bertram and Mr. George strode in.

"We heard squeaking," said Bertram. "Did you have leprechauns?"

Debbie waved toward the dust piles. "Yes, but they won't be bothering us."

"I hear they still can be found in old apartment buildings," said Mr. George.

"Yes, yes, yes," said Debbie, "but what about my Joe? Did you get him to submit? Did you make effective use of mushrooms?" Smoke billowed from her ears. "You didn't up and kill him, did you?"

"Most certainly not," said Bertram. "I sent a mushroom-laden comet through the Earth's atmosphere. That ought to fix him. Ha! Ha!"

"How?" asked Debbie.

"Not entirely sure," said Bertram. "But something really bad is going to happen to Joe. Change his way of thinking, you might say. Ha! Ha!"

"And might it change him?"

"Not entirely sure," said the evil chef, "but oh boy, oh boy, it's going to happen."

"When?" said Debbie.

"Not entirely sure, Mrs. Devil."

"Then Bertram, you have accomplished nothing," said Debbie.

"But," said Mr. George, "he has yet to fail totally."

"That's something," said Debbie as she squirted another red stripe on the wall. She looked at the dust piles and said, "I'll have to get Steve the stock boy in here to clean up this mess."

CHAPTER 5G-GOOD GUYS

"Honestly, Skipper, I didn't mean to blow up the professor's nuclear-powered submarine."

"That's okay, little buddy. I never really meant it when I said, 'I'll rip off your head'."

General Lee watched the credits roll across the screen. Didn't like the sitcom. Found it infantile and predictable, yet he couldn't take his eyes off it. He watched it every day, work permitting. He sighed. Those long, idle months of winter encampments during the war gave everything afterward an aura of fascination.

He spun a $20 gold piece. Did he have time to watch *The Patty Duke Show* before Pedro Erickson came in to discuss Debbie's last thrust at Joe Thorvald?

No.

"*Herr* Lee, what's happening?"

Lee pointed to a comet on the big screen. "It passed through the Earth's atmosphere in the Jurassic Era. Our sensors indicate it's made of Portobellium-235."

"Did it affect Joe?" asked Erickson.

"No, no effect at all," said Lee. "I just don't understand our adversaries. Sometimes, I don't believe they know what they're doing."

Erickson shrugged. "That's my brother Bertram for you." But Erickson in his second incarnation had gone to college in Boise, Idaho in the '80s. He knew what a whiff of Portobellium-235 could do even when released by idiots. But he couldn't tell Lee, a 19th-century Southern gentleman. Besides, it was too late to do anything about it.

Pedro looked at his watch. "Say, Lee, isn't *The Patty Duke Show* on now?

Lee beamed. "Why, yes. Care to join me?"
"Please."

CHAPTER 6--ECCE JOE

The hominids, Uggo and Ugga Ugg, lay face up on the rippling green grass of Olduvai Gorge. Herds of mastodons cavorted, as only mastodons can, on the horizon. The happy couple counted up to two clouds, then stopped. They were content to wait for someone to invent the number three.

"Life is good," said Ugga. She tapped her protruding belly. Suddenly, a baby shot out, Up went Uggo's prehistoric catcher's mitt. Whump! Uggo caught the baby right in the mitt's pocket.

"Wee hee," said the newborn.

Uggo laid the little bundle of joy on Ugga's chest.

"Feel like some boulder tossing?" said Uggo. "I know how you feel like boulder tossing after giving birth."

Ugga laughed. "Silly billy, you know the little one needs to nurse first. When he's done, I'll strap him to my back and THEN we can throw boulders."

Uggo, a particularly handsome hominid, slapped his sloping forehead and laughed. "Oh yeah, guess I forgot. Beautiful baby isn't he?"

Ugga smiled. "Sure is." She stared long and hard at the baby. Her face clouded. Her one enormous eyebrow rose. "Hmm, he really is beautiful. HE REALLY IS BEAUTIFUL! Uggo, dear take a close look, what do you think?"

Uggo bent over the tiny boy for a long time. Finally, he stood up and beamed. "Well, Ugga, you did it. You did it!"

"Oh Uggo, do you really think I produced the world's first human?"

"Oh no doubt about it," said Uggo. "Look at it. He has TWO eyebrows. His head doesn't slope much. He said, 'Wee hee.'"

Ugga smiled. "I think so, too." The smile vanished. "What about our neighbors up the river in Eden? Adam and Steve. Are they human?"

"Dear," said Uggo, "I believe the names are Adam and Eve. But I don't know if they are human. No one can get in to find out. Someone's posted no-trespassing signs all around. Probably their divine friend, 'I AM.'"

"Stuck-up social climbers," said Ugga.

Uggo stroked her hair. "We don't know that, dear. They might be survivalists, fearing general widespread chaos, such as what happens whenever a Portobellium-235 comet reappears."

"The Portobellium-235 comet is just a myth, Uggo. And we're part of a hominid gatherer culture. We have nothing to loot."

Uggo grunted. "Sure, we're far too unsophisticated to produce a materialistic society, or anything other than a catcher's mitt, and as for the Portobellium-235 comet, maybe you're right." He shrugged. "But Adam and Eve might believe that stuff."

Ugga smiled. "Well, I just refuse to let those folks spoil our day. As far our Olduvai Gorge neighborhood, and the rest of the world knows for that matter, we produced the world's first human. So, you just take our birth notice over to the Bible brothers, you know, the story keepers."

"But Ugga dear," said Uggo, "I can't take a notice to the Bible brothers. No one's invented writing."

"Oh honey, you said you'd get around to it."

"One of these days," said Uggo, "but gathering berries takes a lot of time. By the time I'm done I just want to sit back, relax, pop open a nice cold gourd full of thistlewort juice, and watch red ants fight black ants."

"Oh bother," said Ugga, "Well, just run along and tell them."

Uggo's sloping brow furrowed in thought. "We need a name. What shall we call him? How about Uggu or Uggo, junior?"

"No," said Ugga. "look at his little brown eyes. He's definitely a Joe Thorvald. Now, be off with you. To the Bible brothers, go!"

"Sure," said Uggo as he stood up. "Right after I rustle us up some thistlewort berries for dinner."

"Well all right, but don't forget."

Uggo was already loping toward the thistlewort grove.

Little Joe Thorvald was playing Rocks, Flints, Leaves with his sister Uggina. His other siblings: Uggie, Uggu, Uggaz, Uggma, and Bartolomeo Diaz were away collecting thistlewort berries.

But screw 'em; let's go to the important scene where Ugga sat on a cool rock under a tall thistlewort bush. Ugga saw Uggo race toward her.

"Ugga, Ugga, Ugga," he shouted.

"That's my name. Don't wear it out."

Uggo grimaced at the old joke. "Ugga, Ugga, I just found out! God just kicked Adam and Eve out of the Garden of Eden."

"Was it because they used mercury fillings in their children's teeth?"

"No," said Uggo, "they ate an apple."

"Well," said Ugga, "if they ate an apple a day, they would have had no need for fillings, much less ones with mercury amalgam. I just hope the Great Hominid Council outlaws these fillings in our lifetime."

Uggo sighed and held up his hands. "Whoa Ugga, they were kicked out of Eden because they ate an apple forbidden to them by God, not because of their poisonous dental practices. I know because I talked to them."

Ugga jumped from leg to leg. "Did you see them? Were they human?"

"Why yes, dear, they were."

"Then my Uggo, our little Joe Thorvald wasn't the world's first human."

"No, dear."

"Have they told anyone about it?"

"Yes dear, everyone knows. God knows, Mr. Devil knows, their neighbors to the North know, the Bible brothers know."

"Oh no, not really."

"Yes dear. The Bible brothers are memorizing a special set of verses right now. What with God and Mr. Devil involved, it'll be a lot of verses."

Ugga stuck out her protruding lower jaw even more, showing her remaining tooth to the world. "Well, it doesn't matter. The Bible brothers chanted our story first."

Uggo scratched his head, displacing little clumps of dirt and some of the less agile insects. "Dear, I kind of forgot to tell the brothers about that."

"You feral poop, this isn't fair!"

Uggo laid a hand on his sweetheart's shoulder. "Sorry, dear. It gets worse. Childbirth will become long and painful."

Ugga grunted. Her eyes misted. "No more popping out babies with a gentle tap on the tummy."

"No dear, no more."

"Oh," expostulated Ugga.

"There's more, dear. Thistlewort bushes will no longer be plentiful. We will have to plant our own. Their branches will now sport thorns. We shall have to work all day for our food."

"Bummer."

"There's more. Murderous, looting armies, disease, and telemarketers will roam o'er the land."

"Oh Uggo, shall nothing good come out of this?"

"Well Ugga, Adam says he has a word for everything."

The two adult humans approached Uggo and Ugga Ugg's fire. Uggo held out a bowl of roasted thistlewort berries.

"I say welcome to our fire, Adam, Eve," said Uggo.

"But I say, buzz off, you oozing sores," said Ugga. "You fouled our world." She focused on Eve. "Couldn't lay off that one little apple could you, you selfish little bitch!"

Adam turned to Eve and said, "Sweetheart, I sense anger toward us."

"Yes, hon," said Eve, "but it's alright. It's because she doesn't know the whole story." Eve faced Ugga and continued, "Hon, we tried to do right. We really did.

"And Ugga, why would we want to leave? Life was great there. Long, green grass, sex, warm, blue skies, pure, cool water, an abundance of thistlewort berries, more mind-blowing sex, and a funny little man who'd serve us wondrous tacos and meatballs whenever we wanted.

"But then came that evil snake with the tall, black chef's hat. 'Eat that apple,' he said. 'It'll make you smart,' he said. I told him, 'Hon, I don't need to be smart to eat thistlewort berries.

"The next day the snake ate all the thistlewort berries. Ate all the roots so that the thistlewort bushes died. The snake came back. I told him, 'Hon, I don't need to be smart to eat tacos.'"

"The next day herds of taco-eating snakes came to eat all of that funny man's offerings. The evil snake came back.

"'Are you hungry now?'" said the evil snake.

"'Yes, hon, I am,' I said.

"'Hungry enough to eat the apple?'

"I nodded. I ate the apple. God saw what we had done and made us leave the Garden."

"Gosh," said Ugga, "I didn't know that."

Adam whispered to Uggo, "She always leaves out the part about us still having Swedish meatballs to eat."

"Hey," said Uggo, "do you happen to have any of those meatballs on you?"

"Nope, we had to leave Eden in a hurry."

"Ah well," said Uggo, "have some of my thistlewort juice while we take in a red ant-black ant grudge match."

Now back to those kids we so hastily left. But there's more of them now. There's the new little Uggs: Uggub, Uggioh, Uggham, and Willard Scott. Adam and Eve had Abel and Cain. Ah, how the kids ran and frolicked. How the adults humped like rabbits and counted to two.

Then came the evil snake. The return of Bertie.

Bertie slithered over to Uggo. "Yo, Uggo, care for a new taste sensation? Do you want to eat something that makes you say, 'There's a party going on in my mouth and I'm invited.'"

Uggo nodded vigorously.

Bertie smiled as best he could in his snake form. He wiggled his forked tongue. Mushrooms fields sprang up in all directions as far as Uggo could see. One huge mushroom beckoned to Uggo; sang seductive spore songs. Uggo picked it, opened his mouth, and salivated.

Little Joe Thorvald raced toward his father and clutched his leg. "No, daddy, no. No daddy, no. Don't eat that mushroom. No, no, no."

Uggo smiled and patted little Joe's head. "Why not, little one?"

"Because mushrooms are pure evil," said little Joe.

"Aw come on, Joe, how do you know that?"

"God sent me an angel, Daddy. An angel with a tall, white hat handed me a Swedish meatball and told me to never eat mushrooms. That mushrooms are evil and will always be evil, soul snaring tools of Debbie Devil."

"Then," said Uggo, "none of our clan shall eat them."

"I have ways to make you eat them," said Bertie.

"No, no, no," said little Joe, "don't you hurt my daddy." Joe took the flint in his hand and cut off the snake's head.

"Ow," said Bertie.

"Go back to Debbie Devil," said little Joe, "it's a good thing we play Rocks, Flints, and Leaves with real flints."

The two parts of Bertie the Snake faded away.

"What shall we do?" asked Uggo. "How shall we eat? The mushrooms have covered everything. There's only mushrooms everywhere."

"If we have faith, God will feed us," said little Joe.

"Where shall we go? Who will lead us?" asked Uggo.

"God will help us," said little Joe.

Mist appeared in front of them. Out of the mist stepped Robert E. Lee and Pedro Erickson.

Lee bowed low and said, "At your service. If you would be so kind as to follow me. But please, don't eat any mushrooms, only the tacos and meatballs that rain from Heaven."

And Uggo's people did follow. Out of Africa, out of the land of mushrooms they followed, to plant humanity's seed all over the world.

But Cain would become a pimply, troubled teen. He'd eat TWO mushrooms just to rebel against his parents. We all know the rest.

The mushrooms so unbalanced his mind that he killed his brother. Rage and bloody war would stalk humanity to our day.
    Bummer.

CHAPTER 6B-BAD GUYS

"I can't believe Uggo didn't eat the whole thing," said Bertram Blackhand. He held his index finger next to his thumb. "We were so close."

Sweat rolled down Debbie Devil's face and soaked her shirt. "Bless it, we WERE close. We almost had ALL of humanity eating mushrooms for ALL time. I could have had all of humanity for my evil, love toys. And I would have had picked Joe Thorvald.

"I would raised him to be a schismatic Lutheran. Then I would have ravished his soul and his body all day long, for all time. We were so close my loins burned. Shit."

"M'lady, such language. You know you shouldn't swear."

Debbie sighed. "You're right Bertram. First, I tried with my husband to take over everything. Then, I tried to take over the world. Then Thorvald. Now, I'm swearing. Where will this downward spiral end?"

Bertram smiled. "Well, m'lady, you could always get back on track with a little Armageddon."

Debbie poked Bertram in the ribs. "Oh you rascal, you. You're just saying that to cheer me up."

"Yes," said Bertram, "and it worked."

"Ah, Bertram."

"Debbie, why don't we kick loose after you get off work. What do you say we destroy everybody's hard drive in Idaho with a killer worm."

"And, oh Bertram, after that let's plant ant colonies in people's homes."

"Anything you say, Mrs. Devil. We'll get Thorvald next time."

CHAPTER 6G-GOOD GUYS

Darn that beguiling Myrna Loy for recommending Microbarn's *Conflict at Chancellorsville: Lee Versus Hooker.* And darn her impudent attitude, saying she'd treat him to a double-decker cheeseburger and root beer float at *Pete's*. But only if he got good enough to beat her at this computer game.

Lee's blood-shot eyes darted back and forth following the movement of little blue-and-gray squares on the monitor. The muscles in his mouse hand shot messages of white-hot pain back to his brain.

The actress' beckoning smile flashed across his mind. Come on, men, send those blue units to cyber Heaven.

Stonewall Jackson knocked on the open door and strode toward Lee. He stood ramrod stiff holding half of a lemon high in the air. "My respects, sir."

Lee did not look up. He moved the mouse to the left, but the cursor did not budge. "My dear cursor, you were supposed to move west."

Jackson coughed.

Lee shook the mouse to get the cursor to move. It did. To the north. Jackson frowned. "Sir, that square you just moved represented 5,000 soldiers from my command. Are you aware that you just moved it into a prepared Federal position manned by twice as many?"

"No, sir, no," said Lee to the computer screen. "You are not courteous. I made a mistake with the mouse. An honest mistake surely. Please cease this assault."

A red flash on the monitor indicated pitched combat between Jackson's forces and the entrenched Yankees. Lee tried to move the gray square back, but the computer would not let him retreat his engaged forces.

"I'll save you, Jackson," said Lee as he moved the cursor over to a gray square labeled, "Hood."

Jackson came up behind Lee and put his hand on the General's shoulder. "With all due respect sir, your obsession with Myrna Loy and this game do not befit you." Lee's hand twitched at Jackson's touch and the cursor moved. Hood's infantry division moved onto a thin, blue line labeled, "Scott's Run." The gray square blinked twice before being replaced by a death's head.

Lee clenched his fists and thought seriously of pounding the table. "Hood's men all drowned," he sobbed. "My dear Jackson, you are responsible for the death of 5,000 brave souls."

Jackson lowered his head. "My apologies, sir."

Lee was about to reply when three blue squares slipped underneath Jackson's, surrounding the rebel force. Three large, red flashes appeared and the gray unit disappeared. A death's head took its place.

Cheering erupted from the speakers. A picture of a jubilant General Hooker filled the screen. Under Hooker's head ran the words, "Decisive victory for the Union Army."

Lee moaned and bowed his head. "My dear Jackson, this is the 42nd time in a row I've lost at *Chancellorsville*. I have trouble with this confounded Kwestar mouse. I simply cannot get my men to go to the correct places on the screen. I end up drowning my men, sending them off the board, or telling them to sleep for 34 hours. Once your corps went to Tahiti. I still don't know how I did that. Another time they attacked a pig farm."

"Did they win that battle?" asked Jackson.

"Win the battle?" said Lee with a slightly raised voice, "I sent 26,000 battle-hardened veterans armed with muskets against 49 muddy pigs. Of course, they won."

"Sorry, General, one never knows with a computer game."

"But," said Lee, "Hooker took advantage of your men's absence to launch a devastating general assault. He won in 32 seconds. 32 seconds. The game is supposed to be in real time. How real is 32 seconds?"

Lee mentally put his head in his hands.

"Do not take it so hard," said Jackson. "It's just a computer game. Lose here and nothing happens. Win that assignation with Myrna Loy and lose your favored position with God. And don't forget Mary, your wife. It would not be seemly to make her cry."

Lee did put his head in his hands. "Then it is indeed fortunate I keep losing."

"No," said Jackson, "fortune does not obstruct you. It is your good friend, Mr. Erickson. Have you never wondered why you can never order an adequate mouse?"

Lee lifted up his head. "Is that Mr. Erickson's doing?"

"Yes, sir."

"Then he has saved me from a great disaster."

"Take heart, General, you win great victories where it counts, the battlefield for Thorvald's soul."

Lee smiled and extended his hand. "Thank you for your kind words, but I still feel the need for penance."

Jackson lowered his arm and placed the lemon in Lee's outstretched hand. "I believe eating this will help."

"Yes, I do believe it will."

CHAPTER 7-GREEKS WITH GRUDGES

Fwap! Oof!

Huh? By Zeus, Joe Thorvaldes sure itched. He scratched his armpit through a hole in his mammoth-skin tunic. Nope, the itch was still there. But his ass itched more. He stood up to regard a bloody flattened helmet and a bent spear point. And, oh yes, there was a crushed face inside the helmet.

A big, long-haired Argive sprinted across the body-strewn plains toward Thorvaldes. Joe shook his head. Why couldn't he remember a thing? Must have been drinking too much fermented mammoth's milk last night.

The swift-running man in armor came up and put both his hands on Joe's shoulders.

"Fast-falling Thorvaldes, son of Zeus and Atalena, comely shepherdess of Boeotia, you have again brought death to the stallion-breaking Trojans.

"God-like man, your harder than bronze ass has crushed the life out of another Trojan hero. You have slain the spear-throwing Ornitholestes of Lycia."

"Swift-running Odysseus,"--Good, he remembered the name–"how by Zeus did I slay the spear-throwing Ornitholestes?"

Crafty Odysseus, king of Ithaca and spermatozoa of Laertes, roared. "Oh you slay me, fast-falling Thorvaldes, son of Zeus and Atalena, pretending not to remember. By Zeus, son of Cronos, you are far too modest. Sometimes I think you are not truly from Hellas."

"But come," said the noble tactician Odysseus, "let us go back to the wondrous catapult that the great goddess Athena gave us. The battle still rages. Helmet-flashing, stallion-gelding Hector still stalks the battlefield with the tenacity of a door-to-door telemarketer."

The ten-fingered, ten-toed Odysseus pointed toward the Argives' beached ships. "Hark, here comes noble Agamemnon and fierce-fighting Achilles." The noble tactician bent fingers in sequence. "With you and me, they will make four Argives at this bloody spot."

Thorvaldes nodded slowly. "Well counted, gamete of Laertes."

The noble tactician beamed like a royal mother seeing her newborn for the first time. "And fast-falling Thorvaldes, man whose ass is harder than bronze, I can even count up to one and twenty if I am naked."

"Well done, fast-falling Thorvaldes," said the arriving King Agamemnon. "Tell me, what noble Trojan shall you send to his doom when the catapult next flings you over the plains of Ilium? Shall it be helmet-flashing Hector, mighty son of King Priam?"

"Yea, Hector sounds good," said fast-falling Thorvaldes.

But such a choice summoned forth the mighty, burning wrath of Achilles, son of King Peleus and the sea nymph Thetis, from his tent of gold and silk.

Achilles, brave zygote of Peleus and Thetis, strode closer to King Agamemnon. The earth shook under the pounding blows of his hate-filled strides. "Noble Agamemnon, you humiliated me in front of all the Argives when you took the great prize Briseis from me. Now just when I slackened my burning rage to leave my tent to find a Swedish meatball and perhaps afterwards end our mighty quarrel, you dis me by picking fast-falling Thorvaldes for the mighty task."

Odysseus, ten-fingered king of Ithaca, sighed and sat down. Fast-falling Thorvaldes set his harder-than-bronze ass on a rock. These tiffs between Agamemnon and Achilles not only proved fatal to the Argive army, but could go on forever. "How about a game of Rock, Blades, Parchment?" said synapses-firing, idea-laden, well-counseling Odysseus. Ass-hardened, head-nodding Thorvaldes agreed.

"Swift-running Achilles," said Agamemnon, "Thorvaldes never quakes, never holds back when we take him to our catapult to be flung over the plains of Ilium. His harder-than-bronze ass crushes all spears, all swords, all helmets when he falls from the skies to deal doom to one stallion-breaking Trojan after another."

Well-stoked hate blazed from mighty Achilles' eyes. Winging words issued from his mouth, "Bite me!"

"While you," said Agamemnon, "skulk in your tent, nursing your unquenchable rage, as useless to the Argives as a gyro without pita bread."

God-like Achilles' mighty nostrils flared with rage. "King Agamemnon, son of Atreus, brother of Menelaus, I know you are but what am I?"

Crafty, four-limbed, many-celled Odysseus said, "Fast-falling Thorvaldes, how about some games of tic-tac-toe?"

Careful-enunciating Achilles' 32nd grave insult darkened the battle-hardened face of Agamemnon. The noble king of Sparta hurled back the stinging words, "Poc, poc, poc," and flapped his arms like a hen from the plains of Thessaly.

Self-wanking Achilles, tallest and fiercest of all the Myrmidons, put his strong right palm not on its favored place, but on his Trojan-killing sword. "Sez you."

The air sang songs of blood as he pulled his long gleaming sword from its scabbard. "I will make you pay for your insolence, dog!" said swift-running Achilles.

The noble tactician, Odysseus, man of great grammar, made his sixth 'x' in the soil and beat fast-falling Thorvaldes in tic-tac-toe for the twentieth time in a row.

Fast-falling Thorvaldes pouted. "Noble tactician, you have cheated. I can tell just by looking. You have six x's marked in this soil of Ilium and I have but three o's. And as all men of this army know six is greater than three by more than one."

"Noble Thorvaldes," said Odysseus, "fast-falling hero of all the Achaeans and Argives, man whose ass has been hardened more than bronze by the gods, that is why I am called the noble tactician."

Ass-hardened Thorvaldes shrugged.

Crafty, dual-nostrilled Odysseus drew another tic-tac-toe grid in the soil. "Care for another game?"

The fast-falling Thorvaldes shook his head. "My heart is not in it."

"Why is that?" asked the noble tic-tac-toe cheating Odysseus.

"I mean," said the hero with the ass harder than bronze, "why are we here? Why did King Agamemnon assemble all warriors, and those of his many allies to fight here for nine bloody years? Can Helen's beauty be worth the doom of so many valiant heroes?"

Brave Odysseus laughed. "Noble Thorvaldes, it is plain to me that you have never seen loin-stirring Helen. Whooee! The jugs on that beauty! Why if they contained wine, a hundred babes could suckle on her from dawn to dusk and still not drain her." Odysseus laughed again. "And my friend, I would be in line after them."

Fast-falling Thorvaldes shrugged. "If that's what you prefer, crafty tactician. My manhood soars at the thought of comely Briseis' ass. Hers is the ass that could have launched 10,000 ships. I truly understand why the wrath of Achilles flared so when King Agamemnon took her away from him."

Long-ranting Achilles' voice roared over theirs. "God-like Agamemnon, in your dreams."

Crafty Odysseus sighed. "By Zeus, those two are such windbags. Ah, but speaking of outstanding asses, how did you get one of such hardness?"

"A fair question, Odysseus, scion of Laertes. Suppose you're staggering home at dawn after drinking pure wine at your local hostelry and you meet the fierce virgin goddess Athena."

Thorvaldes paused to encourage the formation of his next thought.

"Well?" said the noble tactician.

Thorvaldes, man of slow-firing synapses hung down his head. "Let's just say, it's best not to moon her."

Sure-counting Odysseus slapped Thorvaldes's shoulder. "Don't take it so hard. Valiant Achilles is vulnerable because his mother, Thetis, did not dip both his heels into the magical river Styx."

"Why didn't she dip both heels?" asked the ass-hardened Thorvaldes.

"She suffers from an attention deficit," said Odysseus.

"Brought on by Trojan made mercury-amalgam fillings in her teeth?"

"Yes," said the anchovy-eating Odysseus, "Hector's brother, Oviraptor, put them in and fierce fighting Achilles will not leave the plains of Troy until he avenges that evil dental work."

The noble tactician shrugged and pointed to Agamemnon and Achilles. "Say, are those two men whose anger outlasts the gods still hurling insults?"

Swift-running Achilles, stronger and taller than all the warriors, sneered at the son of Atreus. "You and what army."

Bewilderment clouded King Agamemnon's face. He pointed behind him. "Why, my host of Argives."

"Oh," said slow-thinking Achilles, "well, I have an army of fierce Myrmidons. They shall cut your womanly Argives to bits small enough for dogs to eat."

"Na nana poo poo," said sure-worded Agamemnon, "I guess it's civil war then."

"Well, okay," said Achilles, fierce slayer of Trojans, Danaans, and the lemon-loving Lycians.

The two hate-flashing heroes strode close to each other and raised their gleaming swords above their noble heads.

Suddenly, a silver cloud shot down. Out of the cloud strode Pedro Erickson, meatball-making, taco-serving Chef of Heaven. A joyous goofy grin spread across meatball-making Pedro Erickson's face.

Brave-hearted Agamemnon and rarely-bathed Achilles froze in shocked amazement.

Erickson waved at Thorvaldes. "*Que tal?*"

"What?" said Thorvaldes, man of the ass harder than bronze.

"Excuse me," said the taste-creating chef of Sweden and Mexico, "I'm looking for Thorvaldes. I've come from above to help him battle evil."

Thorvaldes mind flexed in thought. "I am he, but battle evil? I know not what immortal inhabitant of Olympus you may be or what you consider evil, but I am here to restore Queen Helen to her rightful husband and to gain glory on the plains of Ilium."

Sure-spicing Erickson shook his head. "Alas no, good Thorvaldes." He pointed to Troy with its high walls and wide streets. "Helen is not in there."

Agamemnon and Achilles hurled spears at each other and missed. "By the gods, all the force in my mighty toss has been wasted," they said in synchronized complaining.

"But where is Queen Helen?" asked ass-hardened Thorvaldes.

"She is back at Argos, waiting patiently for her husband Menelaus. *Ja caramba*, is she pissed! She thinks Menelaus went off for a loaf of bread. And man, I don't even want to tell you what Clytemnestra thinks of Agamemnon's faux pas of sacrificing their daughter at Aulis."

"But mighty god, if Helen is Argos, then who is the wife of Paris?"

"Oh, that's Debbie Devil, wife of Dave Devil. She is just pretending to be Helen. Man, I tell you she is pure evil, the most evil, powerful being in the world. And I'm not a god. I only serve God."

"Mighty, mighty," said fast-falling Thorvaldes, "you must be mighty of something."

Erickson bowed. "I am Pedro Erickson, mighty creator of heavenly tacos and Swedish meatballs."

"Great meatball maker, how may I serve you?"

"Well," said the salsa-adding Erickson, "could you get yourself catapulted into Troy and kill Debbie Devil?"

Fast-falling Thorvaldes' brain flexed in thought. "Mighty meatball maker, I cannot fly into the broad streets of Troy. Our catapult has not that range. And if somehow I could climb over the city walls, how would I know for sure if I found the evil Debbie Devil? For you tell me she has the power to change shapes.

"And if I did find her, how would I kill her, this mighty force of evil? Me, armed with only a harder-than-bronze ass. Mighty Zeus must be plotting my doom to have sent you here with such a plan."

Sure-spicing Erickson pouted. "Hey, I'm a fast-food entrepreneur." He scratched his head. No plans came forth.

Suddenly, shouts rang out. Mouths dropped in awe and horror. The sky itself darkened with a swarm of little dark dots issuing from the walls of Troy.

Open-mouthed Thorvaldes pointed to the dots. Down, down came the little dots. As they fell, they appeared larger in size--as indeed does everything that falls.

"Oh dear Lord," said Erickson, "they're mushrooms! Troy had no mushrooms! Debbie Devil must have put in an order to George's Mushrooms! Achaeans, Argives, Myrmidons, close your mouths."

But the noble warriors did not, struck motionless in wonder. Mushroom after mushroom plunged down the throats of the open-jawed warriors. Down, down to the ground fell the dying heroes, their hands to their throats, their faces turning purple.

"Close your mouth, Thorvaldes," shouted Erickson. Thorvaldes did not. "If you don't, you'll become a Lutheran love toy to Debbie Devil."

"Huh?" said the open-mouthed Thorvaldes.

"You're the ancestor of a Lutheran hunk," said Erickson. "If you swallow any one of Debbie's evil mushrooms, you'll lose your soul to her. And if that happens, you'll have tilted the whole balance of the universe in favor of evil."

"Huh?" said the open-mouthed Thorvaldes as he followed the downward paths of the mushrooms.

"*Ja caramba*! I must save Thorvaldes myself."

Erickson, two-time winner of the Platinum Spatula, snapped his fingers and a bucket of meatballs smelling sweeter than any ambrosia materialized in his right hand. With his sure left hand the noble Swedish-Mexican chef hurled meatball after meatball at mushrooms heading for Thorvaldes's mouth. Time and time again his well-aimed meatballs brought sudden doom to mushrooms destined otherwise for fast-falling Thorvaldes' throat.

Silenus, an errant painter of ceremonial urns, witnessed this wondrous sight and later painted it. His urn was discovered by Cecil Crisp in 1883, who shipped it to the British Museum of Antiquity. A Colonel Hiram Whelk of the U.S.A.F. saw the urn in 1986.

The painting on the urn inspired him with an idea. That idea provided the basis for the Patriot anti-missile system.

Oh, and by the way, a particularly large mushroom rammed down the gullet of Patroclus, dear and valued friend of Achilles. Mighty rage burst the bonds of Achilles' open-jawed wonder. Swift-running Achilles shook his fists toward the sky. "By all the immortal gods, I am pissed!" The shock of mighty Achilles' voice brought the Argive warriors to their senses.

Yea, plunging mushrooms continued to fell Argives by the hundreds, but Achilles raged on and on. As by long-established custom ass-hardened Thorvaldes and all the other warriors waited quietly, motionless until long-seething Achilles would finish.

". . . and I shall kill Trojans by the dozens, nay, by the hundreds. I shall hack my way to the city walls, stepping my feet in gore all the way. I shall take fast-falling Thorvaldes with me and bash my way inside the city walls."

Everyone looked at each other. Had Achilles truly stopped ranting? No one wanted to risk his life by committing a faux pas.

Finally, brave Thorvaldes, man of the ass harder than bronze, spoke up. "Noble Achaeans, Argives, Myrmidons. Let us shut our mouths. These mushrooms, clearly sent by the Trojan-loving Apollo, have no power unless they get in our mouths. Therefore, let us resolve to shut our wonder-bound jaws."

None did so. They all looked to the swift and mighty Achilles.

Swift-running Achilles shouted louder than thunder on Mount Ossa. "Noble warriors, close your mouths."

The warriors did so.

"Gee," grumbled Erickson, "I wish I had said that."

"Spear-wielding warriors, form your ranks," yelled the crabby Achilles, "form your battalions. We shall avenge these deaths with our spears and swords. We shall sack Troy. We shall not stop until our knees wade through the enemy's blood in the wide streets of Troy. Noble Myrmidons, Argives, Aegeans, can we sack it?"

"Yes, WE CAN!"

Long-striding Achilles brandished his spear above his head. "Then charge with me."

Swift and mighty Achilles took the lead, cutting down one doomed Trojan after another. Their blood splattered his armor, their death cries floated up to Heaven, but the swift and mighty Achilles paid them no heed. "Where is Hector? I know in my valiant heart he had his treacherous hand in the mushroom attack. My soul shouts for his blood on my spear."

Slow-counting, fast-falling Thorvaldes ran panting up to Achilles. He pointed toward a death-dispatching hero standing tall in the midst of a thistlewort grove fighting twenty Argives.

Achilles, listed on page twelve of *The Encyclopedia of Classical Mythology*, ran toward his hated enemy. "Cowardly son of Priam, you despicable wretch. You killed my great friend and lifelong companion with your underhanded mushroom attack."

Helmet-flashing Hector raised his sword. "Mighty, god-like Achilles, I swear by the mighty archer Apollo, that I had nothing to do with the hail of mushrooms that brought widespread doom to your men."

"Helmet-flashing, stallion-breaking Hector, sez you!"

Party-pooping Achilles flung his spear at Hector's exposed neck, but a tall English chef, dressed in Apollo's armor, came out of a cloud to push it aside. The enraged Achilles charged and battered wife-laying Hector with a thunderstorm of sword blows. But no thrust pierced fierce Hector's shield or armor. Bertram Blackhand, culinary son of Basil and Betty Blackhand, saw to that.

Eyes ablaze, mighty Achilles threw down his sword in disgust. "Lucky Hector, cowardly Hector, it is well for you that weirdly hatted Apollo shields you or my sword would have carved out your craven heart."

"Swift and mighty, god-like Achilles, son of Peleus and Thetis," said helmet-flashing Hector, "na na na poo poo."

Eye ablaze, fierce-fighting Achilles cried out to Athena, "Great goddess and great friend of the Greeks, mighty Apollo stands in the way of my great wrath. Will you not help me?"

Pedro Erickson, clad in a dress of silver and wig of gold, whispered into Achilles' ear. "Swift and mighty Achilles, use the harder than bronze ass of Thorvaldes to crush Hector. Hurl him ass first at helmet-flashing Hector."

While clever-spicing Erickson flung a meatball at Blackhand to distract him, strong and mighty Achilles hurled Thorvaldes. Down came the doom-causing ass of Thorvaldes, crushing Hector's armor and body. Helmet-flashing Hector, son of Priam, and fierce protector of Troy died, saying, "That's the second hardest ass I've ever met."

Fast-falling Thorvaldes arose, dusted himself, and scratched another notch on his harder-than-bronze ass. Achilles bent over to strip the bronze armor from the fallen Hector.

Suddenly, an arrow shot out, burying itself in Achilles left heel. "Ow," he said and died.

Swift-counting, wise-counseling Odysseus came up and inspected the arrow in dead Achilles. "Gee, what are the odds of that?"

Fast-falling Thorvaldes grabbed both of Odysseus' shoulders. "Noble tactician, how shall we storm Troy and stop the mushroom murdering ways of Queen Helen?"

"Fear not, fast-falling Thorvaldes, I already have a plan." He turned to the blood-lusting Argives. "Valiant warriors this very day, this very hour shall see us inside the walls of Troy, slaying Trojans by the dozens, enslaving its beautiful women, and carrying off immense plunder. Avenge Achilles. Are you with me?"

The valiant Argives roared their assent. Like Thracian dogs let loose among Attican chicks their flashing swords ate their way through the flesh of the routed Trojans. But not fast enough. The mighty gates of oak slammed shut when they were but twenty paces away.

King Agamemnon, son of Atreus, brother of Menelaus, husband of Clytemnestra, king of Sparta, father of Iphigenia, brother-in-law of Helen, and valiant warrior of Mycenae said, "Oh, pooh."

"Fear not, mighty king," said crafty Odysseus, "I have a plan."

The noble tactician held up his hand and smashed it against the door. The mighty blow echoed throughout the wide streets of Troy.

"Who's there?" said a voice beyond the gate.

Odysseus, the wise tactician said, "I have an olive-and-anchovy pizza for the wise-and-aged King Priam."

"I didn't know he ordered one," said the voice, "but okay." The Trojan guard opened the mighty gate. Like the river Scamander when it floods the plains of Ilium during the spring, so did the Argive army flood through the open gate of Troy.

Crafty Odysseus' sword plunged into the neck of the guard.

"Well," said the dying man, "you're not getting a tip."

Bertram Blackhand, still dressed as Apollo with a tall, black chef's hat, and Debbie Devil, still looking like the beauteous Helen, surveyed the burning city from their tall tower.

Eye-blazing Debbie Devil shook her bony finger at Bertram. "Let's go. Another time, another place. Another blessed victory for the forces of Good."

"Well," said Bertram, "it's tough fighting the foods of God."

Below, the victorious Argives satisfied their manly lusts with the newly-widowed women of Troy and feasted on Pedro Erickson's shredded-beef tacos until Boreas, the goddess of the dawn, appeared.

CHAPTER 7B-BAD GUYS

Debbie Devil glared at Bertram Blackhand. "Well Heaven, sending the soul of Joe Thorvald to the Trojan war sure didn't work, did it?"

"No m'lady, it didn't," mumbled Bertram.

Smoke shot out the nostrils of the Evil woman. "I feel so unused. I guess every English chef but you knows those Trojans and Greeks were all bi or gay. I want to jump that hunky, hetero Lutheran's bones. I don't want anything to do with a gay man."

Bertram's black chef's hat stiffened. "Well, I must say, that not a very politically correct attitude to take."

Flames shot out of Debbie's nostrils. "I don't want to be politically correct. I'm Mrs. Devil, pure evil."

"I'm just disappointed in you, that's all," whispered Bertram.

"I heard that," yelled Debbie. She snapped her fingers and turned Bertram's chef's hat into a dunce cap.

"Hey," said Bertram, "you really know how to hurt a guy."

"And speaking of guys," said Debbie, "where's that slacker Mr. George been?"

"He has the mushroom concession at the national Young Republicans Convention."

"Well, all I can say about this mess," said Debbie Devil. "is that I wish I had your brother Pedro Erickson on my side instead of you. Far more competent."

"Hey, I'm learning on the job," said Bertram.

"And what did you learn?"

"My brother, Pedro, is as you say, quite good," said Bertram. He held his index finger next to his thumb. "Missed getting a mushroom into Joe's throat by that much. Bless that Pedro! Next time no one like him will be around Joe Thorvald's reincarnation."

"Then who will be around Joe?" said Debbie.

"Jesus."

CHAPTER 7G--GOOD GUYS

"Splendid throwing, my dear Erickson. You did a first-rate job of knocking down those mushrooms."

"Gee thanks, General, it was nothing. What do you think we culinary students do all day? Study?"

"Still sir, you did fine work."

"But General you were the one who placed me correctly in the midst of the Trojan war. How did you know?"

Lee almost smiled. "I can see their progression. The first life form, then higher life forms as in dinosaurs, and then the first human Joe Thorvald outside the garden of Eden. They simply looked for the first written story about humanity after that."

"That should have been *The Epic of Gilgamesh,*" said Erickson.

"Yes," said Lee, "but have you read it? It is a joyless, disjointed, boring read. I really think that ten of thousands of Yankees and Southerners took arms in the Late Unpleasantness just to avoid reading *The Epic of Gilgamesh* in public school.

"And if you are the Supreme Evil; well sir, there's no one to make you read it. Now, *The Iliad* is something different altogether. That's a rattling good yarn and that's what those evil people read."

"Well reasoned," said Erickson.

Lee bowed slightly. "Thank you."

"Where will they attack next?"

"I suspect those people are quite frustrated at this point. They'll forget all their training and go for a mindless, frontal assault on our strongest point just like Grant at Cold Harbor."

"Wow," said Erickson, "you really think they'll try to take down Jesus Christ, to get to Joe Thorvald."

"Yes." Lee couldn't decide whether to smile or grimace.

"Then," said the reincarnated Mexican-Swedish chef, "we'll have nothing to do. Jesus, son of Almighty God, can take care of himself."

"I reckon so," said Lee.

"*Ja bueno*, then we can take off a lot of time. What do you say we rustle up several rounds of root-beer floats and break out your complete DVD collection of *The Patty Duke Show?*"

Lee decided it was proper to smile after all. "Only if, my dear Erickson, you allow me to provide the floats."

"*Taks a mikka*, my dear Lee."

But Lee was already picking up the phone. "Hello, Heaven Brothers Root Beer. . ."

CHAPTER 8-BROUGHT TO YOU

The odd couple watched the holy man preach to the immense, hungry throng. Though both were pagan Roman merchants, one tried to walk in the path of goodness and sold grain, while the other sold mushrooms.

"Great Caesar's ghost," said Josephus Thorvaldus, the short, corpulent owner of Thorvaldus Breads, "did you see what he just did? He took only five barley loaves and two little fish from a little boy and fed this crowd of thousands. It's a miracle."

Quintus Fabian, the towering owner of Quintus Mushrooms and life-long friend of Josephus, scowled. "Wasn't the boy carrying lutefisk?"

"He was," shouted Josephus Thorvaldus, "but the bits on the ground are Norwegian salmon. Truly this man is the Son of God."

Quintus ground a cockroach beneath his sandal. "Oh sure, he could be that. But he means something more important to us."

"How's that?"

"Well, my dear Josephus, do you think our good Emperor Tiberius will renew my contract to supply mushrooms to the Imperial Court if this agitator Jesus decides to multiply mushrooms for free?"

"Gee, Quintus, I didn't think of that."

Quintus wiggled his tall black hat at his friend. "And you, my dear friend, what are you going to do if this man mass produces loaves, perhaps even ciabatta, just by passing baskets around?"

Josephus stammered, "Uh, yes. Uh, no, uh, gee, I don't know."

"Will you even have a company if he sets up shop next to you? You know, Josephus, his production costs are zero."

Josephus paled. "Oh my."

"His distribution costs are zero. His customers come to him. Face it, Josephus, he'll bankrupt you."

"Oh no, the Son of God wouldn't do that to me, would he?"

Quintus sneered. "My dear Josephus, if you were the Son of God and you had the power to monopolize the bakery industry, what would you do?"

Josephus sighed and wiped his brow. "Sure is hot, isn't it?"

"Yes, it is. But not too hot."

"Not too hot for what?"

Quintus chuckled. "Oh my dear friend, not too hot to kill Jesus, corporate raider."

Quintus took the sack off his back and removed a silver-plated executive bow and arrow. He drew back the arrow and waited for the annoying worshipers to move away from Jesus. Quintus hated shooting the wrong target. "It's means one less potential customer," he always said.

Josephus stood still. Why couldn't he stop his friend? Why couldn't he ever stop his friend? Act, Josephus, act. Stop this outrage.

The arm that drew back the bow string began to wobble. Quintus pointed the bow to the ground and released the tension. "Rats and plagues, will those people never get out of the way?"

The crowd finally parted from Jesus.

"Now's my chance. Now's my chance." said Quintus. He fumbled his attempt to re-notch the arrow. "More rats and plagues." After two more miscues, Quintus raised the bow.

"Oh great gobs of eel bowels," yelled Quintus, "now his disciples are around him, again. By Jupiter, sometimes it just isn't worth the aggravation to kill a man."

"Son of God," said Josephus.

"Whatever."

Soon, the needy followers parted from a weary Jesus. Quintus re-aimed his bow. Quintus drew back the bow string.

Jesus turned his head and stared into Josephus' eyes. Josephus' heart burned, burning away his sin, burning away his moral timidity, burning away any desire to try mushrooms.

"No, fiend." Josephus' arm shot out and pushed his friend's bow to the side. The arrow missed its intended target by a foot and plunged through the necks of the world's last two unicorns.

"Why did you do that?" said Quintus as he reached for another arrow.

"Because I have a great idea to help you," lied Josephus.

"My dear friend, you?" said Quintus.

"Yes, me. Why don't you merge with the Son of God. Think of the benefits; salvation and zero costs of production."

Quintus stroked his beard. "Hmm, yes. I rather think you have something there, my friend." His face lit up and his eyes sparkled. "By Jupiter, that will work. It will, it will."

He waved his hand across the sky. "I can see it now; angels flying above the Colosseum during gladiatorial contests trailing tapestries. And the tapestries will have a big picture of the Son of God smiling, holding one of my mushrooms. The slogan will be, "For a divine taste, buy Quintus Mushrooms.

"What do you think, my friend?"

"Yes, yes, I like it," said Josephus. "But oh drat, he's heading off to the mountain to be alone again. Oh well, let's go home."

"No," said Quintus. He grabbed Josephus by the wrist. "It was your idea, you're coming with me."

They rushed after Jesus as fast as their panting bodies and flabby legs would take them.

"Hey you," said Quintus, "I require a moment of your time."

Jesus turned around and regarded the mushroom magnate with weary eyes and heart. "Yes?"

"I'd like to make you my spokesman for my campaign to push Quintus Mushrooms to the world's bumpkins," said Quintus.

"Get thee behind me, evil advertiser, mushroom man," said Jesus.

"Is that a no?" asked Quintus.

Jesus waved a hand and the earth shook. A chasm opened between the mushroom magnate and Himself.

"Why do you think I'm evil?" asked Quintus.

"Mr. Devil tempted me for forty days in the desert," said Jesus. "I know his sort of evil and I know your sort of evil, too. Your sort comes from Mrs. Devil."

Quintus spat on Jesus' tunic, spun on his heel, and walked away. Josephus shivered. Josephus' mouth moved. He wanted to say something to his friend. Couldn't. He looked into the gentle eyes of the Son of God. He saw warmth and peace that passed beyond his understanding.

"Well, Josephus," said Jesus, "what will it be? Will you follow the insatiable, empty ways of the Empire and its mushrooms or will you follow me?"

Josephus recognized the full horror of decadent Rome, his grasping friend, and the mushroom. He saw too, a chance for freedom, for pure foods, and eternal salvation.

"Yippee, I'm with you. I shall follow you everywhere. My bakeries shall feed your followers. I shall record your every move."

Jesus smiled.

And so Josephus wrote down in detail Jesus' life, including thirty of Christ's sermons that didn't make it into Matthew, Mark, Luke, or John.

When Josephus died, his brother sent his gospel to the Dead Sea caves. Josephus' account arrived a scant hour after the inhabitants sealed the Cave of Writings. For the want of a priority stamp a gospel was lost to the world.

Oh, by the way, Quintus Mushrooms thrived. Mrs. Devil made sure Romans everywhere developed an insatiable taste for the fungus.

Three-hundred-seventy-seven years later, hordes of lusty meat-eating barbarians crossed the frozen Rhine. Four years later, they sacked and conquered effete mushroom-eating Rome. The Dark Ages descended upon the civilized world. Bummer.

CHAPTER 8B-BAD GUYS

Debbie Devil squirted another ketchup stripe on the wall of the meat locker. "Seven," she said.

Bertram Blackhand strode into the meat locker. "Hello, hello, sorry I'm late. I was doing some freelance work for the Dodgers. Do you think anyone will ever figure out that I'm the one keeping the Cubs out of the World Series?"

Debbie stamped her feet. Fumes shot out her nostrils. "No, why should they when they've seen your latest attempt on Joe Thorvald?"

"Well, I admit I was bit optimistic," said Bertram.

"A bit optimistic," yelled Debbie. "What made you think you, a mere English chef, could take on the Son of God?"

"Have you ever tasted my mad-cow sausage?"

"Auggh," said Debbie, "you stupid fool, you failed, you stupid fool."

Bertram's tall chef's hat stiffened. "Hey, I resemble that remark. Sure, I failed with Joe, but I did plant the seeds for the destruction of the great Roman Empire."

"To Heaven with the Roman empire," yelled Debbie, "I'm horny, so horny for that Lutheran hunk. I want Joe Thorvald. You'd better come up with a better plan to get him, or I'll make your daughter in Cleveland date a theoretical economist."

Bertram paled. He wobbled, bumping into a six-foot high crate of Uncle Jasper's Lard on a Stick. "No, don't."

"Perhaps I should get a hold of Mr. George and see what he would do. Where is he, by the way?"

"He's on a Viking Cruise ship in the Caribbean. He's serving mushrooms to anti-spam legislators."

"Hmm," said Debbie, "good plan. Now, tell me your new idea to get Thorvald."

"It's foolproof," said Bertram, "I'll put him in Viking times. Lots of good ol' pagan chaos back then. I should be able to sneak in and get a mushroom down Joe's throat one way or another."

"No you won't," said Debbie, her eyes flashing red, "this time I'm going; even though it'll mean using up a day of vacation."

"You could call in sick," said Bertie.

Debbie smoothed her uniform. "Oh no, that wouldn't be right."

CHAPTER 8G--GOOD GUYS

Pedro Erickson burped. Lee thought it rude to burp, then thought it better to follow suit and so, eliminate any embarrassment Erickson might feel.

"Urp."

Erickson moaned. "I can't believe we had sixteen root-beer floats, each."

"Yes," said General Lee, "they are mighty fine libations. I'm quite partial to them."

The big board began to flash: DEBBIE DEVIL ON THE WARPATH.

"Time to break camp," said Lee. "I'll put the mugs in the dumb waiter. You put the videos back on the shelf. Hurry, hurry, pure evil has stolen a march on us. We don't even know where or when she'll show up."

Lee worked like three Confederate generals clearing the big table of empty root-beer mugs. He clapped his hands after he put the last one away.

"No, no, my dear Erickson, no. You're not putting the tapes back in order. Now, how do you expect me to find my favorite *Patty Duke* episodes? That one where she runs the school newspaper always makes me smile in times of turmoil. And now because of you, it'll be difficult to find."

Erickson's eyes blinked. His quivered as "I'm so sorry" and "Gettysburg" tried to exit his lips at the same time.

"There, there," said Lee, "it's my fault. My apologies for my unseemly outburst. I'm just upset with myself for not fully anticipating the enemy."

Erickson blew his nose on a monogrammed Belgian-lace handkerchief.

"You know, my dear Erickson, what I'd like to eat now?"

"What?"

Lee sighed inside. "Lutefisk enchiladas."

"Really?" asked Erickson.

"Really."

Erickson smiled. He didn't get many chances to cook haute Swedish-Mexican for the old gentleman.

CHAPTER 9-ROAD TRIP

King Joe Thorvald stood at the bow of the longboat. He ran his rough hard hands over the dragon's head that served as the symbolic eyes of the boat and stared at its gold scales, blood-red eyes, and open mouth, packed with sharp, serrated fangs. Sometimes the dragon's head even scared Joe. Brr!

"Meow." Something soft and warm brushed against his leggings.

The Terror of the North reached down and petted the calico. "Greetings, Eleanor, how fare you this morning?"

Eleanor purred.

Joe squatted to look the calico in the eyes. He sighed. "Oh Eleanor, why do those Britons dread us so? Why must they run to the forests like sheep scenting a wolf? Ah Thor, why can we not act like kin to each other?"

He scratched Eleanor's chin. Eleanor tried to raise her beautiful tail. Couldn't. A flat little stump twitched where the rest of the tail should have been. Eleanor looked up and meowed.

Joe sighed again. "Ah, as usual, you meow truly. Our cheating at chess, egging the townsfolk, writing "Vikings reign" on their monastery walls, and taking their Shetland ponies out for joy rides. Those Britons hold those acts against us."

Eleanor meowed and twitched her stump.

"And they took vengeance against you. Sorry, Eleanor." He reached into his Olaf's-of-Trondheim tote bag that hung by his side and retrieved a loaf of Roman Meal bread.

Joe looked at the loaf with disdain. His lungs hungered for air. His breath rasped. Roman bread was not fit food for a warrior. And it had been hundreds of years since the Romans had been worthy fighters. He felt proud to be a Viking and a Thorvald.

King Joe Thorvald pounded with fists of iron on his barrel chest and yelled his war cry. "Ack! Ack! Ptuie! Ptuie!" Fierce Viking phlegm hurled like a spear from his mouth. Cursed bronchitis!

He pulled out a long white stick from his gray-on-dark-gray designer bag and offered a slice to the cat. Eleanor's wolfed it down in three bites.

Joe looked at the white stick in his hand. "Lutefisk, it looks and tastes so harmless like this."

Bah! But when they boiled it in water, like all the Vikings did, one need not ask the gods why the Norsemen went berserk.

Just thinking of the cooked lutefisk of his companions turned his stomach into a battleground. Lutefisk looked like boiled pus. It smelled like rotting chicks. It tasted like phlegm. It felt like eel bowels. Thank Thor, the vile substance couldn't talk.

Still, by Thor, it was fitter sustenance than mushrooms. Joe's mind harkened back to his childhood, back to when golden wheat waved softly in the fields and peace and harmony ruled the fjords and valleys of Norway.

Then that Frankish mushroom bearer came to his village of Narvik. The monk gave his name as Debevil of Aachen, but Joe doubted the man's devotion to his Holy Trinity, especially when Debevil tried to disrobe him.

Monk?! Man?! Debevil looked more like a temptress with those gentle curves, that golden braided hair, and those lively blue eyes. Yet, with her long, bony nose and those two small gnarled horns on her forehead, she was not his type. Maybe if her breasts had been bigger.

The false god-eater, Debevil, presented her mushrooms to all the villagers. The good folk needed just one look at her offerings to reject her as evil. And by extension, they rejected the monk's Christian god. Perhaps that was Debevil's plan.

Not so for the low minded. Those peasants embraced the new god, or not, on whim. But how they all abandoned themselves to the mushrooms.

Tears streamed down Joe's hardened face. He was but a little boy when the Troubles happened. He recalled how his kingly father spoke with golden words for their great traditions. Hold true to their faith in the old gods! Hold true to their age-old way of trading wheat for tacos with the great seafaring Mayans! But how his stout-hearted father raged like the northern wind against mushrooms.

The village voted in favor of wheat. But the spear through his father's stout-hearted chest gainsayed that decision. All night long the mushroom-demented fanatics pillaged, looted, raped, murdered, and committed other Viking faux pas.

The mushroom men culled the wheat-eating remnant from the village. The gods-fearing homeless folk took to the sea. Four-and-twenty storm-tossed days later, they beached their longboats on the tiny sea-swept island of Kullervo. A small holy man instructed them in the ways of drying and cooking lutefisk. No wonder the holy man lived there alone.

Joe's Narvikans rowed ever southward. On days when they ate fish from the sea, they traded wood carvings. On days when they ate dry lutefisk, they traded insults. When they ate cooked lutefisk, they fought with their fists.

The calico's pitiful meowing brought Joe back to the present. "What's wrong, Eleanor?"

Eleanor's nose twitched. She spun around and fell down. The cat vomited great white waves of lutefisk.

Terrible Fenrir! He smelled it, too. The foul, fetid, stomach-churning, blood-curdling odor of mushroom stew wafting from the south flung him back against the dragon's head.

Joe, his heart as flaming red as his hair, unsheathed his long sword. He screamed his Viking war cry to the heavens until the crew gathered around him.

The men felt no need to ask their king the cause of his fury. Their enraged noses told them.

Joe pointed his gleaming sword to the offending village of Cayeux. "Fellow Narvikans, how my sword thirsts for Frankish blood. Remember what that Frankish monk brought to our village?"

"We do," shouted the Vikings.

"He brought mushrooms!"

"Evil mushrooms," they chanted.

"Mushrooms brought discord, brought death, brought exile!"

"Evil mushrooms!"

"Brought exile to the sea, made us eat cooked lutefisk!"

"Evil mushrooms!"

Joe's eyes blazed as he pointed to Cayeux. "That village cooks mushrooms! It cooks them now! What fate awaits that village?"

"Unslakeable flames for all its huts."

"What fate awaits those mushroom cookers?"

"Bloody death for them all!"

Mushroom-hating rage coursed through the veins of the once placid Vikings, turning them into machines of death, turning them into berserkers.

Splash! Into the frothing surf leaped Erik the Black, he of immense strength, great courage, and limited vocabulary. As the waves swept around his leggings, he unsheathed his trusty sword and yelled so lustily Thor in Valhalla could hear him. "Kill, kill, kill!"

Joe pointed his two-handed axe toward Cayeux. "I must bathe my arms in their mushroom-nourished blood. Follow me!"

Joe leaped over the side. The blade of his axe did not. It impaled itself in the longboat's sturdy gunwale. Joe pole vaulted into the waves.

He burst out of the surf and shouted with the strength of ten gods, "Hoo ha! It's cold. It's really lutefisking cold. Hoo ha!"

That outburst kind of daunted the Vikings on board. "I dunno," said the red-bearded Bengt Bengtson, he of the arms bigger than dragons' necks. "I don't fancy cold water. Couldn't we come back in August when the water is a bit warmer?"

Shame coursed through Joe's stout heart. He could hear the ringing sounds of combat, of Erik the Black alone against one hundred men.

And he was getting used to the water. Fire-eyed Joe freed his axe from the gunwale and whirled it above his head. "Are we not men?"

"We are Vikings!" roared his men.

Valiant Joe needed only one hand to point his death-singing axe toward the huts of Cayeux. "That town cooks mushrooms! What shall we do to them?"

"Evil mushrooms. Kill them all!" shouted his crew.

"Then follow me."

Argon Bjornson raised his gleaming sword and placed his right hand on the gunwale. Blood drained from his face and out of a tiny hole on his pinky.

"Ow. A splinter. By Thor, that hurts." The rest of the crew jostled around, viewing the tiny red dot with ashen faces.

"Gee," said Argon's brother Freon, "that's nasty. You'd better sit down and get your strength back." He shook his head. His long, matted blond hair swayed beneath his helmet. "Besides, I been wanting a chance to discuss plate tectonics with you."

"Oh ho," said the wounded Argon, "so that Mayan priest did talk to you."

"Yo ho," said the vermin-ridden Freon, "he said that Africa and South America were once joined together."

"Oh ho," said the healing Argon, "how did the Mayan know that?"

"Yo ho, it seems they found fossils of the mesosaurus in both continents."

Meanwhile, back at the battlefield, Erik the Black hacked away; Cayeux's peasants armed with cudgels and staves were no match for the fierce sword wielder. "Ha! Ha!" said Erik at length.

Suddenly, mushroom-tipped arrows flew into Argon's and Freon's open mouths. "Oh ho, gmpf, ift," said Freon and pitched forward.

Fierce Joe raged at the shore. "Lucky shots." He turned to his men. "Did you see that? Did you see those evil mushrooms kill the fierce Bjornson brothers?"

"We did," they shouted. "Evil mushrooms. Kill them all." Their blood roused; they bounded into surf heedless of splinters and the icky coldness of the sea.

Up, up raised the berserkers' thirsty swords. Down, down they fell on the peasants' mushroom stained faces. And yet Vikings fell too. For there was that archer, the one in the long flowing, white dress, with the blue rope around her slender waist. With the speed of a Valkyrie she loosed one mushroom-tipped arrow after another into the charging pack of berserkers.

With the fleetness of reindeer spying mates during Lappland's annual-mating day, long-legged Joe, reached the golden-haired archer as she reached into her quiver. Between rasping breaths, Joe asked, "Before my axe drinks your blood, I must know your name so that I may sing of your valiant deeds during the winter campfires."

The fair archer bowed her head. "It's Chlamydia Lipschitz."

Joe's eyes flashed merriment. "And I'm Erik Fatbottom!"

Chlamydia gazed at her Viking foe with the cold eyes of a fjord snake. "My father, a lost Norse clown, stayed just long enough to give me that name. I've hated all Norsemen since. Wanted to kill them all before they could become fathers and give names to their daughters."

She drew back the bow and loosed her lethal arrow. The mushroom splattered against Joe's chest. Chlamydia's eyes widened. "But you're still alive!" she meant to say before Joe's dread axe made her hips lonesome for her torso.

The carnage was over. Joe doffed his coverlet and removed her arrow from one of the many Mayan tacos sewn to his chain mail. "Best lutefisking armor in the world. Tasty too." He took a well earned bite of the shredded beef wonder, sat down, and smiled.

His surviving men flushed with the exuberant energy of youth, decided to party a bit longer by beheading all the town's brown-haired men.

And so perished Cayeux's and Europe's one painter, William the One Painter of Europe. Viking raids would terrorize the God-fearing coasts of Europe for another two hundred years. And it would be 600 more years before the revival of the arts during the Renaissance. And rational discussion of continental drift? Gone for a millennium. Bummer.

CHAPTER 9B-BAD GUYS

Debbie Devil drew another vertical stripe. "Drat! That Joe Thorvald is one tough cookie."

Bertram Blackhand smiled behind his hand. "It's not so easy to get a Lutheran to eat mushrooms is it?"

"No!" Debbie flung out her hands knocking over a stack of Kansan, corn-fed eels. "How did he resist? I didn't see Pedro Erickson anywhere."

"But m'lady, you saw his influence. Tacos were in the village. Just to eat a taco is to reflect on God's goodness. And do you think the Mayans would have even discovered Norway in the 800s without the help of Pedro Erickson and General Lee?"

"No, I suppose not," said Debbie.

"And what about lutefisk?" asked Bertram. "Lutefisk didn't even exist twenty years before their arrival in Norway. That was Erickson's work as well."

Debbie nodded. "Yep, Pedro Erickson is one tough cookie."

"Well, just be thankful you didn't run across Stuffy, The Scourge Of All Evil."

Debbie shivered. "Sometimes fighting Good seems so easy from this locker room. Maybe we should give up with Joe Thorvald. Maybe I should settle for that Unitarian, Steve the stock boy."

Bertie handed Debbie a Twizzler. "Here, m'lady, you look like you could use one. Remember, it's always worth fighting for a truly evil cause. The greater the setbacks, the greater the satisfaction at our eventual victory.

"But enough of this mid-eternal life crisis. Think of possessing Joe Thorvald's soul. Think of his Lutheran manhood inside of you. Excelsior, m'lady, excelsior."

Debbie smiled. "Thank you, Bertie, you've always been a true, twisted friend."

Bertie bowed.

"And sorry for all those times I threatened to destroy your chef's hat and for all those times in the future when I will do it again."

"Oh m'lady, think nothing of it. After all, you are the Supreme Evil."

"Yes, I suppose you're right," said Debbie. "Still I prefer if you handle Joe Thorvald for a while."

"As you wish, m'lady."

"And take Mr. George with you," said Debbie.

Bertie flipped through his appointment book. "No, I'm sorry m'lady. He developing the internet. But have no fear, I shall be quite happy to take up this challenge again."

"Where will you attack and tempt Joe's soul?"

Bertie stroked his chin. "You know I rather fancy spending some quality evil time down in sunny 16th-century Spain."

Bertie flipped through his Entertainment book, stared at a coupon and frowned. "Nope, this 33 percent-off coupon for 16th-century Spain isn't valid until Tuesday."

Bertie flipped some more. "Ah, 16th-century Germany has a 50 percent-off coupon that's expires today. At least, that's the right time period."

He looked at his watch and waved to Debbie. "Evil deeds await."

CHAPTER 9G-GOOD GUYS

"My dear sir," said Lee, "your prescience astounds me. How did you know to start up the Viking-Mayan taco-for-lutefisk trade by the early 9th century? How did you know to create lutefisk in the waters of Norway before that? Inquiring Confederate, military minds want to know."

"Tut, tut, General. I'm not all that smart. From 550 A.D. on I had the Mayans discover every land on Earth and trade tacos with every power on Earth."

"Really?"

"Oh yes," said Pedro Erickson, "in 553 A.D., Justinian the Great of the Byzantine Empire signed a twenty-year trade agreement with Poobah the Mighty of the Mayan Empire."

"Why is it I never heard of this?" asked Lee.

"Well, his successor came to the throne in 565 A.D. and abrogated the treaty. After a brief Byzantine-Mayan naval skirmish off Sicily in 566 A.D. all contact between the Mediterranean and Central America stopped for nearly a millennium.

"As for the Vikings and other peoples such as in Africa, Greenland, and Australia; well, they never kept good records."

Lee shook his head. "Astounding, astounding. But how did you know to put lutefisk off Norway in the early 9th century?"

Erickson smiled. "I didn't. I created lutefisk in every sea at the beginning of every century since the birth of Christ. It's just that the Vikings of that time were the first ones willing to eat the fish. Bit of luck there."

"Not at all," said Lee. "You're too modest. All great generals make their own luck."

Erickson bowed. "Why, thank you."

"But there's one aspect I don't quite comprehend," said Lee. "Why didn't the Mayans harvest their own lutefisk instead of trading for it?"

"Well," said Erickson, tacos became so entwined with the Mayans' everyday and religious life that fishing for food became unthinkable. Then in 925 A.D. mushroom-eating invaders from central Mexico extinguished Mayan civilization with all of its scientific and culinary achievements."

"Astounding." said Lee. "Sir, your work in this last battle was first-rate. Care to join me for some root beer and Dobie Gillis while we plot our next campaign?"

"General, I'd be delighted. Mind if I bring along some caramel popcorn?"

"My dear Erickson, that would be splendid."

CHAPTER 10-A LITTLE TIFF

"Guten *Tag, Herr* Thorvald, how do you fare?" asked Martin Luther.

Josef Thorvald shook his head and pointed to his ears. "My apologies Brother Luther, I cannot hear you. I have wax in my ears."

Luther smiled. "Then *Herr* Thorvald, you had better remove the wax."

The good Czech shook his head. "Sorry, can't hear you. I have wax in my ears."

Luther, a quick study, forbore speaking again. With a burst of inspiration that would shake the world time and again, he walked over and grabbed Thorvald's left hand and raised it to the deaf man's ear.

Thorvald's face erupted into a *Peasant's-Quarterly* smile. Quick as feldspar his right hand shot to his other ear. His pinkies fell to their excavating job with the enthusiasm of a gourmet Andalusian pig searching for bon bons. "Yo ho," said a stout, beaming Thorvald as he flicked away the fearful blockage, "I'll be able to hear you now, Brother Luther."

"I'm glad to hear it," said the corpulent Luther. The two one-time hamlet-to-hamlet traders in pestilence insurance shared a good laugh.

"How do you fare, *Herr Thorvald?*" asked Luther.

Thorvald shrugged. "Like this, like that."

Luther put a hand on Thorvald's shoulder. "You cannot fool me old friend, we sold too many insurance policies together."

Thorvald moved his foot back and forth in the dusty main street. "Okay, I murdered my best friend, slept with his wife, stole his Andalusian pigs, burned down his house, and cheated at checkers."

Judgment furrowed Luther's brows. "*Herr* Thorvald, you've been bad."

Thorvald hung down his head. "I cannot tell a lie. I know it."

Luther wagged his finger at the contrite soul. "I hope you were suitably punished."

"Yes, I was. I paid an enormous fine to my friend's wife. And as she no longer had a husband, I wedded her. As for checkers cheating, I endured seven long days in the public stocks."

"Tsk, tsk," tsked a tsking Luther. "You still have a lot to answer for with your Heavenly Father. It distresses me greatly to know that you are doomed to burn in brimstone for all eternity. Almighty God looks upon adulterous, murderous checkers cheaters with great disfavor."

Thorvald smiled and shook his head. "Yo ho, Brother Luther, not to worry. I purchased these indulgences for twenty golden thalers."

Luther raised his left eyebrow. "What's an indulgence?"

Thorvald reached into his vermin-ridden coat and produced a sheet of Cremonan vellum. "Here."

Luther read aloud the document. "The bearer of this note is hereby absolved of all spiritual punishments for murder, arson, theft, and adultery. Signed, Brother Tetzel."

The great man reread the words. "Hmm."

"Hmm, what?" said Thorvald.

"Well, this document appears noticeably mute about your checkers cheating chicanery."

Thorvald's jaw dropped. His face took on the shade of a fever patient after three bleedings.

"Fear not, *Herr* Thorvald. We shall obtain an indulgence for that from this Brother Tetzel. It should be a simple matter."

Thorvald brightened. "And where does this great man reside?"

"In Wittenburg," said Luther.

"Let's be off to see the great man."

And the merry, half-damned duo, skipped and cavorted on the yellow, dirt road to Wittenburg, singing Top-Twenty Gregorian chants. As they rounded a bend in the road, they heard loud, feline sniffling.

"Sounds like a lion," said Luther.

"Sounds like a cowardly lion," said Thorvald.

"But a lion, nevertheless, with giant teeth and claws as sharp as, as . . ." Luther flung up his hands to Heaven. "Hear me, oh merciful Lord, help me finish my simile."

Thorvald motioned the monk to stand back. "Fear not, while you communicate with the Almighty I shall brain this lion with my trusty loaf of year-old pumpernickel bread."

It's too fearful and gory to describe how Thorvald's pumpernickel battered the lion's brains, so let us move on to the traveler's meal of lion steaks with Bernaise sauce.

Flames leaped from burning straw to the skillet made from a large tin breast plate. Luther's immense Saxon nose flared with delight.

"So, you decided to become a monk," said Thorvald.

"*Ja*," said Luther, "and you, why did you stop selling pestilence policies?"

"Oh that," said Thorvald, "the plague came to our valley. Killed off half the population. All Bavaria Insurance went bankrupt."

"Bad luck."

Thorvald shrugged.

Luther took a long sniff of the sizzling steaks. "Ah my friend," said Luther, "life doesn't get any better than this."

But the great man was wrong. Just then, three bikini-clad damsels from the European Union's Intertemporal Subsidy Program of Agriculture danced toward them and presented them with a tossed salad and a shaker of thistlewort seed. The three damsels curtsied, and vanished with three little pips.

"Wow," said the wide-eyed Thorvald, "what a meal!"

Luther's hands gestured all over the horizon. "But those damsels! Wow!"

Thorvald fixed Luther with a stare that couldn't have been chillier even if his eyes had been gray. "Didn't notice, I'm a one-woman adulterer."

"Hand me another lion jerky, would you?" said Thorvald.

"Sure." Luther removed his rucksack and removed three strips, one for Thorvald, one for himself, and one for the misshapen beggar by the side of the road.

The beggar held out his gnarled hands. "Alms for the poor, alms for the poor."

"Here," said Luther, "have a nice lion jerky."

The beggar took the strip and gummed it furiously. "No good," he cried and he thrust out his hands again.

Luther's eyes misted as he gave the man the sack of thistlewort seed. "Here, friend."

The beggar's eyes became as big as the just-completed dome of Saint Peter's. "Yo ho, I'm rich. I'll sow this and I shall reap this. I shall reserve half of the seeds from each new crop and sow them time and again all over the land."

And lo, he did so, and so did his multitudinous descendants unto this day, which is why bikini-clad damsels from European Union's Intertemporal Subsidy Program of Agriculture are so active. Now you know.

Luther and Thorvald stood before the thick oaken door to Brother Tetzel's ornate house. "Here goes," said Thorvald as he raised the knocker and pounded it against the door.

The door creaked open and the Dominican friar Tetzel peered out. "Yes?"

Luther spoke, "My Czech friend would like to buy an indulgence."

Tetzel peered at Thorvald. "What's he done?"

"Cheated at checkers."

"Cheated at checkers!" Tetzel crossed himself, twice. He stared down his nose at Thorvald. "It'll cost you two sacks of thistlewort seeds."

Thorvald pouted. "Two sacks? That's exorbitant, you rat."

Tetzel sneered. "The Christian church chastens churlish, chubby Czech checkers cheaters."

"That alliteration isn't very Christian," said Luther.

"And what would an Augustinian monk know about doctrine save what we Dominicans tell you?" asked Tetzel.

Luther skulked away. Didn't want to ask the sneering friar for the same answers that wouldn't ever feel right again.

"Oh blast it, blast it," shouted Luther.

Thorvald burst into his friend's room. "What in Heaven is wrong?"

Luther motioned with his dripping quill to the heap of crumpled vellum in the corner. "Nothing is right. Nothing comes out. I know the gist of what I want to say to Tetzel. I've spent all week reading the Scriptures. But nothing comes out."

Thorvald nodded. "You've got writer's block."

Luther smashed both fists onto the narrow writing table. "Yes! Yes! Yes!"

"Mind if I help?" asked Thorvald.

Luther got up and grasped both his friend's hands. "Would you?"

Thorvald nodded and sat down by the desk. He dipped the quill into the ink pot and wrote, "Selling indulgences is bad."

"There," he said.

Luther shook his head. "That's it?"

"Okay," said Thorvald. He wrote some more and read, "1) Selling indulgences is bad. 2) Very bad."

Luther favored Thorvald with a weak smile. "Thanks friend, but I truly have to say it in my own words, sooner or later."

Thorvald nodded and went through the door on his first attempt. He thought over the words on his opus. His heart swelled with pride. If only the Holy Catholic Church could read his compelling words, surely it would reform itself. Surely, a revitalized Church bursting with newfound purity could convert everyone and bring God's holy salvation to everyone.

Zeal fired his heart. He raced out of the inn, across the town square toward St. Mark's Church. He, Josef Thorvald, would save the Holy Catholic Church. He'd just nail his two theses to the church door and . . .

No nail. No hammer. Bummer.

Thorvald wept. He did not observe the portal to Ye New Tavern Shoppe open and a man in a black chef's hat saunter out.

"Say friend," said the man in the black hat, "what sorrow troubles your soul?"

Thorvald dried his eyes with his dirty sleeve. "Good sir, I have here words to save the Holy Church but I have no hammer nor any nails."

"Let me see," said Bertram Blackhand.

Thorvald handed over the document, his creation. As Bertram read, his hat wilted. Why, anyone reading this would have to agree with its sentiments. There could be no possible grounds for argument and worse, no cause for everlasting division within the Church.

"I'm sorry friend," said Bertram, "but I have neither hammer nor nail upon my person. But fret not, come with me to the tavern and have a piping hot bowl of mushroom stew while I look for them."

"Get thee behind me, Debbie Devil," said a scowling Thorvald.

Bertram blinked. "But how did you know I work for her?"

"I once sold insurance policies. Our actuaries knew who scourged God's people with mushrooms. I will never partake of your evil brew."

"Then you will die." The evil chef shoved the greatest post-Renaissance mushroom down the good man's throat.

As Thorvald's life ebbed, he saw Jesus walking down a golden staircase, arms extended, ready to give him a hug and a taco. Bertram sneered at Thorvald's contented still face, burned the two theses, and vanished.

"*Ja caramba, ja caramba*," said a figure racing across the town square toward the fallen Thorvald. He knelt beside the lifeless man and removed the evil mushroom, his brother's evil calling card. "*Herr amigo*, you have my profound apologies for arriving too late." Erickson put a luminous white card with golden writing in Thorvald's left hand. "Here, when you get to Heaven give this coupon to Saint Peter. It's good for a Blessed Meal at his 50's-style diner, Pete's. Great burgers. And the tall root beers served in chilled mugs are to die for."

The weeping Pedro Erickson wished he could do even more for Thorvald. He looked half-heartedly for the man's two theses, but he knew in his heart Brother Bertram had already taken them.

Meanwhile, back at the inn, Luther prayed for a sign for what he should do.

Whap! A Swedish meatball splattered on Luther's window. The meaty mess took on the image of Thorvald flying up to Heaven. The impact of a second meatball produced the sign of the cross.

Luther moved toward the window and traced fingers along edges of the image and the sign. God had blessed him with two messages, but what did they mean? Luther bowed his head and prayed for more guidance.

"*Hola*, lardass," yelled a voice from the square below. Luther blanched and pointed to himself. "Yeah you, you potato sausage," said the hidden voice, "get off your Teutonic butt and write theses decrying indulgences and corruption in the Church. Then nail your work to the church door."

God's will is unusually clear, thought Luther. He staggered back to his desk and set down to write.

Luther nailed his words to the church door as the cock crowed. The undeniable soundness of his arguments compelled many to protest indulgences and the worldliness of the Church. But Luther's 95 theses had not the soothing simplicity of Thorvald's two and the unmasked anger of the great theologian's passionate words drove many to reject lardass's views altogether.

Protestant and Catholic views grew and hardened out of the discord inspired by Luther's document. One hundred years later, Protestants and Catholics would slaughter each other by the thousands in the Thirty Years War. Mushrooms would grow for decades in the untended, depopulated farmlands of Europe. Bummer.

CHAPTER 10B-BAD GUYS

Debbie Devil took off her fuchsia slingbacks and plunged her feet into the tub of hot water. She sighed. Just thinking of this had kept her going all morning. And the day promised to get even better. The manager of Hungry Hank's had just promised her a six-percent raise in March. Yes, life could be good for the Supreme Evil.

She scarcely felt like opening the ketchup packet in her hand and squirting another red stripe on the meat locker wall. When she felt this good, she really didn't feel up to unleashing Armageddon on the world.

She heard someone knock on the door. "Come in."

"Good afternoon, m'lady," said Bertram.

She smiled. "So, you failed again. No matter."

Confusion clouded Bertram's face. "You're not angry?"

She waved her right hand. "No, not really. You split Christianity in two. So we got something out of it."

Bertram smiled. "Thank you, m'lady." Whew.

"Besides, I could never get really angry when I'm giving my feet a hot bath."

Bertram's smile vanished. He pointed to her feet.

Her glance darted downward. "Blessed Heaven! I hate it when this happens. Blessed water froze again."

Bertram coughed. "Well m'lady, you are in a meat locker. Things tend to freeze in here."

Debbie clapped both hands against the ketchup packet. A red stripe appeared on the locker wall. Why the Heaven should she hold back on Armageddon if her feet were frozen? Bah! She could toast the world right now!

She readied the fingers on her right hand for the Snap, the snap that would conjure the end of the world.

"Checker needed up front," said the voice from the loud speaker.

Debbie sighed. The customer always came first. She gave a tiny snap at the tub and the ice melted. "Today the tub, tomorrow the polar ice caps."

Bertram took off his black chef's hat to produce a box of Belgian chocolates. "Here, m'lady, for you. You may be the Supreme Evil, but you're still a woman."

Debbie took the box and smiled. "Thank you, Bertie."

CHAPTER 10G-GOOD GUYS

"Oops," said Pedro Erickson.

"I share the same sentiments," said Lee. "I sincerely expected Bertram Blackhand to show up for the Spanish Inquisition. How could I have made such a blunder?"

"Well, General, you didn't buy this year's Entertainment book from Elizabeth Ann Seton's daughter. If you had, you would have seen that for this year they added a 50%-off coupon for 16th-century Germany.

"Debbie Devil's small income makes such a bargain irresistible."

Lee sighed inwardly. "Mr. Erickson, it is all my fault."

"Don't take it so hard, General. You spent over half your monthly retainer buying Girl Guide cookies from Betsy Ross's little girl, Zilla."

Lee nodded. "Yes, I did that. But I could have spent less on root beer."

"Then you would not have been Lee."

Lee lowered his head. "My dear sir, I have a confession. I did not have the money to buy the Entertainment book as I had already used it to pay a three-day late fee for the movie rental, *Beach Blanket Bingo*. Can you forgive me, Mr. Erickson?"

Erickson clasped Lee on the shoulder. "That I can, and that I will. We all make mistakes. Besides, although we didn't prevent division in the church, I still got there in time to rid it of its worldliness.

"But enough of such talk. How about watching *It's a Mad, Mad, Mad World?*"

"I'm afraid, my dear sir," said Lee, "I am financially embarrassed. I cannot afford to rent another DVD at the moment."

"Then allow me to present it to you as a gift," said Erickson.

Lee turned away to hide a tear. "Thank you, sir."

"And let me fix up a hot steaming bowl of *menudo*."

Lee raised an eyebrow. "Isn't *menudo* innards?"

"*Sí.*"

Lee's tear evaporated as his stomach churned. He faced Erickson and said, "Much obliged."

CHAPTER 11-THE PIT, THE PENDULUM, AND THE MUSHROOM

or

HOLY TOLEDO

Señor Jose Thorvald followed close behind his liberator General DeSalle. Jose didn't know how a French army had fought its way all the way to Toledo, fairest city in all Spain. He did not care. He was just grateful.

DeSalle turned to the troops behind him. "*Soldats, allons y, toute suite!*" The French infantry began to trot, their hard shoes clanging against the street's Jurassic cobblestones.

Jose lagged behind. His body cried for more strength than his daily bowl of skim soy-milk had given him. The cramps in his legs stopped all motion. He fell nostrils first to the street. "General DeSalle, I've fallen and I can't get up."

"Then alas, *Señor* Thorvald, I must send you my heartfelt regrets and apologies. Don Burrito and his army are but five minutes away. *Adieu!*"

"But, most excellent General DeSalle, since when is the mighty French army afraid of anyone?"

A still trotting DeSalle yelled back, "This is but a small detachment foraging for rare spices so that our armies might prepare chicken a hundred new ways. I trust this intelligence does not inconvenience you."

Not inconvenience him! Jose's head swirled. He'd outfoxed the Inquisition twice. Once with the pit. Then with the pendulum. He surely would have been Thorvald *flambé* but for the fortuitous intervention of DeSalle and his raiding party.

How long before the long arm of the Inquisition grabbed him? How long before . . .

"Listen up, *Señor*," said the figure in the black-hooded robe, "this is Spain here, and in Spain we don't let our heretics get away from us. Boils our good Holy blood, it does, even on this fine April day."

Jose peered at the figures on the black robe. Golden figures of monstrous mythical animals abounded surrounded by red pentagrams, crosses, and mushrooms.

Something about his captor bothered Jose. Perhaps it was his black chef's hat. "*Señor* Inquisitor, are you from our country's western lands?"

"*Sí, Señor* Thorvald, how did you know? No doubt, it was my accent. Well, I am Don Juan Vano from Saint Augustine, in Florida, the fairest land of Our Most Catholic King Philip III."

"Really," said Jose, "I heard it is beautiful in Florida. I hear that the streets of Saint Augustine are lined with gold."

Vano laughed. "My faith, you are a funny fellow. There is no gold in the streets there. But when the sun sets over the beach the sand, the sand, it looks like gold." He sighed. "My faith, I wish I were back there."

"Must be a wonderful land," said Jose.

"*Sí*, it is," said Vano. The Inquisitor thumped his chest with his massive right fist. "I tell you what. After this is all over I'll take a vacation; I have six months coming to me. Come with me to my plantation in Saint Augustine."

Jose's grin grew ever wider during this speech. Then it vanished.

"Why the sad face, heretic?" said Vano, "You know it takes fewer muscles to smile. Come on, *Señor*, be a good fellow."

"Well," said Jose, "after this business is all over. I'll be dead."

Vano again roared with laughter. A minute later, he wiped the tears from his eyes. "Oh you heretics, you'll be the death of me yet."

The Inquisitor extended a helping hand to the still prone Jose and lifted him up. He bowed and said, "After you."

"No, my dear Vano, I'd prefer to go after you."

The agent of Holy Terror scratched his head. "My dear *Señor*, I confess I don't understand you."

A huge goofy grin appeared on the Inquisitor's face. He slapped his thigh. "I see. You are a funny fellow. You mean you wish to die after me."

Jose thought, Geez, sadists and killers always have a slow wit. He said, "I'm a tough man to kill."

"You are that," said the Inquisitor, "you are that. You have been my greatest challenge."

Jose blushed. "Aw gee, you're just saying that."

"No, no. You have no idea how much we inquisitors look forward to the death of a clever heretic. Most of our victims just fall into the pit after seeing the "latrines here" sign on the far wall. Those inconsiderate heretics are no challenge; giving us nothing to talk about on our days off in the monastery."

The Inquisitor guffawed and slapped his thigh. "But you, *Señor* Thorvald, my grandchildren will be telling your story." He extended his arm again. "But come, we have work to do."

The duo walked arm in arm back to Thorvald's dungeon room, their budding friendship marred only by religious hatred and an unstoppable desire of one to torture and kill the other.

They approached the Inquisition's castle. The drawbridge lowered. Bells rang. Pink and white confetti rained down from the battlements. Beautiful maidens with raven-black hair and fiery eyes and smiles danced along the drawbridge toward Jose. They twirled around Jose, their flimsy, long, white Belgian-lace gowns fluttering in the gentle breeze.

A lovely *señorita* with milk-white skin and hair the shade of Aztec gold approached Jose. She extended a silver tray to him. Atop the tray lay a scented envelope with lettering of real gold.

"For me?" said Jose.

The *señorita* smiled and nodded. Her eyes beamed forth all that is soft and warm with humanity.

Vano elbowed Jose. "Take it, *amigo*."

Jose picked up the envelope. He looked at Vano. "Is it all right to open this?"

Vano smiled. "*Sí*, no hard feelings."

Jose broke the wax seal, opened the envelope and perused the letter. It read: "Congratulations! You are our one-millionth customer. Please do us the honor of accepting a beach-front mansion in Cartagena in His Most Catholic Majesty's New World.

"And that's not all, you will travel in style in your very own stateroom on the luxury ship Aguacate Verde. *Bon voyage, Señor.*"

Jose's eyes misted. "Gee, my dear Don Vano, I don't know what to say. How may I ever repay you?"

Don Vano sneered. "By dying, my dear heretic, by dying."

"Hey, no fair!"

"April fool."

"Geez," thought Jose, "how come I didn't see this coming?"

The inquisitor snapped his fingers. The maidens gently removed their lace to reveal naked bodies of steel.

Oh my God, thought Jose, the notorious, naked, wrestling, weightlifting virgins of Toledo.

The comely wrestlers reached into lavender pouches that hung from golden braided belts to remove the biggest, baddest grayest mushrooms of the Counter Reformation.

"Last chance, Thorvald," said Don Vano. "Do you wish to confess your heresy and eat mushrooms?"

"Mushrooms are pure evil," said Jose. "Those who grow them, reap them, or distribute them are pure evil. Swedish meatballs are the true food of the true faith."

Don Vano spat at Jose's face. "Recant your heretical culinary tastes. Eat mushrooms."

"Never," said Jose

"Is that your final answer?"

"*Sí.*"

Don Vano nodded to four deceptively minute maidens who knocked Jose to the ground and pinned his limbs. A fifth beauty pried open Jose's mouth. The golden-haired *señorita* shoved one mushroom after another down Jose's throat.

Consciousness began to ebb from Jose. Just before the first mushroom reached his stomach, he saw Pedro Erickson coming down from Heaven holding a bowl of Swedish meatballs in his right hand and a platter of tacos in his left. Bertram quickly waved the soul of Joe Thorvald to a new body, a new place, and a new time.

Meanwhile, back at the Inquisition, the sign above the gate now read, "One million served."

CHAPTER 11B-BAD GUYS

Debbie Devil sat on a stack of Topeka Tom's Corn-Fed Pig Balls stuffing fistfuls of Twizzlers into her mouth. Her stomach protruded grotesquely out of her blue Hungry-Hank's shirt. Hundreds of Twizzler wrappers lay strewn around the meat locker.

Bertram knocked and entered. "Wow, m'lady, you've gone on the mother of all Twizzler benders. Still I understand what caused all this. We did come close."

"Close, Bertie, close. We came closer than the diameter of a Twizzler to getting a mushroom into Joe's stomach. He would have lost his soul. To me!"

"I'm sorry, m'lady. But I did manage to transfer Joe's soul into a new body before Erickson spirited him away to Heaven."

"Oh my culinary demon," said Debbie, "Erickson wasn't taking him away to Heaven. It's not his time. They just wanted to give him a vision of what awaits him in the afterlife and they succeeded. It'll be tougher than ever now."

"Sorry, m'lady."

"It's tough being a horny devil," said Debbie. "We were so close. I could really feel Joe inside me. And I needed it so much that I used up an entire packet of Farmer Jasper's Mystery-Meat Hot Dogs. But you know . . ." Debbie wept.

Bertie put an arm around her. "There, there. There, there."

Debbie stopped crying, removed Bertie's arm, and snapped her fingers. Her belly went back to normal. The Supreme Evil can get away with binge eating, you bet.

"Well, Bertram, it's time to get back to work. Any chance of help from Mr. George on our next attempt?"

Bertram consulted his red appointment book. "I'm afraid not m'lady. He's mislabeling dress sizes at all Nordstrom's in America."

"Well then, Bertie, what are your plans?"

"I thought I'd try to terrorize Joe in Paris during the French Revolution."

Debbie clapped her hands. "Ah, Paris during the Terror. My favorite place, my favorite time. Oh, how I remember sitting outside a quaint, little *café* sipping a demitasse, munching on a fresh baguette and watching the guillotine cutting off one head after another. Paris, it's calling me. Bertie, I'm going with you, and I have the cutest yellow chiffon butcher's apron that I have been just dying to wear."

Bertie frowned. "Sorry, m'lady, but I'm afraid you cannot go to Paris."

Debbie pouted. "And why not? I'm the Supreme Evil."

"Yes, m'lady, but they're French and they have their regulations. You're *persona non grata*, I'm afraid. It seems that two years ago, you left Paris without paying your hotel bill. So, the French aren't going to let you in."

"But, I want to see The Terror in 1794," said Debbie. "The French would be barring me for something I wouldn't do for another two centuries. They can't do that."

Bertie flipped through his *Imbecile's Guide to French Bureaucracy*. "Oh, but they can. In 1982, President Mitterand established the Intertemporal Alien Debtor Agency to keep out all bill skippers from *La Belle* France throughout the entirety of French History."

Debbie sighed. Bureaucracy was usually such a good friend to her. "Well, Bertie you had better go. Watch a few beheadings for me, will you?"

"Yes, m'lady."

CHAPTER 11G-GOOD GUYS

Lee removed a carefully folded, monogrammed handkerchief to mop his brow. "Good heavens, that was close."

"*Ja, sí,*" said Pedro Erickson, "that was close. *Taks a mikka* to God, I got there is time."

Lee allowed himself to drum his fingers for one second. "Yes, but Mr. Erickson, I find it my painful duty to remind you that you could have stopped the young women before they put a single mushroom in Mr. Thorvald's mouth."

Erickson shuffled his feet. "Well, I admit it. I was watching the young women. A bit too much, I guess."

Lee raised his left eyebrow a sixteenth of an inch.

"Oh come on, General. Those young women were the notorious, naked, wrestling, weightlifting virgins of Toledo. Wow, what honeys."

Lee spoke gently to Erickson. "My dear Pedro, we all have our weaknesses. Mine is *The Patty Duke Show*. But still, we are in Heaven. We owe it to our Heavenly Father to do our duty first."

Pedro managed a weak grin. "I suppose you're right. *Ja caramba*, I guess my tepid Swedish blood almost lost Thorvald's soul to Debbie and so brought on the victory of evil over good. I guess you should replace me with someone who is immune to such temptations. You'd better call God and see if He could send you Stuffy."

"There, there," said Lee, "you'll do much better next time. We shall speak no more of this."

CHAPTER 12-AN UNBEARABLE LIGHTNESS OF BEING

No one ever talks about how Parisian life-insurance companies suffered during the French Revolution. And neither shall we.

A man dressed in fine clothes entered the shop of Citizen Thorvald. *"Bonjour*, do you by chance have any meat for sale?"

Joseph Thorvald gestured to the dubious lump of meat on the counter. A week ago, it had been lamb. Now, even the few flies that approached it buzzed away disgusted.

The nobleman leaned over. *"Merde!* Did that come out of you?" The man's outraged nostrils danced a minuet before marinating the meat with great gusts of Gallic goobers.

"Sacré bleu, Comte de Couchon, look what you have done!" Joseph wrung his hands. "Oh, but sir, you have ruined my meat. I cannot sell it now."

The *comte* took some snuff. It appears to me that I have rather improved the meat's appearance."

"Mais non," said Thorvald, "it is against all the new regulations to sell meat with goobers on it, even your noble goobers."

The *comte* shrugged, withdrew a ten-assignat note from his pouch and tossed it in Thorvald's general direction. "That should cover it." The nobleman left without even saying, *"Au revoir."*

Madame Louise Thorvald's sabots clip-clopped down the circular stone staircase to the shop. "Joseph, you idiot, what was all that about? Did you sell the last bit of meat?"

Joseph shook his head. "No, but I got ten assignats."

"Ten assignats, only that?" Louise's visage took on the anger that made her the natural leader of any riot. *"Monsieur,* you imbecile, you fool, now how am I supposed to buy bread, eh?"

"But *ma chèrie*, this is not my fault. The *comte*, he sneezed on the meat. That's all the *comte* gave me."

"You stupid husband," said Louise, "you always have a ready excuse for this stupid business. The dullest street urchin can see you're in a dead-end profession. Everyone but you knows that the farmers don't have any meat to sell. Why don't you get a better job?"

"I would but *ma chèrie*, it is not so easy to find another job in these times. How would I look?"

Louise sneered. "Bah, more excuses! I suppose I must try and find some wild mushrooms in the alleys. If they are not all picked over." She withered her husband with a stare of disgust and left.

Joseph fingered his ten-assignat bill. "*Sacré bleu*, how I wish a good job would show up at my doorstep."

Thud!

Joseph opened the door and picked up that week's *Le Paris Assignat Saver*. The bottom headline read, "Mushroom shortages in Paris." The middle headline read, "Remove blood stains from silk shirts." However, the top headline got his attention. "Become a guillotiner, Impress your neighbors. Earn big assignats. No experience necessary. Must be a people person."

Joseph put down the paper and scurried over that very moment to the guillotine job fair at the Rue de la Paix. He chuckled at the banner over the entrance proclaiming, "Come get ahead with us." He marveled at the displays of bloodthirsty French ingenuity. The good butcher wandered around open-mouthed. A fly buzzed in. A fly buzzed out.

Citizen Thorvald halted before a gleaming iron guillotine from the city of Nice. Above the death machine hung a banner that read, "Join the Guillotine Corps and See the Riviera."

The noisy clambering of the twelve neighboring Framboise kids destroyed Joseph's pleasant reverie. Each giggling kid in turn put his head down in the slot at the bottom while another of the urchins pulled hard at the rope to release the giant blade.

But none could get the beckoning blade to budge. But try, try, and try again. Joseph smiled at their youthful exuberance. Then came Gaston's turn. Gaston Framboise, a strapping lad of eighteen, possessed arms like anvils. He pulled the death rope with ease.

Down came the sharp, heavy blade. Off came the head of little Jean, a snot-nosed whining brat.

"A thousand pardons, brother Jean," said Gaston, "I hope that makes it up to you."

Dead Jean looked the other way and said nothing, for he was beside himself.

Little Henri tugged at his mother's tattered black dress. She scowled at the nuisance. She wanted nothing more but to calculate how many assignats dear little Jean's death would free up for the family budget.

Henri tugged harder at Mama's dress. "My little brat, what do you want now?"

"Mama," piped up Henri, "could I have Jean's bed? He won't be using it anymore. And I'm tired of sleeping with Robert."

Mama raised an eyebrow halfway. "You share a mattress with Robert?"

"Yes, Mama, and he has head lice."

"Very well, then."

Joseph took in the whole scene. The guillotine worked! It had helped Robert. Little Jean didn't suffer at all. Truly, the guillotine was an instrument of mercy!

Joseph looked around to sign up, but being twenty minutes after noon, the good executioners of Nice were out eating lunch.

The good butcher investigated the alluring guillotines, the pride of over eighty Francophile cities. Sometimes the sun hit a blade at the right angle producing a wondrous rainbow on the ground. Sometimes a wooden platform took him back to the sweet-smelling trees of the Argonne Forest.

But really, Paris, his own Paris, possessed the guillotine that truly curled Joseph's nostril hairs. It soared an extra six feet taller than any other. Paris disdained the unimaginative angular design of the blade in favor of a cheery semi-circle resembling the broadest of smiles. Some wag had even painted a happy face on it.

But the executioners. What mistress magnets! How they oozed self-assurance. How they reeked of the finest garlic. And their enormous necklaces of expensive, firm mushrooms around their necks! *Sacré bleu*, no other tradesmen could afford even one.

Joseph shuffled over to the recruiter. The job-seeker coughed. The tall, austere recruiter looked up.

"*S'il vous plaît, Monsieur*, I would like to become a guillotiner for Paris."

"You would, eh? And why? Do you believe in the Revolution? Did some nobleman wrong you? Speak up, little man!"

"*Eh bien*," said Joseph, "I am but a poor butcher, and just this very day a nobleman sneezed on my last piece of lamb."

"Did he compensate you?" said the recruiter.

"Yes, ten assignats."

"*Merde*," shouted the tall man, "he should have given you twenty. Bastard nobility! I can see why you would want to join us."

Joseph took a half-step forward. "Then you will give me a job, *oui*?"

The recruiter straight-armed the butcher's chest. "A moment, citizen, we have so many applicants, the number of resumes limited only by Paris's general illiteracy. Citizen, you must show us that you can do the job. I, Robespierre, leader of the Terror, hire only the finest angels of death."

Robespierre launched into his usual mind-numbing diatribe about the virtues of decapitating the nobility.

Joseph's head slumped. He snored like a student at the *Université de Paris*. "No," thought part of his brain, "bad interviewing technique. Wake up, Thorvald." Joseph opened his eyes and forced a smile. "*Mais oui*, isn't that something?"

"Yes it is, citizen," said Robespierre, "but you must find the parasitic noblemen yourself. You must decapitate them yourself. Show me you can do that and I'll give the job."

"What?" said Joseph. "You want me to find and kill a nobleman before I even start work?"

Robespierre shook his head. "*Mais non*, for this purpose a little dog with monarchistic tendencies shall suffice."

Joe scoured the quality sections of Paris for a quality dog. But he found only mangy mutt after mangy mutt. Joe picked them all up and looked them in the eye.

Their big, brown runny eyes gazed back at him. "*Et tu*, Citizen Thorvald?" they seemed to say. So, Joseph redoubled his resolve to find an aristocratic dog, a dog that deserved to die.

He found that dog at the intersection of Rue Jambon and Rue Oeufs eating chocolate-covered truffles out of a golden bowl. The poodle sported a white chef's hat and a pink ribbon. A gold medallion hanging from the ribbon proclaimed the dog's name to be *Le Roi des Toutes*. *Oui*, he could kill that dog.

Joseph ran back with the dog to Robespierre just as fast as his vitamin C, vitamin B12, and vitamin B6 deficient legs would carry him.

He found the Paris guillotine. He did not find Robespierre. "Probably at a wine-and-head-cheese party," thought Joseph. The good butcher showed initiative and climbed the steps with the white-hatted pooch.

Joseph nestled the dog's soft neck gently onto the chopping block. "There, there doggie." Joseph inspected the blade at the top. "You know, Thorvald," he thought, "this guillotine blade isn't much different than your meat cleaver, just bigger that's all. *Oui*, your great transferable skills make you a natural for this position."

Joseph pulled the cord. Down came the blade. The dog's head flew into the waiting Christian Dior basket. Out of the *Café* Dindon sprinted Robespierre.

Robespierre took the steps of the guillotine two at time. Sweat ran from his beet-red face. "You fool, you have ruined everything!"

Joseph arched the middle of both eyebrows. "But how?"

Robespierre pointed to the inert dog head. "That's no ordinary dog."

"I know," said Joseph.
"That poodle belonged to Barras."

Joseph shrugged.

"Barras is a man of great influence in the opposition. Your killing his dog shall rouse him to action. Oh yes, he'll blame me for this. He'll seek my death to avenge his little poodle.

"Oh you, great fool, can't you see you have brought down me, the Terror, the Revolution, brought on the Royalist counter-revolution, military dictatorships, and plunged France and Europe into bloody chaos that will last over a hundred years?"

Joseph shrugged; he'd botched this job interview. He walked with measured pace down the steps. Perhaps, General Bonaparte needed a good butcher. As the brilliant strategist always said, "An army marches on its Swedish meatballs."

CHAPTER 12B-BAD GUYS

"Rerun the video, please," said Debbie.

Bertie Blackhand rewound the tape and pressed the play button on the VCR. "You know, m'lady, you are the Supreme Evil. You really should get a DVD player."

"But," said Debbie, "I always have trouble with new technology. I used to get the newest computers, but they'd always freeze, get worms, or just plain not work at all. Now, I just get the cheapest computers. Better to throw out a no-good cheap computer than an expensive one."

"But m'lady, you, Mr. George, and I are all responsible for all those computer problems."

"I suppose you're right, Bertie. Hand me another bowl of popcorn, will you?" She rested her head against a stack of head cheese and propped up her feet on a carton of sweetmeats.

Bertie pressed the play button and the screen came to life. "FBI warning." Then the title, "What I did on my Paris Vacation by Bertram Blackhand."

Down, down came the guillotine.

"There, there," said Debbie, "did you see how his blood spurted? Ah, Paris, Paris."

The guillotiner held the head by the neck and showed it to the crowd.

"Look," said Bertie, "a smile really is a frown upside down."

Debbie beamed.

"And m'lady, it doesn't take more muscles to frown than smile, when you're dead."

"Oh Bertie, you'll be the rebirth of me yet."

Debbie Devil fell on the floor laughing. Bertram giggled. And back in Europe, Norway launched a preemptive nuclear strike on

Britain. Norway didn't have any nuclear weapons—still doesn't, the slacker--so no one noticed the attack and life went on.

Citizen Thorvald occupied the screen and Debbie licked her lips. She cried when Thorvald didn't get the guillotine job.

"Oh bless it," she cried, "what good is it to unleash a bloody revolution when its very chaos makes it impossible for a Lutheran hunk to buy mushrooms? How could I be so careless?"

"Ssh, ssh," said Bertram, "Paris does that to everyone. Why don't we forget all about it and watch *Spartacus*?"

Debbie sniffled. "That would be fine."

CHAPTER 12G-GOOD GUYS

Lee smiled. Erickson and he had beaten those people again.

Pedro Erickson walked into the room carrying two loaves of limpa bread and a jar of lingonberry preserves. Lee's smile vanished.

"Hey *Herr* Lee, why the long face for me?"

"Rest assured sir, my sadness is not from your presence."

"Then from what, General?"

Lee sighed. "We keep beating them, sometimes easily as in this last case."

Erickson slapped Lee on the back. "Then lighten up, *Herr* Dude."

"But," said Lee, "they kill people even when they fail. With this French Revolution, they killed thousands of innocent people. But those people do not care, they keep trying to get Thorvald to eat mushrooms.

"What if they exhibit the same tenacity, the same willingness to see countless thousands of good people die that the Union did during Lincoln's war? What if they win?"

Erickson's white chef hat drew itself up to its full height. "General Lee, if you had honored your pledge and stayed in the Union, had become the Union's commander, then the Civil War would have been over in less than a year and with a fraction of the deaths. Na, na, na, poo, poo."

"Na, na, na, poo, poo to you, too, sir" said Lee, "I was only doing my duty to Virginia."

Erickson opened the jar of preserves and scooped out a handful. He prepared to throw it at Lee.

The red telephone rang. Lee and Erickson froze. "Permit me to answer it, sir," said Lee. Erickson nodded. Lee picked up the phone.

"Yes, sir, Robert E. Lee, speaking."

Lee's left eyebrow shot up a tenth of an inch.

"Yes, sir. As you say, sir."

The right eyebrow joined its companion in its elevated state.

"You'll have my full cooperation, sir."

Lee handed the phone to Erickson. "It's Stuffy. He'd like to speak to you."

Color drained from Erickson's face. "Yes sir, I'd just like to say . . . Yes Stuffy, I agree. We should forgive each other, yes sir. Especially up here, in Heaven. You have my word, sir."

Erickson hung up the phone and wiped his sweaty forehead. "Whew, General, it appears to have gotten hot in here."

Lee nodded. "It does, indeed."

"Nothing a few rounds of root beer with crushed ice couldn't fix?" said Erickson.

"Sir, that would be a fine idea," said Lee. "Perhaps the situation calls for Messieurs *Rowan and Martin's Laugh In* and two bowls of lutefisk?"

"Sounds wonderful," said Erickson, "but oh dear, I'm afraid I'm all out of lutefisk. How about if I go to my kitchen and return with honey-glazed Virginia ham and sweet potatoes."

Lee smiled, relaxed even. "Thank you, sir, I would be much obliged."

"You're welcome, General."

"Sock it to me," thought the Southern gentleman. One of these days he might even be able to say it.

CHAPTER 13-THE TRAIL OF THE LONESOME PINE

"Bloody 'ell!" The shock of the injury numbed the throbbing pain. It could not numb his horror at the blood geyser erupting from his thigh.

Charlie put both his hands on the gaping wound. Great gouts of blood spurted up through his fingers. "Bloody 'ell, I want to live, I do."

The good infantryman grabbed handfuls of mud and shoved them into the enormous red hole. Thank God, the constant shelling and rain made mud as far as he could see. What the hell was he thinking? If it weren't for the shelling and rain he'd be safe and comfortable.

The same scene held for thousands of other Tommies unlucky to be on the Somme front on July 1, 1916. Many would die.

Would the mud staunch Charlie's flow of blood? We'll never know as our story really takes place 53 years earlier in Gettysburg, Pennsylvania. But hey Charlie, we're pulling for you.

General Pickett adjusted his hat an eighth of an inch before addressing his fellow officer. "Good morning, General."

"It is indeed a good morning, sir," said General Joseph E. Thorvald. With practiced ease he brushed a bit of shrimp scampi off his much-stained tie. "To what do I have the honor of this visit?"

"Sir," said Pickett, "I wish you to ready your brigade to attack the Yankee line."

"Yippee! Yippee! I can't wait to tell my men," said Thorvald before taking off. Pickett yelled at the running man, "General, I require a moment more of your time."

As Thorvald turned and raced back, Pickett cringed inside. Dang, that man was an idiot. Always running off half cocked. And how the blazes did he get so many marinara stains on his new uniform? Lee's Army of Northern Virginia hadn't eaten spaghetti-with-marinara-sauce in over a year. Still, if you could point him in the right direction at the right time, there was no braver man, no one more likely to inspire his men to victory.

"At your command, sir," said the gasping Thorvald.

"General Thorvald, our attacks of the previous two days failed. My division is the only fresh one left. We shall be attacking the Yankee line. Your brigade is my division's largest. It has the most veterans. Your performance today can make the difference.

"If we succeed, if you succeed, the South will get foreign recognition and independence will certainly follow. If you fail, we'll have to skedaddle from Pennsylvania like licked dogs. Do you understand?"

"Yes, sir."

"Later today, at my command," said Pickett, "I wish you to lead your brigade against the Yankee line. Your objective will be that tree yonder on Cemetery Ridge."

"Which tree?" asked Thorvald.

Pickett paused. Tarnation, he saw another tree, big and leafy, with lots of shade. Too tempting for picnic-loving Thorvald. So, Pickett pointed at a stand of trees. "Do not, my dear sir, under any circumstances attack toward that other pine tree, a half-mile to the right."

Thorvald searched for the incorrect tree. He guessed, pointing to the right. "Do you mean not that tree?"

Pickett rolled his eyes. These blasted gourmet generals. "My fault for bringing it up. It does not signify which of those yonder pine trees I don't want you to head toward."

Thorvald stiffened. "It does to me sir. I wish to get it right. Do you wish me to avoid that one?"

Pickett sighed audibly. All right. "Yes sir, I mean avoid that one over there. Avoid that one."

Thorvald grinned. "Very well, my men will not attack toward that tree."

"Good," said Pickett.

"But General, what about the other trees around it? Do I avoid those too?"

But Pickett didn't respond. He had already trotted off muttering in search of a tall, thick tree. He wished to bash his head against it.

General Thorvald addressed his lieutenants, "Gentleman, we attack the Yankee line after our bombardment stops. Our objective won't be that tree over there, the one with the sign, 'Men, don't attack this tree.' I put the sign up an hour ago."

"Brave deed, sir," said Lieutenant Tracton, "We were wondering what the blue bellies were shooting at."

Thorvald waved his hand quickly. "Oh, it was nothing. In the meantime, let's have a nice lunch. We're apt to be famished after a long charge across that open field with all those Yankees firing cannonballs and grapeshot at us. And I don't expect those folk to feed us gourmet food when we get there either."

"And it would be a shame to lie bleeding to death in that field without one last gourmet meal in your belly," said Sharpton.

"So, men," said Thorvald, "let's eat caviar and drink *L'Oiseaux Gris* '49 to our hearts content while we can."

And so they did. So much so, that the overly contented men felt rather inert when the bombardment ended.

Thorvald drew his sword and waved it wildly.

"Ow," said Thorvald's aide de camp.

Thorvald whispered to him, "My most sincere apologies." To his men he yelled, "For our glorious cause, charge!"

Lieutenant Sharpton held up a hand. "A thousand pardons, sir, but the men and I are feeling a mite bloated after our fine repast, and we were wondering if we couldn't make do with a purposeful walk instead?"

"Yes, yes, yes," said Thorvald, "only let's get going. For our glorious cause, walk purposefully!"

His men gave the Rebel yell and strode toward their appointment with destiny.

Well, sort of. Sure, every man knew which tree to avoid, but not which one to head toward. So by the tens and twenties, Thorvald's soldiers careened toward various spots in the Yankee line. Some rebels headed the wrong way entirely. One small group was even spotted in western Greenland in 1869 before vanishing from history altogether.

An hour later, only 122 men remained with the vacillating General Thorvald. Lieutenant Tracton gestured toward the rest of Pickett's men being cut down in front of the Yankees' center. "Perhaps we should come to their assistance?"

Thorvald shook his head. "No, Lieutenant, we have our orders and we will follow them. If only we knew what tree." He shook his fist. "Will no one show us the correct tree?"

"What ho," said the man in the tall, black chef's hat as ran toward them. "Bertram Blackhand at your service. Here, my card, sir."

Thorvald took the card and read, "Bertram Blackhand, Tree Locator on Battlefields since 1187."

"Mr. Blackhand, sir," said Thorvald, "I'd be greatly obliged if you would point out the correct tree."

"Certainly, General, I ask only one favor in return."

"And that is?"

"Well, I have strong aspirations to become a gourmet chef and I would rather like to have your expert opinions on some Shiitake mushrooms I've cooked in a lemon sauce."

Thorvald's jaw dropped. "You want me, a God-fearing gentleman, to eat a mushroom? No sir, I will not do it."

Bertram shrugged. "Then I won't be able to point out the right tree for you. And I'm afraid the absence of your little band will mean this great attack will fail. And with that, your precious Confederacy with its glorious cause will be destined to defeat."

Thorvald paused. Refuse the mushrooms and lose the war. Make the sacrifice of 100,000 Southern soldiers be in vain. Or, eat the mushrooms that all the faithful knew damned a man's soul to Hell.

Suddenly, a shot rang out. Actually, the 423,000[th] one. But this one hit Lieutenant Tracton in his right eye, flinging bits of gore everywhere. Tracton collapsed dying to the ground. "Ow."

Thorvald trembled as he addressed Bertram. "Sir, I shall eat your blasted mushrooms."

Bertram beamed. "Right ho, one serving of Shiitake mushrooms for the General."

Bertram never noticed the Swedish-meatball bombardment belching from Battery 13G of Hancock's II Corps. But General Thorvald did. "God in Heaven, a sixteen-pound Swedish meatball sure does rip the head off an English chef." If Thorvald had looked at the Yankee gunners he could have seen a Mexican-Swedish man jumping up and down and waving his white chef's hat.

But Thorvald did not look that way. He faced his men and yelled, "For our glorious cause, charge!"

And they did. But they still had differing opinions about the correct tree. None of them even made it within a hundred yards of the Yankee line before the retreat sounded. And so they just wandered off into historical oblivion.

So, the South did lose the war, but America and the world would preserve their souls.

CHAPTER 13B-BAD GUYS

Debbie Devil stamped her size 6 ruby-red slipper on the floor. "Bless it, you failed again. You failed again."

Bertram's black chef hat drew itself up to its full height. "Madam, I came close. I got him to agree to eat a mushroom."

"But Erickson killed you before you could get Joe to actually eat it!"

"Madam, he cheated. He bombarded me with Swedish meatballs."

"Then," said Debbie, "why didn't you counter with a mushroom bombardment?"

"My brother," said Bertram, "was in the Union Army in his first life. I was only a chef while alive and the curriculum of the London School of Culinary Arts is noticeably deficient in such matters."

Debbie pouted. "But you directed such a great bombardment of mushrooms with catapults at Troy?"

Bertram bowed. "Thank you, Madam, all culinary schools, except those in France, teach their students to use catapults."

"Why?"

Bertram scrunched his eyebrows. "Can't rightly say, but I believe it might have something to do getting rid of infected meat during the days of the Black Plague."

Debbie jumped up and down and clapped her hands. "Ooh, ooh, just think of all the chaos I can create by giving catapults to all those fast-food chefs in all those slums."

"Sorry, Madam, but Taco Bell, McDonald's and company do not teach catapulting to their employees."

Debbie stamped both slippers. "Well, why not?"

"Well, O.S.H.A has rules against it," said Bertram.

"Blessed goody two-shoes," said Debbie. "Then you teach them, Bertram."

"I will not. I am a chef, graduate of the London School of Culinary Arts. I do not keep the company of short-order cooks." Bertram's hat shuddered.

"Oh all right," said Debbie. "I went too far with that suggestion. Back to the main chase. Have any suggestions for getting Joe?"

"Yes Madam, I do. I'm going to isolate him for years without any sweetheart, without any company at all. He might go crazy enough to do something drastic, something irrational, such as eating our mushrooms."

"That might work," said Debbie. "Bless it, I know I'm going to unleash Armageddon if I don't get Joe for my love toy." Her eyes misted.

"Oh Madam, how can anyone be sad in such splendid slippers?"

Debbie managed a small smile. "These old things. Do you like them? I got them off a little Kansan girl who chased one too many tornadoes."

CHAPTER 13G-GOOD GUYS

"Mr. Erickson, sir, you have my most profound admiration. Your first-rate Swedish-meatball bombardment hit only Mr. Blackhand."

Erickson bowed. "Thank you, General. Battery 13G performed with dispatch."

"When did you develop such a skill?" asked Lee.

"In my second incarnation. I was just starting my chain of Swedish-Mexican fast-food franchises in Boise, Idaho when *Swedish Mundo* came into town."

Lee frowned. "I seem to remember hearing about them."

"That's because they were ruthless scum. They come into town and drove out all the Swedish-Mexican competition with super low prices. Then when they were the only ones left, pow, they jacked up the prices and demanded tax relief from the municipal government."

"That's ungentlemanly behavior," said Lee.

"*Ja caramba*," said Pedro Erickson, "and they used nutmeg instead of allspice."

"The scoundrels," said Lee.

"*Ja señor*," said Erickson, "they were that. So, my board of directors and I bombarded them with Swedish meatballs made with allspice."

"Didn't the police arrest for you for firing cannons in public?" asked Lee.

"No, Mayor Magnus Magnusson appreciated my never asking for tax relief."

Lee fought down the urge to raise one eyebrow. "At any rate, well done, sir. I believe this calls for a round of tall, ice cold root beers and a platter of mini tacos."

"And some slices of Virginia ham," said Erickson.

The Southern gentleman bowed. "Thank you, sir." He looked the Swedish-Mexican chef in the eye. "And by the way, you may straighten up. You need not continue bowing."

Erickson grimaced. "I can't straighten up. My back went out."

"Then sir, we shall eat on the low card table."

CHAPTER 14-DRIFTING ALONG WITH THE MUMBLING MUSHROOM DEEDS

Old man Thorvald looked out the way station's window at the newly arrived stage coach. Company!

A man dressed in black and topped with a tall, black chef's hat jumped off the driver's seat. The man carried two Colt .45s in his holsters.

The man had five notches in the mushroom-inlaid handle of one of his Colts. Thorvald waited for someone, anyone else to get out of the coach. No one did. So, the man in the chef's hat must have killed them.

Still, he was company! Company!

Thorvald ran out to meet the man. "Howdy stranger. Welcome to Dry Water Gulch."

The man managed a perceptible nod.

"Well come on in, come on in," said Thorvald.

They walked inside. The man bellied up to the bar. Old man Thorvald went behind it.

"Well stranger, what'll it be?"

The stranger stared at Thorvald, turned his head and spat into the spittoon twelve feet away. He faced Thorvald again and growled, "A glass of your finest Chardonnay, and smile when you serve it!"

Thorvald scratched his long, white beard. "Ain't never had Chardonnay around these parts. How about something else?"

The man spat again into the spittoon. "All right, give me a bottle of Merlot."

"Nope, ain't got that either."

The man spat again. "Chianti?"

"Nope."

The man had no more spit. He'd have to drink something, anything. "Mogen David?"

"Nope."

"Annie Green Springs?"

"Nope."

"All right, Old Man."

"The name's Thorvald, Joe Thorvald."

"All right Thorvald, what do you have?"

"Whiskey."

The man in the chef's hat sighed. "Okay, Joe Thorvald, I'll have a bottle of whiskey and a bowl of shrimp scampi."

Thorvald shook his head. "Ain't got none of that neither. Could rustle you up some rattlesnake, though."

"Could you, could you please, sauté it?" said the man.

"Sure thing, stranger." Thorvald headed back to the kitchen. "I always got plenty of spit."

The man put his head in his hands and groaned. Blessed tough to be a gourmand out here. Still, it might make his task easier.

The man looked around. The tablecloths on the two tables in back of him were of the finest Belgian lace; perfectly white. Actually, the immaculately maintained Queen Anne furniture everywhere bespoke of a degree of gentility rarely attained in this stretch of the Western desert.

The man gazed at the two exquisite French tapestries on the far wall and drank in the full length portrait of the woman in between. He stared and stared and stared. So beautiful. So beautiful.

"I say stranger," said Thorvald. "Your sautéed rattlesnake is ready." He plopped the bowl down by the visitor.

The stranger pointed to the picture. "Who is that woman?"

A smile spread across Thorvald's face, calling into action several dormant muscles. "That's Molly. My wife."

"May I pay my respects to her?" said the man.

"Nope," said Thorvald. "Cain't do that. She's been dead for quite a spell now."

"Well, your wife is quite beautiful."

Thorvald snorted. "No, she ain't pretty now. Are you deaf? I just told you she's dead. She's just a pile of bones in a box. That ain't pretty, is it Mister?"

The stranger's eyes examined a particularly edible chunk of rattlesnake. "No, I would venture not."

"Heck fire," said Thorvald, "I 'spect even a few weeks after she was a-properly buried and all, you would have found her right ugly if you had a-hankerin' to dig her up and open her coffin.

"She would have been a fiercesome sight with worms going in and out of her deterioratin' eyes and all."

The man took a deep breath, looked Thorvald in the eyes and said, "But she was a beautiful, *live* woman once, yes? How did you meet her?"

"Yep," droned on Old Man Thorvald, "she was the prettiest durn filly west of the Pecos. Her real name was Molly McNamara, but she went by Molly McNamara because she was wanted by the police back east. Smart one, that Molly, figured she'd be the only outlaw with an honest alias."

The man stirred his rattlesnake chunks. "You must miss her quite a bit, a fine woman like that."

"Mister," said Thorvald, "I miss her somethin' fierce. Shoot, that Louis XIV bed of mine gets mighty big on them cold winter nights. And them hot summer ones, too. And them temperate spring and fall nights, too. She'd make me laugh all day long and she was the best rattlesnake catcher and antique rustler ever."

The stranger gazed anew at the room. Appreciated all the feminine touches. "A place like this needs a woman. A man needs a woman like that, too."

"Shoot," said Thorvald. "I know that. Sometimes I get all het up and figure I'll just saddle up Ol' Paint and head over to Wet Water Gulch forty miles to the west."

"Well, why don't you?" said the man.

"Can't do that, mister. I'm a-contracted to run this way station. If'n I head over to Wet Water Gulch, who's gonna take care of any stagecoach that comes by? Tell me that, Mister."

The man didn't tell Thorvald there would be no stagecoaches, ever. There had been no stagecoaches for eight years. The railroad twenty miles to the north had seen to that. The man had to ambush this stage far to the south just to get here.

"Hey, old man, what would you say if I'd told you I had a fine lady of great beauty in the stage coach just itching to marry a man like you?"

"I'd call you a gol' danged liar and a mean one to boot, making fun of an old man like myself."

"I'm not lying," said the man. He snapped his fingers and touched his chef's hat.

A woman appeared outside the stage. Thorvald walked over to the way station's door. "Why, she's the spittin' image of Molly. And you say she wants to marry me?"

"She does," said the man. "She knows of you. Your reputation as a kind husband and a fine culinary artist runs all over the West."

"Shoot," said Thorvald. "Well bring her on in. I can't wait to meet her."

"Sure thing," said the man. He got off his chair and walked to the door. Old man Thorvald spat on his fingers and ran them through his long, rebellious hair.

"Wait, Mister," said Thorvald.

The man stopped and turned around. "Yes?"

"I ain't got nothing to give her but antique furniture and rattlesnakes," said Thorvald.

The man smiled. "Ah, but she has something to give you."

"And what would that be, Mister?"

"Mushrooms. She wants to feed you mushrooms. Lots of mushrooms. She'll only marry you if she can feed you mushrooms."

Tears streamed down Thorvald's leathery face. "I'm a God-fearin' man. Mister, I cain't eat no mushrooms, not for any woman."

Old Joe Thorvald looked the stranger in the eyes. "Mister, I reckon you're evil, yourself."

The stranger doffed his black chef's hat. "Bertram Blackhand, English chef."

Old man Thorvald ran screaming out into the blazing desert sun. Didn't even take a canteen.

"Oh, poo," said Bertie.

CHAPTER 14B-BAD GUYS

Bertie Blackhand opened the door of Hungry Hank's meat locker with his right hand behind his back.

Debbie hung her head. Tiny, evil tears rolled down her cheeks. The horns on her head cried out for their daily polishing. "We failed again. Oh Bertie, if a long-time, woman-needing, woman-deprived man won't eat mushrooms, then what chance do we have?"

"M'lady, I have another idea."

"Oh Bertie, all of your plans fail. Even the good ones. It's all so useless."

"M'lady, I have something for you."

Debbie looked up. A shaky grin appeared. "Bertram Blackhand, what do you have for me behind your back?"

Bertram withdrew his right hand to display a bouquet of deadly nightshade. "Just this."

Debbie squealed and clapped her hands. "Oh Bertie, Bertie, thank you, thank you." She wiped her eyes and cheeks. "Here I was sitting on a stack of Happy Face menudo feeling sorry for myself, and you come into to remind me that there is still so much that is evil in the world. So much that I caused. Thank you Bertie, thank you for again making me feel that I matter."

Bertie bowed. "Thank you, m'lady."

"Tell me, Bertie, what is your plan for your next attempt on Joe's soul?"

"Well, m'lady, we've been rather nice to Joe lately. Erickson and Lee will be expecting another nice attempt. So, I thought we'd outfox them with a nasty, vicious attack."

An evil peace swept across Debbie's face. Somehow, all would soon be wrong with the world. "See to it, Bertie."

"Yes, m'lady." Bertie turned to leave.

"Wait Bertie." Bertie turned back. Debbie pressed a little grayish, white button behind seventy-six boxes of German pigs' knuckles. A door behind the boxes opened.

Whiffs of cigar smoke wafted out. Someone in the room beyond said, "Ha! Got the Princess Frostine card. You're toast, Fred. I can just smell that thousand dollars."

Debbie gestured to the open door. "Bertie, how about a game of Candyland before you go?"

"Yes, m'lady, with a dollar a point and a doubling cube?

"Yes." Debbie smiled. "Is there any other way to play?"

CHAPTER 14G-GOOD GUYS

"That old man Thorvald sure was a strong, moral character," said Pedro Erickson.

General Lee nodded. "A fine man."

"I was behind the Bayeux tapestry the whole time," said Erickson, "but I never felt the need to intervene."

Lee nodded again. "A God loving, mushroom-shunning man brings joy to Heaven. You can be sure that a thousand singing angels will greet Thorvald's soul when it finally reaches here."

"Say," asked Erickson, "do you think Patty Duke will make it to heaven?"

"I hope she does," said Lee. "I hope all the stars from her era make it up here. We'd have so much to talk about."

Erickson doubted that. Lee had never been able to carry on an easy conversation with any of those stars already in Heaven.

Oh sure, Lee would be gracious. He'd offer the dead celebrity an ice-cold root beer. Then he'd become star struck and stammer out mangled comments and questions about '60s sitcoms. Soon, in a desperate attempt to appear lucid, Lee would invariably lurch into an interminable discussion on how he won the Battle of Chancellorsville in 1863.

At that point Erickson would offer to take the grateful star on a tour of Heaven's kitchen--the very ones where they multiplied the fishes and the loaves of bread.

"Maybe some day you could greet a writer from that era," said Erickson. "Mel Brooks, perhaps?"

Lee smiled. "I've always wished to make that gentleman's acquaintance. He's quite droll. I wish I could have been funny. When I was a young man, I spent two years, whenever I could find the time, writing the words for a minstrel show."

"What happened?" asked Erickson.

"Oh," said Lee, "I showed it to the manager of one of those shows and he said he'd seen more laughs at the funeral of a two-year-old girl dead from smallpox."

Lee sighed. The hurt in his heart had never gone away, never abated. It never would. Thank goodness for the all-encompassing mercy and compassion of almighty God.

"So I joined the army and the rest is history."

CHAPTER 15-WHISTLE WHILE YOU WORK

Sergeant Joe Thorvald sat tied to the sturdy, wooden chair. Another hour in this sweltering tin hut. Was he going to die? Was his year of hiding in Bataan's jungle living off wild thistlewort berries in vain? God, he could use a frosty cold root beer and a crispy shredded-beef taco! A giant frosty mug, bigger than an oil barrel, shimmered at Joe's leather-tough feet.

"Look up, Joe," drawled his brown, round-faced interrogator, "ready for another talk?" Joe's eyes met Lieutenant Shiitake's piercing gaze.

"Ready if you are, Shitcake, you miserable son-of-a-bitch," snarled Joe. Actually, the come-as-you-are Joe only disliked Shiitake for the pistol-whippings and the cigarette burns administered to his armpits. Joe shrugged. Ah well, war just brought out the worst in some people.

Shiitake strutted around the room, officer's baton in hand. "Well, Joe, what would you like me to do now? Tell me?"

Joe smiled. "Well, I'd like you to put me under a beach umbrella at Catalina with Betty Grable. We're sipping an ice cold root-beer float, one glass, two straws, then we look up. Our lips meet and . . ."

Shiitake's baton crashed hard against Joe's collar bone, hard enough to splinter bone and baton. Joe's eyes hurled back a disapproving bolt.

"Okay. Veronica Lake, then."

The lieutenant clenched his hands. "You, you, every hour you say the same thing."

"Well, every hour I want to do the same thing. Have you ever seen Betty Grable? Great legs, yes?"

Shiitake spat in Joe's face. "You smug American, I want to know about your activities as an aircraft observer."

"Well, you didn't ask me that. How was I supposed to know you wanted to know that?"

The lieutenant removed his pistol from his holster and waved it inches from Joe's face. "I want to know the location of your radio transmitter and to whom you reported."

Joe stared at his tormenter. "Gosh, lieutenant, 'to whom.' How'd you ever learn English so well?"

The faintest smile appeared on Shiitake. "I went to school at Texas A&M."

Joe's eyes widened. So did his grin. "Couldn't get in Stanford, Berkeley, or even Southern Cal, huh?"

The lieutenant snarled, "No, my grades weren't good enough."

Oops, thought Joe, you went too far with that humiliation. Armpits, say hello to Mister Cigarette.

Shiitake did not light a cigarette. He unsheathed his samurai sword and sliced off Joe's right ear. The officer pounced upon the ear and thrust it at the sergeant's quiet, quivering lips.

"Eat it, Joe."

Joe turned his face away.

"Eat it, Joe," shouted the red-faced Shiitake, "or I shall cut off your other ear."

Joe faced the ear and wrinkled his nose. "It's raw. I can't eat sushi. I'll break out in hives. Besides, it's not even spiced."

Shiitake's face flexed in thought. A minute later, he dropped the ear in a pan of sizzling sake. Dang, that fried ear sure smelled good.

Joe's brow furrowed. Aren't human ears considered meat for gourmet purposes? Shouldn't his torturer be cooking his ear in red wine?

The blood trickling down his cheek into his mouth reminded Joe of his mother's Swedish meatballs awash with marinara sauce. He'd promised his less-than-Julia-Child mother at age twelve never to let his lips touch alcohol. And the torturer's sake was definitely alcohol.

"Joe, Joe, pay attention. Your feast is ready."

Joe's eyes focused on his sizzling ear en brochette, except that Shiitake had impaled it not on a stick, but on a bayonet.

"No, thank you, I'm a teetotaler."

Shiitake pushed his bayonet a quarter inch into Joe's gut. Blood soaked the sergeant's shirt.

"Joe, Joe, that ear is getting into your stomach by your mouth or by bayonet." He poked Joe's gut again.

Ouch. Perhaps cooking burned off all the alcohol in the rice wine. Joe reasoned his mother would never know and just this one time, what the heck?

Joe opened his mouth. The chef inserted the cooked delicacy. Joe chewed and chewed. He swallowed.

The lieutenant laughed, leaned forward. "So Joe, how do you like your ear?"

Joe smiled. "Great, tastes like chicken."

"Aieee!" Shiitake gripped the sword with his black glove, lifted the weapon high above his head and drove the blade deep into Joe's neck.

As Joe's smile and life drained swiftly away, he thought, "Perhaps the man's heard that old joke one time too many."

CHAPTER 15B-BAD GUYS

Debbie Devil opened another packet of ketchup and squirted another red stripe on the meat-locker wall.

"Doesn't the manager of this locker ever wonder about the ever increasing number of red stripes?" asked Bertram Blackhand.

"Nah," said Debbie, "we get so many mission and vision statements around here. He just thinks it's tracking some corporate goal."

"Tracking the number of attempts before Armageddon is a corporate goal?" said Bertie.

"He doesn't need to know that."

Bertie shrugged his right shoulder. He would never understand the corporate world. He felt thankful for simple, unadorned evil.

"And speaking of goals, what did you possibly gain by cutting off Joe's ear?" said Debbie.

"Well m'lady, I thought that maybe if Joe liked his own ear enough, he'd ask for Shiitake's."

"Then what?" said Debbie.

"Shiitake would give it to Joe to eat as a gesture of good will."

"Okay, okay," said Debbie, "then what?"

"Joe would eat Shiitake's ear, not knowing that Shiitake was actually a mushroom that had its DNA altered here and there to become a Japanese officer in World War II.

"And then Joe would have eaten a mushroom. His soul, his Lutheran body would have been yours. Clever, huh?" The evil English chef giggled.

Debbie stamped her slingback on the floor. "Then how come Shiitake tried to kill Joe?"

Bertie's black chef's hat wilted. "Oh that. Shiitake had an evil will of his own. If only I had could have bought *Genetically-Modifying-*

Shiitake-Mushrooms-to-Produce-Controllable-Evil-World-II-Japanese-Officers for Idiots. But the bookstore was always out of the bestseller."

Loud pounding sounds rang out from the locker door.

"Blessed Heaven," said Bertie, "it's the guys from P.E.T.A."

The door flew off its hinges. But as so often happens, a particularly tall stack of Scottish haggis and other disgusting innards from European animals stopped the door's fall.

A grayish ogre squeezed sideways through the doorway. He pointed a thick, wart-ridden finger at Bertie.

"Animal killer, I'm going to make you eat tofu until you switch to vegetarian cuisine."

Bertie's chef's hat stiffened. "Never. I'm an evil English cook. Serving offal is what I do."

Debbie snapped her fingers and the ogre turned into a pile of dust. "And I hate rude ogres. Next time say, "Excuse me, please."

CHAPTER 15G-GOOD GUYS

"I can't believe," said Pedro Erickson, "how Bertie expected Joe to find his own ear appetizing."

"I can," said Lee, "I had an English luncheon at Gettysburg." His stomach churned at the memory.

The result of that meal is well-known history. Lee ran to the outhouse and dropped trousers. Longstreet knocked on the outhouse door requesting the day's orders. Lee moaned and said to come back later.

Longstreet came back in an hour. Lee, his bowels erupting like Krakatoa would twenty years later, gave orders for Pickett to charge the center of the Union line just to get rid of Longstreet.

Pickett's men fell by the thousands in that doomed charge. The defeated, decimated Army of Northern Virginia never recovered. Two years later, the South lost the Civil War.

Lee's fingers gripped an ice cold mug of Heaven Brother's root beer until his knuckles turned white. English food at Gettysburg! General Sherman had it right. War was all hell.

CHAPTER 16-WHEN YOU WISH UPON A REX

"Thank you for flying Leaping Cow Airlines," crackled the pilot's voice over the intercom. "We're beginning our final descent into San Diego. It's quite pleasant down there as long as you don't get eaten by Teddy T-Rex."

Square-jawed Joe "The Terminator" Thorvald clicked his seatbelt together and shook away the flutters Bertram Blackhand had placed in his mind. He took a last sip of *sake*.

Joe remembered how San Diego had acquired this distasteful reputation. Of course he did. He belonged to the paramilitary arm of the San Diego Tourist Board. He and his fellow regulators squashed forty stories of Teddy T-Rex devouring tourists. Too bad there were forty-one such news items.

And just how many natives were reported eaten at Petco Park? He didn't know. Those munchings didn't make the national news. Thank goodness, the Padres' Bill Basker chose that game to strike out twenty-one Dodgers. So the local media tended to downplay the night's unpleasantness.

Joe winced at the memory. Blood just doesn't wash out of a $500 shirt. How did these annoyances start? With those Canutes.

Thorvald walked with Sven Canute and his six-year-old boy, Jan, inside the Natural History Museum at Balboa Park. Joe couldn't say he liked either of the Swedes, especially little Jan, who talked only about dinosaurs and never admitted to being wrong.

Joe glanced at the reconstructed skeleton of a Tyrannosaurus Rex and scowled. "That phony isn't a predator, just a timid scavenger, ate mushrooms mostly, bah."

Little Jan had to argue. "No ho, you're clearly not a competent paleontologist. It's not a scavenger you're seeing, but a warm-blooded, flesh-ripping, flesh-eating machine of terror." The boy sighed. "I wish it were real. That would be fun."

Joe scowled. "Be careful what you wish for, Jan. You just might get it."

The skeleton raised its upper part off the support bar. Flesh and muscles sprouted up and down the skeleton. Skin raced across the flesh. The T-Rex opened its mouth and roared, just like Joe's ex-wife.

But only briefly. Its powerful jaws snapped shut on Jan's head. Blood spurted from the unencumbered neck like ketchup out of a squeezable Heinz-57 bottle. Jan's ungainly remnant danced the limbo. How low could it go? All the way to the floor.

"See?" Joe said to Jan. Jan's headless body gave our hero the cold shoulder.

"See?" Joe said to Sven. However, the screaming, gibbering, convulsing father showed signs of distress, so Joe let the matter drop.

Something tugged hard at our hero's mind. Was he supposed to bring ketchup home from the store or was it meatballs? Joe couldn't remember; the stampeding crowd shrieked too much.

The T-Rex shook the building as it strode to the exit. It smashed its head against the wall above the door. It ducked on its second attempt to leave.

Clearly, the builders of the museum never considered that a live T-Rex would ever want to leave or they would surely have printed a height warning above the exit. In all fairness, the T-Rex couldn't have read the warning anyway what with English being a second language to it.

Anyway, Joe looked at the blood-spurting, truncated Jan and at Sven. Our hero thrust out his hand.

"Sven Canute, I, Joe Thorvald, am not too proud to admit when I'm wrong. The Tyrannosaurus Rex is a predator. Let this reconciliation be the start of a new and great friendship.

"Tell you what," continued the genial Joe, "want to go to Starbucks? On me. Better yet, let's go to Tony Roma's for some of their all-you-can-eat ribs."

Joe waited patiently for a response. Finally, the laconic Swede summed his tumultuous feelings, "Yuk!"

"Yuk, indeed." Joe grabbed Sven's hand and shook it. "You know, Sven, I got a feeling this is going to be a start of a beautiful, one-sided friendship."

The odd couple walked arm in arm to the eatery.

"Wait, Joe, wait," yelled Bertram. "Sorry I was late. Wait, wait."

But Joe did not hear Bertie and continued on. Bertie looked at the retreating duo. He knew he'd have to do something no self-respecting chef would ever want to do. Move quickly. He had to catch Joe.

See Bertie run. Run, Bertie, run. See a tyrannosaurus rex block Bertie's path. Block, tyrannosaurus rex, block.

Bertie cursed and reached deep into his black bag of mushrooms. He removed a particularly big, unwholesome one, removed the stem, and chucked nature's little grenade as high and hard as he could toward Joe.

But the T-Rex intercepted the mushroom and swallowed it. The T-Rex roared. Its skin turned red.

Oh dear, thought Bertie, it's getting horny and it's looking straight at me. I sure hope I'm not its type."

Bertie didn't need to worry about that. It's a common myth among English chefs that a carnivorous dinosaur's scales turn red only when they get sexually excited. But as we all know, the scales also turns red when the carnivore becomes highly enraged. Makes dinosaur dating exciting, you bet!

Disappear, Bertie, disappear. Bertie did so.

Suddenly a taco shot out. The T-Rex swallowed it in mid-air. A man in a white chef's hat shouted, "*Ja bueno*," and pumped his left fist in the air.

The T-Rex chewed the taco. It considered the awesome delicacy. Great, just great. How did it live through the Cretaceous period without Mexican spices, Mexican food?

The T-Rex bowed to Pedro Erickson. The chef returned the bow, doffed his white chef's hat, and disappeared.

The dinosaur remembered the earlier mushroom. The horror, the horror. For the first time, the T-Rex knew the difference between good and evil. Like wow, it thought, time to become a force for good.

That's just what happened. Oh sure, there were those silly, unavoidable mistakes, like all those innocent people it devoured at that ball game. But the biggest mistake of all was that Teddy T-Rex was actually an allosaurus, a dinosaur from an entirely different era. Little Jan had known that. Oh God, why must all the good paleontologists die so early in the chapter?

But on the bright side, Teddy, as the TV stations came to call him got pretty good at eating only mushroom eaters and standing up for taco eaters everywhere. And the Swedish throng crossing illegally via Mexico found a welcome ally in Teddy T-Rex. But that is another story.

CHAPTER 16B-BAD GUYS

Debbie Devil stamped her dainty monogrammed Red-Wing slingback. Smoke billowed out her nose and ears. "Bertie, just what the Heaven were you doing down there? Letting Joe get away like that."

Bertie Blackhand cleared his throat and offered Debbie a Twizzler.

Suddenly, a lightning bolt flew out of Debbie's right-index finger incinerating the innocent candy.

"You went to such trouble," said Debbie, "to harden Joe's heart, then you let him off the hook. You let him become a nice guy!"

Bertie averted his eyes. "Sorry, m'lady."

"I should hope so," yelled Debbie. "He turned nice without the help of a taco or a Swedish meatball. He was so ready to eat a mushroom, but you were late. You'll never again get him in such a favorable body, situation, and time."

"Sorry, m'lady," mumbled Bertie.

"Just one question, Bertie, before I send you to that lecture, "The Changing Role of Allen Elasticities of Substitution on Post Keynesian Theoretical Microeconomics from 1979 to 1986."

Bertie paled. His chef's hat went limp. "Oh no, m'lady."

"Why the Heaven were you so late at that last attempt?" yelled Debbie.

"I was watching the World Series of Cooking on the Food Channel. It was Scotland versus Wales, and oh my, you should have seen the haggis that Scottish cook made."

Debbie snapped her fingers and a box of Hersheys with almonds materialized in her right hand. She sat down on a crate of Rocky Mountain oysters, looked at the new ketchup stripe on the meat locker's wall, and cried. Bless it, why was it so hard for a gal to get a Lutheran Hunk before Armageddon?

Bertie took this opportunity to sneak out of the locker. He glanced at his watch. He still had time to rush over to Wellesley's Bar and Grill across the street. Sure, Wellesley's was a hotbed for Methodist ministers wanting a quick beer after work, but if he never told them he worked for Debbie, The Supreme Evil, everybody could get along okay for an hour.

CHAPTER 16G-GOOD GUYS

"I feel constrained, Mr. Erickson," said Lee, "to mention your lateness in those people's last attempt on Joe Thorvald. May I inquire of the cause?"

"I was watching the World Series of Cooking on ESPN5. It was Sweden versus Mexico. Sorry General, I know the fate of good versus evil hangs on Joe Thorvald, but it was shredded-beef tacos versus Swedish meatballs, made the correct way with allspice! Allspice, General, allspice."

Lee signed inwardly. "My dear Mr. Erickson, we all make mistakes, but we must learn from them. We must resolve never to repeat . . ." Lee's eyebrows rocketed up a sixteenth of an inch. "I thought the World Series of Cooking was on the Food Channel."

"Part of it is, General, but some of it is on ESPN5 as well."

"I didn't know cooking was considered a sport," said Lee.

"Yes, it is."

Lee sighed audibly. What would have Stonewall Jackson said about this?

Erickson continued, "But the main things are that Bertram Blackhand and Debbie Devil failed again and that San Diego is being made safe from mushrooms."

Lee frowned. "My dear Erickson, I'm not entirely sure having a tyrannosaurus rex, however endearingly named, rampaging through supermarkets and restaurants devouring mushroom sellers and eaters is the best way."

"Perhaps," said Erickson.

"Then you will remove the dinosaur?" asked Lee.

"You mean terminate its existence? Kill it?" said Erickson.

Lee nodded.

"No way!" said Erickson. My parents never let me have a pet, not even a turtle, and now that the networks have given it a name, I just don't have the heart to do such a thing. And Teddy has the biggest brown eyes."

Lee sat down and rubbed his temple.

"Would a root-beer float help?" asked Erickson.

"It would indeed, sir. I'm much obliged."

CHAPTER 17-THE RAINBOW DINOS OF GRAFTON COUNTY

The little freckle-faced boy licked his grape lollipop. Contentment coursed from his busy mouth to his ever-moving body. Remnants of other purple lollipops on his white shirt shouted to the world his preference in sweets.

The boy, Billy, looked up at the towering T-Rex. "Gee, Mom, that's a big di'saur. Wouldn't it be neat if it was alive, huh, Mom? Make it alive, Mom!"

Mom smiled. "Oh my little silly Billy, Mommy can't make a T-Rex come to life."

Billy stamped his size-4 Bob-the-Builder shoe on the floor. "Oh gee, I wish it was alive."

The T-Rex slowly turned its head to Billy. Billy's scream drowned out the slow creaking of the dinosaur's neck. The little kid scurried behind Mom and hid his face in Mom's skirt.

Joe Thorvald stepped out from behind the base that supported the T-Rex. Joe regarded Mom's ashen face and shaking body. "Gosh, ma'am, I suppose I scared you some. But there's no need to be alarmed. I was just testing out the sound effects and mechanics for our new, 'End of the Dinosaurs' show. Didn't know anybody was still here. We're supposed to be closed."

"W-e-l-l, I-I-I-I g-u-e-s-s we-we-we-we were a bit slow-slow getting o—u—t," cried Mom. Billy sobbed into her dress.

"I suppose all of us lose track of time sometimes, Mrs., um . . ." Joe slapped his forehead. "Where are my manners? Here I am scaring a mother and child half to death and I haven't even introduced myself." He extended his hand. "The name's Thorvald, Joe Thorvald. I'm the curator of this museum."

As Mom jumped back from the hand, she said, "Mrs. Sally Plankton. And this is . . ."

Billy let go of Mom's soaked dress, looked Joe up and down, wiped a booger from his nose, ran to Joe, shook his hand, squeaked, "I'm Billy," and ran back to Mom.

Joe wiped Billy's gift onto the railing around the T-Rex. He looked at Billy and said, "Billy, do you know what type of dinosaur this is?"

Billy puffed out his chest. "Sure do, it's a T-Rex."

"That's right. You're smart."

"I want to see a live dinosaur. Was this one alive? Was it alive yesterday? Was it alive today? Did we miss it walking around?"

Sally smiled and Joe chuckled. "No, Billy," said Joe, "dinosaurs died out over 65 million years ago."

"Wow, that's a long time. Mister, did you see this one alive?"

"Oh, Billy," said Mom, "don't be rude to the nice man."

Billy looked up at Mom and said, "Gosh, Mom what did I say?"

Sally whispered a bit too loud into Billy's ear, "I'll tell you later."

Joe chuckled again and waved his hand. "That's okay, Mrs. Plankton. I'm sure I look pretty darn old to a young kid."

"How did all the di'saurs die?" said Billy.

Sally raised her hand as if back in class. "A massive meteor wiped them out." She smiled, proud to display knowledge in an area that mattered to her son.

Joe smiled. "No, that's what we used to believe. We now know dinosaurs became extinct within a ten-year period because all the female dinosaurs became lesbians all at once."

Sally gasped and put her hands over little Billy's ears. Billy squirmed away.

"What's a lesbian di'saur?" asked Billy.

Mom made a grab for Billy, but he evaded her with a move that would have made any Spanish matador proud.

"Mommy, what's a lesbian di'saur?"

Sweat beaded on Sally's forehead.

Billy asked, "what's a lesbian di'saur?"

Sally opened her mouth but only a gurgling sound came out. She closed it, paused, and said, "You see, Billy, when a female dinosaur loves another female dinosaur very much . . ."

"Oh, I see," said Billy, "it's just mush for lady di'saurs."

Sally looked down at her son and sighed in relief. "Yes, Billy, it's more mush."

She glared back at Joe. "You were joking about the dinosaurs, weren't you? Just a bad joke, right? A meteor really did annihilate the dinosaurs, right?"

Joe shook his head. "Sorry, ma'am, rampant lesbianism did in the terrible lizards."

Billy went over to investigate the control box for the T-Rex.

"How can you say that to my boy?" growled Sally. "How could you possibly know that?"

"Fossils."

"What fossils?" asked Sally. "I haven't heard of any lesbian fossils. Where did you find such fossils?"

"Right here, in New Hampshire."

"Oh come on," said Sally, "there haven't been any diggings in this state. You're just making a sick joke. I'm going to complain to the State Tourist Board."

"Ma'am," said Joe, "I'm telling the truth. You're right in saying there haven't been any digs in New Hampshire. But you're wrong in saying we didn't find any fossils."

"Oh yes, then where did you find the fossils?"

Billy flipped a combination of switches and the T-Rex's mouth opened and shut.

Joe said, "Just up the road. You must have heard how that granite formation known as the 'Old Man of the Mountain' fell down not too long ago."

"Yes, I have reason to remember."

"Well then, about six months ago a hiker by the name of Chester James noticed one of the fragments had an image of a dinosaur on it. We investigated the find and found dozens and dozens of complete fossils at the site.

"About a third of them showed pairs of female dinosaurs engaged in lesbian sex. The other two thirds showed solitary males.

For all types of dinosaurs, too, tyrannosaurus rexes, brachiosaurs, triceratops, ornitholestes, pteranodons, you name it, that type of female dinosaur whooped it up with one another. And you know, no heterosexual dinosaur sex, no dinosaur babies."

"How can you be so darn sure of the lesbian sex?" said Sally.

Billy flipped another set of switches. The T-Rex began to breath huskily.

Joe spread out his hands, "Gee, Mrs. Plankton, lesbian sex is lesbian sex, whether it's portrayed in a movie or caught on a fossil."

"Really," said Sally. She shook her head. "No, I don't want to hear any more." She paused and surveyed Joe. She smiled. She traced a line with the tip of her right shoe. "So, what made the lady dinos act that way?"

Joe smiled at her. "About 65 million years ago a tail of a massive comet swept over the entire earth and turned all the female dinosaurs into raging lesbians."

"Oh, how?" Doubt furrowed her brow.

"We found fragments from that comet in California. Those fragments contained high levels of the metallic compound Portobellium-235. And do you know, Mrs. Plankton, what Portobellium-235 can do to female elephants?"

"Turn them into lesbians?"

Billy flipped some more switches and the T-Rex said, "Come here, big girl. I won't bite."

"Right," said Joe. "Ten years back, we tested what few samples we had of the compound at zoos in Guam."

"I didn't know Guam has zoos," said Sally.

Joe shrugged. "Sure, now."

Sally clenched her right hand and shook it in the air. "Aha, aha! I was right. A meteor did cause the extinction of the dinosaurs." Knowledge unfurrowed her brow.

Joe nodded. "I guess you were right after all."

Sally grinned.

"I'll tell you something else, Mrs. Plankton. We're five-million years overdue for another Portobellium-235 laden comet."

The thought of that comet returning, causing another mass extinction, and providing steady work to fellow paleontologists 65 million years hence gladdened Joe something considerable. Sally warmed, as all women do, to the effects of a paleontologist's smile.

Joe said at her beaming face, "You're beautiful."

"Oh, thank you."

"Is there a Mr. Plankton around?"

"No, he died when the Old Man on the Mountain fell on him."

"Ouch," said Joe, "that's quite ironic, isn't it?"

"Yes," said Sally, "I miss him. Heck fire, I miss having a man if you know what I mean."

"Gee, that's great," said Joe. "Oh no, I mean that's horrible. Oh gosh, would you like to make hot monkey love in the fossil room?"

Joe grinned.

"But what about Billy?" asked Sally.

Joe pointed to her son. "That control box will keep him occupied for hours."

The paleontologist smiled from ear to ear.

Sally licked her lips. "Take me, big boy."

Joe, Sally, and Billy took the Cog Railway up to Mount Washington. Billy stuck his head out the window the whole way.

"Thank goodness, he's entranced," said Joe between long, wet kisses.

"He's a real train nut," said Sally before biting his right ear lobe.

The train soon reached the top and disgorged its human contents.

"So, why did you bring me up here?" said Sally as she placed her hands on the zipper of her sweater.

Joe said, "Today is the 1st annual tutu race up Mount Washington."

"A tutu race?"

"Yeah, the New Hampshire Appalachian Women Hikers Club is staging its first annual Tutu Frolic up Mount Washington. The first woman to run up the steep 6,288 foot climb in a pink tutu wins one of the Museum's lesbian fossils.

"Look," said Billy, "here they come."

Sure enough, the lead runners of a long pink line came snaking up the mountain trail.

"How come they all have white wings on their backs?" asked little Billy.

Joe tousled the kid's sandy hair. "Billy, those wings represent the souls of the lesbian dinosaurs floating up to Heaven."

Little Billy gazed into Joe's eyes and said, "Do you think there are really lesbian dinosaurs in Heaven?"

Joe put a hand on Billy's shoulder. "Why, yes Billy, I do."

"I'm glad," said Billy.

Sally shivered. "I'm getting cold."

Billy said, "I'm getting cold too."

"Gee," said Sally, "it's sure getting cold in a hurry. And it's September!"

"It can get cold in a hurry up here on Mount Washington, Why, temperatures can drop over forty degrees in less than an hour."

He scowled. "A plunge in temperatures can mean a big wind coming up. Big winds come out of nowhere here and . . ."

The loudspeaker blared, "Attention, attention, please be advised that our weather station reports a 240 mile-an-hour wind will hit Mount Washington in five minutes. Attention, attention, a 240 mile wind in five minutes. Please get inside the visitors' center and make your way down to the basement. Attention, attention, you have five minutes."

Everyone atop Mount Washington made his way to safety. Not so for the tutu-sporting hikers. One by one, the gale lifted the kicking, flailing hikers by their outfits' white wings. Up, up they went, filling the sky like pollen from a pink-and-white dandelion. Down, down the frigid tutu-clad corpses rained in nearby Bretton Woods.

New Hampshire tutu-hiking would never recover. However, tourism in Bretton Woods--already strong due to its one room devoted to the economics accord of 1944--would pick up even more with the building of a Ripley's-Believe-It-or-Not Museum. So, some good would come out of it.

Only the lead tutu hiker marched unfazed up the path and into the building. The T-Rex of feminine beauty stopped in front of Joe. Joe's blood pounded in his ears.

"Hi, handsome," said the woman hiker. "Guess who won."

"Guess you did," said Joe.

"Gonna give the winner a kiss?" She leaned forward.

Joe let go of Sally's hand and stepped toward the winner, and gave the sort of wild, passionate kiss that only a paleontologist can give.

"Want to go with me to Tahiti?" said the hiker.

Joe nodded like a bobble doll.

The hiker reached into her backpack and retrieved two sticks of jerky. She held one out to Joe. "Say, I'm hungry," aren't you?"

"Sure am." Joe smiled.

"Ugh."

Joe looked back at Sally's red, scrunched-up face.

"You're leaving me for that ugly woman. An ugly woman who's feeding you mushroom jerky, of all things."

Joe thought, "Leaving you. What ugly woman? What mushroom jerky?"

Joe held the jerky to his nose. Took a good, long sniff. It was made of mushrooms. The horror, the horror.

Joe looked at the woman hiker. How could he have ever found her beautiful? Those two bumps in her head. That long, bony nose. A monster. Ugh.

And he'd been ready to leave Sally for that monster. Joe looked at the panoramic window. Saw his disgusted reflection. Spat at it.

Joe sprinted up the stairs. "No, Joe, no," yelled Sally. But Joe kept going. Sally raced after him. Joe flung open the door and went out. Before he had even taken two steps, the wind swept him up and flung him head first into a pile of rocks.

Sally did not weep. She strode back down the stairs, her hands fists of granite. She'd show that man-stealing hiker. But she didn't find her foe. And no one in the visitors' center had noticed the winner leaving.

"Billy," she said, "we're going back home."

"Why?" asked Billy.

"Because dear, this state of New Hampshire is mighty hard on good men."

No one even noticed Bertram Blackhand swirling around Joe's body. Unlike Sally, Bertram possessed second chances to get things right with Joe.

CHAPTER 17B-BAD GUYS

Oompah, pah, oompah, pah, went the German band in Hungry Hank's meat locker. The band concluded its performance an hour later, after a series of apparently identical songs.

"Thank you," said a tall, wiry man. "And now it's time to call the All World School Board to order."

"You're not Principal Bunkum," said a voice from behind the stack of calf livers.

"No, I'm Mr. Blather, the acting principal. Bunkum has been placed on administrative leave for listening to a joke and for letting Sandra Reynolds stay in school despite missing more than twelve days in a row."

"She was in a coma," said the calf-livers man.

Blather shrugged. "Her parents knew the school policy when they let that meteorite fall on her."

"Not fair!"

"On the contrary," said Blather, "we've always enforced this policy. Why, there was that time when we had to expel that Jesus boy for missing forty days. Said he was in the desert talking to his father. Well! He didn't even bring back a note from dad. . . Moving on to our 122nd order of business."

Suddenly a shout rang out from Debbie Devil, "Oh shut up." She snapped her fingers and the entire school board turned into tidy little piles of dust.

Bless it, thought Debbie, those people needed to have gotten laid. She eyed the picture of Fen the Fishermen on the carton of Fjord Fish Sticks. Bless it, Fen was nearly as handsome as Thorvald, but alas, woefully two-dimensional.

Bertie Blackhand knocked on the door, entered, and sneezed. Ashes from the school board flew everywhere and especially onto

Debbie's Hungry Hank's uniform. "Bless it, Bertie, look at this. How can I face MY customers with the vice principal all over me?"

"Sorry, m'lady, but we did come close again. Joe almost ate that mushroom jerky."

Debbie sighed. "Yes, so close."

"And, m'lady, you were right about the portobellium-235 meteor. It did absolutely nothing to make Joe Thorvald eat mushrooms. Just wiped out all the Cretaceous dinosaurs."

"Oh that, don't give it a second thought," said Debbie, "I don't mind mass extinctions. Let's focus our positive energies on Joe Thorvald."

"Yes," said Bertie, "and if you'll give me your uniform I think I'll have just enough time to get it clean before your lunch break is over. Might even toss in another attempt on Joe's soul."

"But I'll be half naked until you come back," said Debbie as she handed over her uniform. "What if someone comes in while I'm like this?"

The evil chef winked at her. "And maybe that someone will be a Lutheran." He bowed and left.

The sometimes ravishing force of Evil sighed. Her confidence evaporated. It just doesn't matter if you're the Supreme Evil or not, try as a woman might; it's plain hard to find the right man. She had only eleven more attempts before Armageddon. That's what the stripes on the wall said.

CHAPTER 17G-GOOD GUYS

Lee permitted himself a slight frown. "Mr. Erickson, how was it that you found yourself unable to come to Mr. Thorvald's aid on Mount Washington with a timely taco or Swedish meatball?"

Pedro Erickson hung down his head. "Sorry, General, but I was at Bretton Woods' exhibit of fixed exchange rates and lost track of time. When I finally stepped outside, I found myself in the middle of New Hampshire's 1st Annual Taco Barbeque.

"Hundreds of people came up to me. A few dozen said I looked quite well despite having been dead for more than a decade. But they all wanted me to sign autographs and share a grilled taco. I didn't want to be rude and, well, I stayed a little longer."

Lee sighed inside. "Astounding."

"Sorry, General."

The Southern General held up his hand. "We'll say no more about it. Come, let us anticipate those people's next move."

"Those people," said Erickson, "are awfully hard on dinosaurs. Thank goodness for my Teddy T-Rex. He's the last of his kind."

"My dear Erickson, I have some rather bad news about Teddy."

"Oh, no!"

"Sorry, sir," said Lee, "but Teddy drank some flouridated water and spontaneously combusted."

Erickson collapsed sobbing on the big table. "Damn dentists! Please leave me, I want to be alone."

Lee went to the refrigerator, retrieved a cold root beer, and placed it beside Erickson. He gave the Swedish-Mexican chef a manly pat on the shoulder. "Sir, there are no dentists in Heaven. I hope that provides solace to you."

As Lee left Heaven's war room he heard Erickson shout, "Oh Teddy, my little Teddy, they never loved you."

Astounding thought Lee, that twentieth-century chefs could get so emotional over their pet dinosaurs.

CHAPTER 18-PLATO AT THE AIRPORT

Bertram Blackhand flitted back to Mrs. Devil, leaving a groggy Joe Thorvald with yet another body, another life.

"Good evening, it's two o'clock at San Diego's Lindbergh Field," came the heavily accented voice behind Joe. "Got goatsmilk?"

Thorvald's head throbbed. He whirled around intending to deliver a few choice words in Swedish to the airport bum. Instead, he froze. Right in front of him stood Plato, the great but long-gone Greek philosopher, sporting a spiffy Ronald McDonald's toga. Had he, Joe Thorvald, really been in the check-in line long enough to die and go to Heaven?

"I could really use some goatsmilk," croaked Plato.

Joe didn't know what to say so he made small talk. "Aren't you Plato, the founder of the famous academy in the grove of Academus and the developer of an idealistic paradigm with mathematics as the model of reality, and a renowned barbequed-ribs lover?"

"That's me. Got goatsmilk?"

"Oh sure," said Joe, "I have some in my carry-on bag." Joe removed his thermos. "Plato, how do you speak English so well?"

"It's a long story," said he.

"Plato, we're at an airport. We have plenty of time."

"Well, I went to Pella to give Alexander the Great a copy of *The Idiot's Guide to Conquering the Persian Empire* for his eighth birthday. My voyage back to Athens got canceled when a pirate fleet plundered and sank the incoming trireme. I took my ticket to Acropolis Lines. They honored it but routed me through their port hub in Miletus. Fog caused the ship from there to run aground in Rhodes. Couldn't get out of that port for six years because of a blockading enemy fleet. I took the first ship out. It went to Alexandria, Egypt."

The nondescript people in the next line nodded along with Plato's story.

"Well, one natural, or manmade, disaster bounced me from one city to another. Spent all my life in ports, stagecoach stations, train stations, and airports reading scrolls, reading newspapers, and watching television. My favorites are CNN and the Children's Channel. Love that Barney. He's super dee dooper."

Plato sighed. "But my luggage never did catch up with me."

Thorvald favored the learned man with a long look. "It's amazing you're in such great shape after all these years."

He straightened and smiled. "It's my diet. Olive oil, bread, and goatsmilk. I recommend it to everyone."

Plato and Joe bellied up to the counter. The ticketing agent flashed her warmest smile, the one she reserved for famous-and-really-ought-to-still-be-dead-Greek-philosopher customers and their friends.

"And where will we be traveling today?" the representative for Leaping Cows Airline asked Joe.

"I'm traveling to Madison, Wisconsin," said Joe.

"Doesn't everyone, Mr. Thorvald?" The agent took Joe's ticket and punched in 3,236 letters and numbers. She looked up from her keyboard and asked, "And now, Mr. Thorvald, did anyone else pack your bags?"

"No."

"Were your bags at anytime out of your possession?"

"No."

"Did any Frenchmen ask you to carry mushrooms for them in your bags?"

Joe's face reddened something considerable. "Why, you think I'm carrying French mushrooms in my bags. Hell no! I'm a God-fearing American. You, you, you . . ."

"I'm sorry, Sir," said the agent, "we live in dangerous times. Those French, you know."

Joe grunted.

She looked at Joe's gray-haired companion and his cheery toga. "And where will you be traveling?"

"To Athens," said Plato.

She waited for him to produce his ticket. He did not.

"Mr. Plato," she said, "do you have a ticket?"

Plato padded his toga frantically. He shook his head.

"I'm sorry, sir, but you must have a ticket to board our airplanes."

"He doesn't have a ticket," said Joe. "I'd like to purchase one for him."

She favored Joe with a you-idiot-can't-you-read-the-big-sign-above-my-head scowl. "Well, I don't know. This line is for ticketed passengers only."

Joe flashed a retaliatory I'm-still-upset-you-thought-I-might-be-smuggling-mushrooms-for-those-French frown. "But, he was probably contemplating the dichotomous natures of the seen and unseen universes and wandered into this line."

"It's still the wrong line."

Joe pointed. "But there's no one behind us."

"Well, okay," she said.

Plato bowed in appreciation. "Super dee dooper."

"Mr. Plato, what would you like?"

The Greek said, "I would prefer to board the very first trireme leaving port."

"What's a trireme?" asked the agent.

"It's a boat with three banks of oars on each side manned by galley slaves," said Plato. "Do you have one of those? It's still the only civilized way to go."

She shook her head. Her shoulder length raven-black hair swished from side to side. As she did so a gigantic, goofy grin erupted across Plato's stoic face.

Plato fell in love with her, in Lindbergh Field! And the Cubs had just won their division. What a day!

Anyway, the smitten philosopher probably didn't even hear her say, "Oh no, Leaping Cow Airlines wouldn't have anything like that, not with all those new FAA regulations."

"Do you fly to Athens?" said Joe.

"Oh yes," she said, "Leaping Cow only goes to San Diego, Albuquerque, Madison, and Athens."

"Any non-stops to Athens?"

She made 1,722 keystrokes, frowned at her computer, and said, "No, none from San Diego, but . . . " She made 789 clicks, looked up, and smiled, "there is a nonstop to Athens from Albuquerque. Hmm, I could get him on the next flight to Albuquerque. It leaves in 47 minutes."

"Great," said Joe, "he'll take it."

She looked at the main man of Western Philosophy. "Mr. Plato, I'll need to see some identification."

Plato straightened, put his hand over his heart and said with noble voice, "I am Plato. I swear this by the goddess Athena."

The agent scowled. "I'm afraid sir, that won't do. I must have proper identification."

As contrived luck would have it, Joe spied a copy of Plato's Republic by the agent's left elbow. "Look at that."

She glanced at the book and said, "Yes, that's Plato's Republic. I read it whenever there's no line. It gives me enough perspective to deal with those difficult mimes."

"Amen to that," said the tall man behind the next ticketing counter.

"They take so long to gesture their final destination. The only one I get right away is Chicago, the Windy City, and we don't fly there. Yep, Plato gets me through the day."

"Yes, yes, yes," said Joe, "the book's great, but look at the cover. That's Plato." Joe gestured to Plato. "Can't you see this man is Plato?"

She looked twice at the book cover and at Plato. She asked the opinion of the nearby ticketing agent. He agreed; Plato was Plato.

"Okay, Mr. Plato," she said, "I'll issue you the ticket."

Plato burst into tears. "No one has ever been so kind, and to me, an eternal traveler. I love you. What's your name? Would you be, could you be, my wife?"

Tears streamed down the agent's makeup like the Big Muddy in flood season. "No one, kind sir, has ever been so nice, so thoughtful, so appreciative to me, ever. Oh, I love you, too. My name is Katie McIntyre, and yes, I will marry you."

Plato leaned over the counter and embraced his love. They kissed wildly, passionately until the adjacent agent made a great show of clearing his throat.

The two lovers looked up at the throat clearer. The man pointed ahead and said, "Katie, you have a long line, a long line of mimes."

Katie brushed away her tears and said, "Well, Plato, I'd better issue you those tickets to Albuquerque and Athens. That is if you still want to go."

The nemesis of millions of bored students in philosophy classes through the centuries sobbed. "No! I don't want to go. I don't really want to go. There's no one for me in Greece anymore. They've all been dead for 2,300 years."

She smiled. "You don't have to. Stay, stay."

"Excuse me, Katie," said Joe, "but Plato's old enough to be your hundredth grandfather."

She fixed Joe with an icy stare. "Look, Mr. Thorvald, Plato's young at heart. You'd better let true love flourish or I'll send your luggage to Tokyo."

Her fingers poised over the keyboard.

"You're right," said Joe, "he has a kind face."

Katie smiled in triumph, but Plato frowned.

"How will we live?" said Plato. "I have no employment. All my pupils are dead. I have no more savings."

Katie's eyes misted. "I barely make enough for myself." Her lower lip protruded.

Joe tugged at Plato's sleeve. "Plato, I can get you a job teaching Swedish at the University of Wisconsin. I'm the department head."

Plato shrugged. "It's been over two millennia since I've had a steady job. Just lost my job as a walking billboard for McDonald's. Yes, Mr. Thorvald, I'd be honored to teach Swedish for you."

He extended his hand and they shook.

"Katie, my love," said Plato, "I won't be going to Athens after all. Please, get me on Mr. Thorvald's flight to Madison. Will you wait for me?"

She pouted the pout of the brokenhearted. "No," she said, "I finally meet the man of my dreams, a man who charms my heart and invigorates my mind and what does he do? He walks out of my life leaving me to deal a mob of useless mimes."

The waiting mimes gestured outraged protests.

Katie yelled at them, "Oh, go stick your hands in your pockets." She collapsed sobbing to the counter.

The nearby agent came over and put his arm around her shoulder. "It's okay, Katie, it's okay. Go to Madison with Plato. We're hiring lots of ticketing agents there. I'll take care of these mimes."

She looked up at her rescuer. "I'll always be grateful, Robert. I'll always remember this."

Robert favored her with a regal nod, went back to his counter and addressed the mimes, "Over here, please."

A mime walked up to Robert.

"What is your final destination?" Robert hoped it was six feet under home plate at Petco Park.

The mime demonstrated an asthmatic rhino making an over-the-shoulder-catch in center field. Robert gripped his Plato's Republic with white-knuckled hands.

Joe arched his eyebrows. Did all the employees read that book? No wonder Leaping Cow was known as the literary airline.

Meanwhile back at our counter, Katie said to Plato, "We'll be together. Can you believe it?"

"Super dee dooper, I cannot wait to teach you about philosophy."

Katie leaned forward, stroked Plato's cheek, and smiled. "And I can't wait to teach you about the mile-high club."

Plato ejaculated, "Super dee dooper."

CHAPTER 18B-BAD GUYS

"Oh, crap," said Debbie Devil as she squirted another stripe of ketchup on the locker's wall. "We used up another incarnation of Joe."

Bertie Blackhand thrust a spanking clean uniform at Debbie. "Here it is. Did you get lucky while I was away?"

Debbie stamped her foot. "No! Only Steve the Stock boy came in and he is but a Unitarian. A shy one at that."

Bertie turned away as Debbie put on her clothes. "Sorry, m'lady."

Debbie finished with the last button. "You may turn around, I'm done.

"And speaking of failures, Bertie, I noticed in this last attempt on Joe, you weren't even there to tempt him with a mushroom or anything. How the Heaven, did that happen?"

"Well, m'lady," said Bertie, "I slept in."

"You slept in?"

"Yes," said the evil chef, "I set my clocks back one hour last night instead of ahead an hour. I'm afraid I'll never get Daylight Savings quite right. But it won't happen again. I went right out and bought myself a watch that sets its time to radio waves from the National Center for Time."

Bertie proudly displayed his new wristwatch to Debbie. The Supreme Evil sat down on a crate of Belgian escargots and sighed. She wondered, did the watch count ketchup stripes?

CHAPTER 18G-GOOD GUYS

"Well, General," said Erickson, "that was easy. Bertie and Debbie never tried anything on Joe. I had no evil to fight."

"So what did you do with your time down there?" asked Lee.

"Well," said Erickson, "I went to the Saranac soda factory in New York, and brought you back an ice-cold case of Saranac Root Beer."

Lee smiled and bowed. "I'm much obliged, sir. Did the Pearly Gates Customs Station give you much trouble?"

"Nah. Oh, and I looked up Clint Eastwood and got a signed, glossy 8" by 10" photo of him as Rowdy Yates."

Erickson produced the photo and gave it to the general. Lee's eyes misted.

"Oh, and I almost forgot," said Erickson, "I got Patty Duke to sign one as well."

Tears rolled down Lee's cheeks. He tried to speak, but couldn't. He even thought of hugging the good chef.

CHAPTER 19-THE WAYS OF MEN

Chief Inspector Henri Champignon and his wife, Deputy Inspector Charlotte, strode toward the unexpected noise. Years of experience told him that a stand of trees overlooking the beach does not, no not ever, party wildly in English, especially not in the inert seaside town of Cayeux. Must be people behind them.

Charlotte tugged at Henri's sleeve.

"Hallo," shouted Henri. "Who is there in these trees?"

The trees became mysteriously quiet.

"This is Chief Inspector Henri Champignon. Come out. I know you are there. I heard your loud voices talking."

"Oh, bugger," said one voice.

"Oh now you've done it," said another voice. "He'll never believe we're not here now that you've talked."

"He might have passed it off as the wind whistling through the trees, if you hadn't confirmed it," said the first voice.

Henri turned to his wife. "*Mais oui*, I was right. Men are hiding in those trees."

Charlotte tugged at Henri's sleeve.

"*Eh bien*, Charlotte," said Henri, "you wish to say something?"

Charlotte pinched her husband's hand. "*Mon chère* idiot, I wished to whisper something. I wished to creep up on these men and see what they were up to."

Henri shrugged and walked toward the raucous Englishmen. "Come out here. This is the law."

"Bugger off."

"We are the inspectors of Cayeux," said Charlotte. "Come out or we shall arrest you."

"Oh bloody hell, Joe," said one Englishman. "The frog law has a woman in it."

Joe Thorvald, the tall, blond nobleman with the physique of a pumped-up Hercules, rushed out from the trees into the clearing. Henri Champignon grabbed his pistol and fired. Bullets peppered a nest of once nearly, now totally, extinct Picardian Gnatcatchers. But this was France, so the Champignons shrugged.

Joe pointed a dirty finger, his in fact, at the law. "Now see here, I can take a man trying to kill me, but we don't want any woman around when we have dug a fifty, or so, mile tunnel just to get away from women."

"You hate women so much?" asked Charlotte.

"No, we love them. All but me are married."

"You are not? *Pourquoi?* But you are so handsome."

Joe blushed. Henri clenched his fists. The rest of the Englishmen emerged.

"He has an ugly woman chasing him," said one tall man. "Bony nose and two tufts of golden hair. Not like you dear lady. You'd be a right proper sweetheart for Joe. Quite the dish."

Charlotte smiled. Henri raised his right hand and stepped forward. "*Ça suffit.*" He addressed Joe. "Who are you and what are all you English doing here?"

Joe straightened. "I am Sir Joseph Thorvald of Brambleborough. I have the honor of being the chairman of Her Majesty's Branch of the European Union's Thistlewort Counting Association."

"But *Monsieur* Thorvald," said Henri, "I see no thistleworts with any of your men, only those bottles of beer."

Joe waved his hand. "Oh, it's been a bad day for counting thistleworts. Haven't counted one. Better luck tomorrow, what?"

Charlotte raised one eyebrow, Henri raised two and pointed beyond the Englishmen, "You dug a tunnel here?"

"No," said Joe, "we started from Dover. Completed it exactly ten years ago. That's why we were celebrating."

"*Mais monsieur,*" said Charlotte, "why did you dig to here, to Cayeux? Calais is so much closer. Why did you not dig to Calais?"

A ruddy man named Chester raised his glass of ale. "What, and ask someone for directions?"

"*Mais messieurs*," said Charlotte, "why did you not tell the world? England and France spent billions completing the tunnel from Dover to Calais. You could have saved everyone so much time and money."

"Well, *madame*," said Joe, "then we would have let our women in our secret hiding place."

Charlotte rolled her left eye. "You dug a tunnel over eighty kilometers long, for who knows how long and for how many years! *Sacré bleu*, but why?"

"So we could do things our women wouldn't let us do," said Joe.

Chester belched. "Like having a few pints in the morning."

"And playing darts and wearing yesterday's clothes," said a redhead bloke called Thomas.

A small smile appeared on Henri's face.

"Not picking up our food and dirty socks," said Joe.

"Swearing up a storm," said Chester, "and forgetting the year."

Charlotte sneered. "You imbecile, the year, it is 2001."

Thomas, who knew it to be 2000, kept his gaze on Henri. "Winning arguments with our Missus."

Henri stepped a bit closer to the Englishmen. "But *messieurs*, you do not have your wives with you."

Joe smiled. "That is why we win."

"Bloody right," shouted Chester, "we don't stand a chance at home."

A broad grin appeared on Henri's face.

Joe swept his arm toward the trees. "*Monsieur*, our tunnel lies this way. Would you like to take a look? We'd be most honored to show you."

Henri bowed. "*Certainment*, after you."

Charlotte scowled. "And what about me, eh? Do I not go with you?"

Henri waved both his hands toward her. "Oh but no, *ma chèrie*, stay here. These men are quite dangerous." He turned back to the Englishmen. "You are dangerous, no?"

"Oh, quite," said Chester.

And so Her Majesty's Branch of the European Union's Thistlewort Counting Association led Henri away to the tunnel entrance.

Henri wept. "*Mon Dieu*. It is so beautiful."

Henri's eyes surveyed the well-lit tunnel; its state-of-the-art ventilation, two-lane road, titanium train tracks, saloon paintings of nude women, mountains of beer bottles, beer cans, half-eaten sandwiches, empty bags of crisps, and dirty sweaters whose colors couldn't match any to be found in the known universe.

Henri's nose surveyed decaying ham sandwiches and mugs of stale beer. The Frenchman tried to speak, but the words would not come. His tears flowed.

Joe laid a hand on Henri's shoulder. "Welcome home, Man."

"I have always dreamed of such a place," sputtered Henri. "But you English, you, you have created paradise."

Joe smiled. "Thank you, we're rather proud."

Chester walked right up to the Frenchman's face and belched.

Henri's nose twitched. "But, you are allowed to burp a liver-and-onions sandwich in another man's face?"

"Got it in one," said Thomas, "that's why we moved millions of tons of dirt and bedrock. And we get to do this too." The redhead put his left hand down the front of his plaid pants and scratched his bum with his right.

Henri clapped. "*Liberté*."

Thomas bowed. He sneezed on his left hand and wiped it on his pant leg. His face contorted with concentration as he treated the ensemble to a thunderous fart.

The fart echoed for minutes before it disappeared into the far reaches of the tunnel. No one spoke a word until the noise stopped, each one savoring the magnificent timbre and resonance. Henri wept anew as the tunnel's ventilation system kicked into high gear.

"Dear friend," said Joe, "we'd be honored if you favored us with a blast of your own."

Henri shook his head. "Oh no, *mes amis*, I could not do such a grand thing."

"What did you have for lunch?" asked Thomas.

"Oh my Charlotte, she made me a magnificent bacon, onions, and egg omelette."

Thomas looked at his watch. "Then, Mister Inspector, I suggest you are armed and ready."

"*Oui*, I am." Henri clenched his jaw, clenched his fist, unclenched the muscles in his buttocks and let loose a Gallic bombardment sounding very much like *La Marseillaise*.

Thomas shook hands with Henri. "For years, I was the best. But I saw no successor, no apprentice. Now I hand off the baton to this worthy man."

The Frenchman bowed. "As your Sir Isaac Newton said, 'If I see farther, it is only because I have stood on the shoulders of giants.'"

"Well said," said Joe. "In just five minutes, we'll guzzle ale, eat peanut-butter-and-onion sandwiches while telling rude, crude, pointless jokes. My dear Henri Champignon, would you like to join our little society?"

"*Monsieur*, I would be most honored."

"Capital," said Joe.

"But I have just one small question," said Henri.

"What is it?"

"*Eh bien*, where did you put all that dirt from the tunnel?"

Joe shrugged. "Oh that, we put it in a small parcel of land between two shires. If it's not in someone's jurisdiction it doesn't exist."

Henri sighed. "It is the same here in France."

Henri shrugged. Joe shrugged. The other Thistlewort Counters shrugged in solidarity.

"We meet here the first weekend of every month," said Joe. Can you come?"

"*Mais oui.*"

"We tell our wives we're doing vital work for Her Majesty's Branch of the European Union's Thistlewort Counting Association," said Joe. "What will you tell your wife?"

The Frenchman shook his baton. "I shall tell her that I am on a secret mission to stop criminals from smuggling American electronics into *La Belle* France. It shall be a lengthy investigation, no?"

Joe put his arm around Henri. "Henri, this is going to be the start of an odoriferous friendship."

CHAPTER 19B-BAD GUYS

Debbie Devil stared at the new ketchup stripe adorning the locker wall. She counted them. Eighteen. She yearned for a bag of Twizzlers, but didn't have the energy to go back into the store and buy one. Debbie even had to get Steve the stock boy to open the ketchup packet and make the latest stripe. She sighed. Time to count those stripes again.

Bertie Blackhand knocked, opened the locker door, entered, and smiled. Debbie tried to raise her eyebrows at Bertie, but the force of gravity proved too strong today. Bertie gauged her listless state and felt tempted to be sarcastic. He quickly killed the idea. Oh sure, he could probably get away with it today, but then tomorrow she'd turn his surviving daughter into a used-car saleswoman. He shuddered inside. Instead he reached into a large, white canvas bag and produced a sack of candy.

Debbie's nearly closed eyes focused on the sack in Bertie's right hand. They opened up. She smiled. She giggled. She clapped her hands.

"Oh Bertie, chocolate covered Twizzlers. You know what I like."

"Yes m'lady, I really know what you like," said Bertie. He produced a Venus flytrap. "One of your favorites, I believe, m'lady."

"Flowers, for me!" said Debbie. "Why, thank you."

"And of course, m'lady," said Bertie, "I brought some food for it as well." He reached once more into the sack to retrieve a plastic bag of newly stunned Portugese flies.

"Oh Bertie, you can be so thoughtful after you fail so stupidly."

"Sorry, m'lady, but I really thought I was being clever this time. You see, the mushroom was Henri Champignon. I thought *Monsieur* Champignon would make friends with Thorvald. Then they would go to eat at a French restaurant, and as you know, Supreme Evil, the French can't help but put mushrooms in everything they make.

"Joe Thorvald would eat the mushroom-ridden food and, *voilà*, you'd have your saucy, Lutheran boy toy."

"Good plan," said Debbie, "except for a few small details. One, the name Champignon only means mushroom in French, it does not make him one. Two, the good inspector tried to kill Thorvald. Three, Champignon did not convert Thorvald to French food; Thorvald converted the French inspector to English fare.

"Now, not only did you fail to get Joe Thorvald to eat a mushroom, there is one fewer Frenchman eating that fungus. Perhaps his wife Charlotte will stop eating them as well. Maybe millions of Frenchmen will no longer garnish everything with mushrooms."

Debbie leaned forward. Steam roiled just inside her ears. "Bertram Blackhand, do you know how much time I've spent over the centuries to get the French to eat mushrooms? I've tried so hard with those people and now, and now . . ."

She buried her head in her hands and sobbed.

"M'lady, I knew how you would feel about that, so I took the liberty of getting you this. Debbie raised her head. Bertie reached into his white bag and produced a small glass bottle.

"Bertie, you got some perfume for me?"

"Yes m'lady, but not just any perfume. It's *Sueur de Beau Lutheran*."

Debbie clapped her hands. "*Merveilleux*, where did you get this? I could never afford *Beau Lutheran* on my salary. Oh, you should have."

Bertram's hat relaxed somewhat. "You know, m'lady, why don't we forget this little setback and add random fees to millions of bank statements?"

"And I'll splash on some of this *Sueur de Beau Lutheran*, eat chocolate covered Twizzlers, and feed stunned flies to my flytrap," said Debbie.

Still, Armageddon might be near. Debbie reached into her shirt pocket and retrieved a small red book full of phone numbers. She flashed a smile at Bertie. "And I might have a surprise for you as well."

CHAPTER 19G-GOOD GUYS

"You're a great tactician, General," said Pedro Erickson.

Lee bowed. "Thank you my dear Erickson for your kind remarks."

"You're welcome," said Erickson. "but how did you know Bertie Blackhand would try to use a French inspector to get Mr. Thorvald, the head of a women-fleeing, cross-channel tunneling society, to eat mushrooms after failing to get Plato to give mushrooms to Mr. Thorvald at San Diego's airport because of confusion over how to reset one's watch at the onset of daylight savings?"

"Well," said Lee, "those people are easy to predict."

Chef Erickson didn't find those people's actions obvious, but he reckoned it was such mental acumen that made Lee a great military leader.

"But," continued Lee, "you frustrated the enemy without recourse to your formidable tacos or Swedish meatballs."

Erickson shrugged. "Ah that was easy. I used my brother Bertie's own English food against him. I knew Inspector Champignon would join our side when presented the opportunity to fart without nagging from his wife. Don't all married men yearn for such freedom?"

Indeed, Lee's wife, Mary, never had approved of his post-dinner blasts. It didn't matter that he couldn't help it. And so he had requested posting to Mexico in 1846 right after eating her cucumber-and-thistlewort-seed soup.

His brilliant scouting brought on one stunning military success after another as he and the American Army tooted freely all the way to Mexico City. And America gained by this campaign as well, acquiring the territories of New Mexico, Arizona, and California.

Then in early 1861 General Winfield Scott offered Lee the command of the Union Army for the upcoming Civil War. He almost accepted, but Mary made such a face when he passed gas after eating her ham with honey-and-thistlewort-seed glaze.

That command in Washington, D.C., would be just across the river from his Arlington home. Mary would certainly want to eat dinners with him. And she certainly wouldn't let him pass gas afterward. Oh, the pain of trying to keep it in.

So the gastrointestinally-challenged general went upstairs after that very dinner to resign his commission in the Union Army. Later, he got offered the command of the Army of Northern Virginia. His brilliant leadership against overwhelming Union forces prolonged the war for years, ensuring that 600,000 men would die.

Ah, well.

Lee nodded. "But, my dear Erickson, how did you know Mr. Thorvald's friend would favor Inspector Champignon with a sufficient enough, um, um, um . . ."

"Fart," said Erickson.

"Yes thank you," said Lee, "to impress a Frenchman."

"I'm a chef," said Erickson. "I made sure the friend ate plenty of peanut-butter-and-onion sandwiches and good old English sausages. Of course, it didn't hurt that I heavily spiced the food with thistlewort seed."

CHAPTER 20-LAUGH OR DIE

Joe the Clown removed his big red nose and inhaled deeply. His clown face registered as much satisfaction as a clown face could. He'd win the prestigious Poway Clown Barbeque Cookoff. He always had the best rib sauce, made with English thistlewort.

His red clown nose rang.

"Oh bloody, fucking hell!"

As Joe ripped off the red telephone nose and placed its left nostril to his white-painted ear, the shocked look on the judges' faces told him not to expect many points in the congeniality section. Didn't matter, though. He knew he would have to leave this contest.

He spoke into the red nose's right nostril. "What's up, doc?"

The cheery voice from the phone nearly curled Joe's rubber lip. "Oh hi, Joe. Hope I'm not interrupting anything."

Joe snarled. "Just the Poway Clown Barbeque Cookoff."

The voice said, "Sorry Joe, but we have two serious ones."

"I'm not going, you fathead. Let the damn doctors heal their own damn patients with their own damn medicine. Oh, botched punch line; every doctor wants a piece of my funny bone."

"Have you forgotten," said the voice, "that you're a charter member of the Healers of Ha?"

Joe sighed. "I'll be there."

"Good." The nose clicked off.

The clown stomped toward his limited edition, Rolls Royce Ha Ha 303. He got in and sped off. Atop the car, big ears on a plastic clown's head flashed red and blue. An eerie "Pull over. Ha, ha, ha," sounding like two mating armadillos emanated from the clown's head.

Most cars did pull over. A fresh-off-the lot BMW did not. Its driver gave Joe the one-fingered salute. Joe pushed a red button. The

Ha Ha 303 catapulted a custard pie onto the BMW's windshield. Danged scofflaws. Fantastic high-arc shot.

Joe burst through the hospital's emergency entrance. The receptionist looked around her tower of admittance forms. "Well hello, Joe. Good to see you again. Got anything for me? A diamond ring, perhaps?"

Joe patted his outfit. Shook his head. Patted some more. Reached into his top pocket and smiled. "Ah, here it is."

The nurse beamed. Joe gave the rubber ball in the shirt pocket a good squeeze. Water squirted from his fake flower, drenching the nurse. The nurse's dripping face erupted into a smile. She collapsed laughing into the tower of forms. Her ha-ha storm burst across the waiting rooms, spreading good will and releasing endorphins everywhere.

Even a weary mother, barely holding onto her unconscious, hastily bandaged daughter, chuckled.

Joe smiled again. Laughter always felt good. "Where are the patients?"

The nurse looked up. "The first is in E.R. 2," she wheezed. "He's dying to meet you." She gave a mighty whoop of laughter and fell off the chair. "Ow, ha, ha, ha."

Joe tightened the grip on his bag of tricks and took off down the hall just as fast as his oversized shoes would let him.

He burst through the emergency-room door. "Howdy, howdy, howdy, did someone call for a Healer of Ha?"

The doctor's head hung down and the head nurse's lip quivered. "Oh Ha Healer," she said, "it's bad. We took him off anesthesia, so you could help him. You're our last hope."

"How bad is it?" asked Joe.

"Real bad," said the doctor, "his appendix burst an hour before getting here."

Joe put his hands to his bright-orange cheeks. "Gosh."

"It gets worse. In his pain, the man put his hand into his table saw. Cut his hand right off."

"Zowie."

"It gets worse. The hand flew off and up. Gave him the finger--to his eye. Poked it out."

"Yikes."

Joe and the nurses bit lips to stifle giggles; no healing properties in unsympathetic laughter.

Joe gazed down at the patient and fluffed his red tufts of clown hair. "Hey guy, look at me. I'm having a bad hair day."

The patient didn't smile. Didn't even try. Joe sucked in air. He told the one about the kangaroo going through customs.

"Bye bye," said the patient as his eyes closed for the last time.

Joe's eyes misted. Humor had let him down. "Damn."

Another nurse came into the room. "Joe, Joe, you're needed in E.R. 1."

Joe glared at her. "Do you really want a failure to help?"

The intruder scanned the room and the clown. "Now see here, Joe Thorvald, I have no time for your self pity. Get your sorry clown ass over there."

Joe shuffled after her and into the next room. "Thank goodness you're here," said the head doctor.

"What's up, doc?"

The doctor tilted his head toward an impossibly pale man on the examining table.

"He ate a bad batch of George's mushrooms. We pumped his stomach, but his vitals are still falling. He should be fine, but he's just plain given up."

Joe walked over to the table and looked. He felt the weight lift from his shoulders. "Why he's dressed as Lex Luther. This should be easy. A few classic jokes and he'll be laughing in no time."

The head nurse put her hand on his shoulder. "There's something you should know. He's a Young Republican."

"Shit," muttered Joe, "he's dead meat."

The doctor wept. "Don't give up, Bozo. I've done all medical science can do. I'm not a clown. I'm a doctor, dammit!"

"Okay, okay, I'll do my best."

The nurse managed a weak smile. "The angels themselves can't do more than that."

Joe screwed his mirth to the sticking point and gazed at the young man. He told the one about the hero sandwich and the blimp. Nothing. He presented the knee slapper about the Albanian artichoke in Cleveland. Nothing. Joe sighed.

He let out all stops pantomiming a rhinoceros giving birth to twins. The patient stared at him and whispered, "Are these jokes?"

Joe wiped the sweat from his brow. Facial paint ran down his gloves. "I'm sorry, doc, the man has no funny bone. He's a goner."

The doctor slung down his head. "He's my patient, too."

Joe's left hand became a fist and struck the palm of his right hand. "No, it's not going to happen to us. I am so stupid. It ain't pretty, but I know what will make this man laugh."

Joe leaned close to the man's ear and whispered, "Hey, Lex Luther, why did Bill Clinton cross the road?"

Sparks flashed in the patient's eyes. Joe continued, "To have sex with an intern."

The corners of the young man's mouth turned up. A smile began to spread across his face. Teeth appeared. So did faint sounds. Were they? Yes, they were, they definitely were "Heh, heh." Soon, a mighty torrent of "Har dee har hars" crashed over the whole room.

Nurses, doctors, the anesthesiologist, and various mystery attendants of the emergency room grabbed each other and danced with wild abandon.

The Young Republican sat up and shouted, "I want to live. I want to live. Thank you, Bozo, thank you."

Joe just sprawled in a chair by one of the pinging machines, and reached into his vest pocket. He retrieved a packet of candy cigarettes and removed one. He stuck the stick in his mouth, took a long lick, and blew off the powdered sugar.

Yes, life was worth living after all. He mattered. In fact, he wouldn't change his life with anybody in the world.

But a dark fog swirled toward Joe as a man in a black chef's hat put a hand on Joe's shoulder. Joe would indeed change.

CHAPTER 20B-BAD GUYS

Debbie squirted another ketchup stripe on the wall of Hungry Hank's frozen-foods locker. How many more stripes before Armageddon? Twenty-six stripes minus nineteen is . . . Hmm. Time for mathematical assistance.

She grew sixteen more fingers to make a total of twenty six. The Supreme Evil furrowed her brow and vaporized nineteen fingers, one for each ketchup stripe. She started counting the remaining fingers. Yes, in *seven* days she'd unleash . . .

Loud banging issued from the other side of the door. "Blessed handle won't work," came from the great unfrozen beyond.

Bertie materialized through the door. His black chef's hat stood erect, pulsing with red streaks.

"I must most vehemently protest, m'lady," said Bertie. "You ran the last attempt on Thorvald's soul without me. I looked at the tapes and you weren't there; just some short, swarthy bloke."

"Yes, that's right. My helper hails from India. His name is Singay Orissa. But his phone name is Art."

"Singay Orissa. But why?" asked Bertie.

"I outsourced your job," said Debbie. "It's sure tough trying to defeat God for Joe Thorvald's soul and manhood, and oh, dominion over everything in the universe on what Hungry Hank's pays me. Singay doesn't oversleep and was willing to work for a lot less."

"But m'lady, Singay Orissa, . . ."

"Call him Art. That's his phone name," said Debbie.

"Whatever, the point is that he failed," said Bertie.

"So have you, Bertie, so have you. Eighteen times, in fact."

"But m'lady, Singay will fail in exactly the same way, time after time, if you let him. I know, I set up the system. Damned or not, they'll all look through their manuals.

"In this case, Singay looked through his '1,001 Evil Uses for Mushrooms.' It's standard in India. The closest thing in there to 'Hex Lutherans' is 'Lex Luther.'

"And where does an evil-outsourcing-Indian find his living Lex Luther? At a comic-book convention. So, he shoved Mr. George's evil mushrooms down a comic-book conventioneer's throat."

"Was that the Young Republican that Joe Thorvald rescued in the Emergency Room?" asked Debbie.

"Yes, m'lady." Bertie threw his red streaked hat to the floor. "It was. We didn't even get a random soul out of it."

Debbie offered a conciliatory bag of pork rinds to the English chef. "Singay, or some other Indian could try again."

"I'm telling you, m'lady, they'll look at that '1,001 Uses' manual and find the same entry for Lex Luther and another conventioneer will head to E.R. M'lady, you can't afford to have the same old failures. You've got to use me."

"Okay, then," said Debbie, "eighteen minutes of time out for you. Then you're back on the job."

"Very good, m'lady." Bertie picked up his hat--which was totally black again, having regained its composure--and left the locker.

Debbie reopened her red book of phone numbers, just in case Bertie didn't outdo Singay.

CHAPTER 20G-GOOD GUYS

Lee scratched his chin. "Those people astound me. Their mercenary, Singay Orissa, didn't accomplish anything. In fact, my dear Erickson, those people didn't give you anything to do."

"Nope," said Erickson, "No need to make any tacos or Swedish meatballs. Didn't have to go into my kitchen at all."

Lee looked at the room's big message board, then at Erickson. "Sir, I strongly suspect those people need to regroup." He sighed. "Still, I'd be grateful if the message board favored us with some scouting reports."

"No problem, General." Erickson arose from his chair and walked to the board. He punched it with his fist. "We should have bought the extended warranty. After all, we have an eternity up here in Heaven."

The board crackled and fizzled. Words on it came into focus. "Sinister plan of Evil in complete disarray."

Lee smiled. Erickson threw his white chef's hat into the air and whooped. "It'll take days for my brother to come up with a new plan to get Thorvald."

"Can we rely on that?" said Lee.

"Absolutely," said Erickson, "Bertie's an English chef. When was the last time they came up with a new food?"

Lee digested this intelligence and reviewed those people's latest string of feeble failures. He knew, just knew, the next attempt would be serious. But for now, Erickson was right.

"Yes, my dear Erickson, "it appears that those people have given us a chance to take a furlough. What place appeals to you?"

A furlough, a vacation. Erickson grinned until his facial muscles hurt. Where to go? Where to go? "Oh, I know, I know, let's go to

Paris and eat at Maxim's. Then we can go to the Folies Bergère and watch beautiful half-naked women sing and dance."

Lee frowned.

"But in the most tasteful way possible, General."

The frown remained.

"Or, we could go to NBC studios and watch shows being taped."

Lee shook his head. "No, I fear that wouldn't do, either. I do appreciate your kind offer, but *The Patty Duke Show* and *Dobie Gillis* appeal far more to my tastes than do all these new reality shows. I say, my dear Erickson, have you ever seen *Bachelor Economist*, *Fundamentalist Island*, or *Bikini Vice President?*"

Erickson shook his head vigorously. He had seen all of those back on Earth during a bout of insomnia, but he didn't want to disappoint the old gentleman by saying so.

"Then, where would you like to visit?" asked Erickson.

"The map of the world, please," said Lee.

The map appeared on the right wall.

Lee walked over to it and put a finger on Honolulu. "My dear Erickson, I've been thinking of spending some time here."

"What would we do?" said Erickson.

"Oh," said Lee, "we'd sit on beach chairs just a few yards from the ocean and sip ice-cold root beers. And the mugs would have little pink umbrellas in them. We'd just sit there and watch the waves roll in and out. And I'd watch my cares and responsibilities wash out with them."

A tear formed in Lee's right eye as he faced Erickson. "I never got to leave those on Earth, ever. Nor up here. I need to be carefree, just once, if only for a few days."

Erickson gave Lee a big hug. Lee's arms hung rigid. Then he too gave Erickson a tentative hug. They unclenched.

"Oh course, General, of course. but you can't go to Hawaii wearing that."

Lee inspected his outfit. "Would it not be appropriate?"

Erickson whistled. "Oh no. It's been well over 100 years since a Confederate General's uniform was hip. And you don't even want to be anywhere near heavy wool clothes in Hawaii."

Lee nodded. "I place my sartorial selection in your capable hands. What do you suggest?"

Erickson snapped his fingers and a pair of green shorts with palm trees and an orange tee-shirt with white flowers appeared on the table before Lee.

In spite of his best efforts, Lee groaned. "My dear Erickson, you don't actually wish me to wear these?"

"Don't worry, General, you'll fit right in."

"But," said Lee, "they're not me."

"Oh come on, General. Live a little bit. You did say you wanted to be carefree."

Lee bowed. "I did. If you'll excuse me, I'll go change in the next room."

"Fine," said Erickson. He extended to Lee a pair of Ray Bans. "You'll need these, too."Lee frowned at the sunglasses. "The root beer shall be A&W and the mugs frosted?"

"Oh absolutely, General."

Lee took the sun glasses. "Sir, we have an agreement."

CHAPTER 21-SILENT MIMES

The man in the orange trench coat on the steps of the Natural History Museum stood as inconspicuously as he could. He wished he had brought his faux orange tree to hide behind.

He dismissed the notion. The good people of San Diego would surely notice an orange tree on the steps to one of their museums. Ah, but would they care? He decided not to chance it.

The man produced his Bushnell 303 Mime Finder binoculars: also orange so as to blend in with the trench coat. He focused on the Orange Mime, Olaf, who performed in the square by the fountain.

No San Diegan ever suspected Olaf was a Norwegian Orange Mime. How could they tell? Did they even try to tell?

Ah well, that was all for the better, for then they would never even suspect that Orange Mimes were the most powerful secret society in the world. Oh sure, there was that time when the Illuminati were number one, but then the Norwegian Orange Mimes beat them in a winner-take-all game of Candyland.

A rare Andean condor pooped on the man's orange overcoat, disturbing his reverie. The white splotch also brought about unwanted attention to the orange undercover man. Fortunately, the crowd returned its attention to Olaf the Norwegian Orange Mime.

Joe Thorvald was in the crowd watching Olaf. The man in the trench coat trained his binoculars on Joe. Joe removed his clown's nose, looking embarrassed. The man in the trench coat spoke into his cell phone. "Governor Erickson, Mr. Thorvald removed his clown's nose. Tell Iowa to secede from the Union."

"But it's lunch time in Iowa," said the governor. "Can't secede on an empty stomach."

The man in the coat sighed. "After lunch, then."

And Iowa seceded at 1:01 p.m., but happy and fed.

Olaf mimed a man trying to pump up a bicycle tire. Joe smiled. The man in the orange coat dialed. One minute later, on the New York Stock Exchange, shares of General Mills jumped 83%.

Olaf pantomimed a rendition of "Take Me Out to the Ball Game." Joe didn't get it, frowned. The man in the coat spoke again into his cell phone. One minute later, the Joint Chiefs of Staff decided to invade Peru.

Olaf pulled out all stops with his version of two ant colonies fighting. Joe laughed and laughed. The man spoke again. One minute later, Hank Fletcher, the richest Iowan anywhere, announced a $500 million donation to the Salvation Army.

Olaf pretended to throw a pass to Joe. Joe went deep. And at the Super Bowl, Homer LaFong caught a long bomb for a touchdown.

Olaf laughed silently at Joe. Joe struck Olaf on his big, red nose and walked away. The man spoke into his cell phone and a minute later, Jamaica performed a successful test of an atomic bomb.

Olaf and the man in the trench coat went to a Taco Bell for chicken chalupas. Joe headed home. A man in a black chef's hat detached himself from the crowd; he'd been well hidden until then.

Bertie, the evil English chef, caught up with Joe just near the Model Railroad Museum. A mime, Mike, with an orange cell phone and orange suspenders, stepped out from its entrance and followed the two.

Bertie ran in front of Joe and puffed. He held out his hands. "Whoa, there stranger. Let me catch my breath."

Joe stopped, but he really would have preferred Bertie to be female. Joe, a typical American male, found that huffing, puffing female English chefs always made him horny. Oh dear, I've given away *Cosmopolitan*'s deepest secret.

Bertie regained his breath. "Thanks. I saw what that mime did to you. Outrageous."

Joe nodded. "It makes my blood boil. I wanted to have words with the pus bag, but he was a mime." Joe shrugged.

"So you settled for punching him in his nose, but then his big orange honker absorbed the blow."

Joe nodded.

Bertie put his arm on Joe's right shoulder. "You know, friend, there's only one thing for you in this situation. You need to eat as many fried mushrooms with salsa as possible."

"You know," said Joe, "I really could go for a big sizzling bowl of fried mushrooms with salsa. Lead on McDuff." The Orange Mime called and Taco Bell added chicken tortas to its menu.

Bertie smiled at Joe's useless literary reference. They walked arm in metaphorical arm toward the Prado Restaurant. They could see people playing Frisbee on the lawn before them. And a minute later, John Deere announced it would be starting a line of combination golf carts/lawnmowers.

Suddenly, a Frisbee shot out, hitting Joe in the face. An old white-haired and whiskered gentleman clad in green shorts with palm trees and an orange tee-shirt with white flowers ran toward Joe. Erickson followed.

Lee took off his sunglasses and said to Joe, "My dear dude, I most humbly apologize for the errant throw of my Frisbee."

Joe rubbed his face. "Think nothing of it, old man." Lee winced. Joe continued, "Nice clothes."

Lee bowed. "Thank you, sir. And again, please accept my apologies."

Erickson stepped forward and addressed Joe, "Hey, want to join my friend and me for lunch?"

Bertie sneered at Erickson. "So, the old 'Frisbee-to-the-face-from-an-elderly-Southern-general-in-Hawaiian-clothes-then-whisk-my-guest-away-to-your-own-lunch trick.' Well, I'm not falling for that one again. C'mon Joe, your fried mushrooms await."

Bertie and Joe took a few steps toward the restaurant. Erickson placed himself in front of them.

"Out of my way, goody two shoes," said Bertie.

"Over my dead body," said Erickson.

Bertie's face went blank. "But you are dead, twice."

"Oh yeah," said Erickson, "I meant sez you."

Bertie raged. Erickson danced. "Ha, ha, I win the argument. You must yield to my superior reasoning."

"No," said Bertie, "I will not."

"Hey, no fair," said Erickson. "You lost the argument. I said, 'Sez you' first. You should give up Joe and step aside."

Bertie laughed. "Oh bite me. I work for the Supreme Evil. I can do what I like."

Erickson's head bowed and his shoulders sank. The good chef tasted defeat. He could never get his tacos and Swedish meatballs down Bertie's throat for he well knew that Debbie Devil provided an anti taco-and-Swedish-meatball force field to all her minions. Sort of like a human employer giving his workers a 401(k) plan.

Joe paid scant attention to this debate of a surprisingly high level between two dead chefs. He gazed past them, into the restaurant where two mimes, one orange and one green, were hand signing obscenities at each other.

Lee did not see mimes. He did see that Joe was about to eat mushrooms. Then Debbie Devil would win Joe's body and soul and the entire forces of Good would be in permanent retreat.

Still, he declined to rush in. After all, good manners are never out of style. He coughed. Erickson just stood there, his head hanging down.

Bertie made a clever tactical move and walked around the inert Erickson. Joe followed.

Lee coughed again. Erickson paid him no heed. Bertie signaled for a maitre d'. "My dear Erickson," said Lee, "snap out of it."

But Erickson did not snap out of it. Bertie and Joe sat down at their table. Lee tugged at Erickson's sleeve. Erickson did nothing.

Bertie and Joe ordered fried mushrooms with salsa. Erickson stood still. Forces of decorum and necessity raged within Lee.

Lee's fist shot upwards. "Cowabunga." He grabbed two small glass jars from Erickson's ever-present belt pouch. Lee walked briskly toward Bertie, jumping over a pair of mimes attacking each other with Bowie knives.

Lee placed himself beside Bertie and summoned as much dignity as an elderly gentleman in sunglasses and Hawaiian clothes can muster.

He addressed Bertie. "Sir, I must insist you leave Joe and this restaurant forthwith."

Bertie sneered at Lee. "Pish."

Lee frowned. "I can plainly see that I am not dealing with a gentleman."

Bertie giggled. "Duh." Joe giggled out of confusion, but Denmark did not invade Norway a minute later.

The two mimes drove their long knives into each others' throats. Temper, temper.

"Then so be it," said Lee. He turned his hands around to reveal a long glass spice jar of cumin and another one of allspice.

Bertie paled. "Taco and meatball spices. What are you going to do with those?"

"I must insist again that you leave Joe, now," said Lee.

"No way, I won," said Bertie. His hand twitched, knocking over his glass of water.

"Then I am afraid I must do this." Lee made a cross with the two economy-sized spice jars designed for the on-the-go chef in eternity.

Bertie trembled. "No, no," he squeaked.

Lee said nothing but unscrewed the tops of the spice jars. Bertie whimpered.

As Lee showered cumin and allspice over Bertie he intoned, "In the name of the Father, Son, and Holy Ghost."

Bertie became smaller and smaller. "Help me! If I was only good."

All that remained of Bertie was a pile of loose sausage meat soaked in grease.

"My dear sir," said Lee to the evil chef's remnants, "You should have said 'If I *were* only good'." He paused and bowed to the pile. "My humble apologies. Perhaps this is not the best time to amend grammar."

Joe looked at the offal heap. "Boy, I thought I was having a bad day." He shrugged; just another afternoon in San Diego's Balboa Park.

Joe motioned for Lee to sit down "So, would you like to join me? There's two orders of fried mushrooms coming up."

Lee grimaced. "No thank you, sir. I would prefer to eat elsewhere."

Joe pointed to the dying mimes. "Don't let that spoil your appetite. Those green and orange mimes have been killing themselves by the dozens lately. Nobody seems to know why."

"Have you ever asked them?" said Lee.

"Oh no," said Joe, "they're mimes. They won't talk."

"They might for me," said Lee.

"More power to you," said Joe. Lee smiled inwardly and walked over to the gurgling mimes.

Lee knelt and addressed the green mime. "Kind sir, please confide in me. I come from Heaven and have the ear of our Lord, God."

A raspy voice issued from the green mime. "I am Tobor Hobias, from Hungary. I am a member of the Illuminati."

"The most powerful secret society on Earth," said Lee.

"We used to be." Tobor laughed twice. "First the Orangies won secret supremacy when they beat us at Candyland. But that wasn't good enough for them.

"Soon, orange mimes started killing off our members one by one. We formed our own army of green mimes, but it was too late. We are doomed to extinction."

With that, Tobor gave a death rattle and died.

Lee shuffled over to the orange mime and said, "Kind sir, please confide in me. I am here to help."

"I am Sam," said the orange mime. "I am a member of a society so secret that I don't even know its name."

"How do you remain anonymous when other secret societies fail?" asked Lee.

"We act randomly," said Sam.

"Randomly?" said Lee.

"Yes," said Sam, "that's how we avoid detection. All the other societies have an ultimate purpose, and so behave with a distinct pattern. This pattern ultimately becomes known to another society no matter how much the first society tries to hide it. We act randomly and so never display any pattern. This is our foolproof armor against detection."

"But," said Lee, "I must ask how you pick your random event generator."

"Oh that," said Sam, "we pick an individual, in this case Joe, and follow him. Every one of Joe's actions has consequences for the world according to our master handbook.

"Why just today, Joe's actions made shares of General Mills go up, moved America toward war with Peru, affected the Super Bowl, and made Jamaica a nuclear power.

"Before that we watched Tim Thorton. When little Timmy cheated on his arithmetic test in 1933, we put Hitler in power in Germany. When Tim dented his neighbor's Ford in 1939, we told Hitler to invade Poland."

"Amazing," said Lee. "What would Mr. Thorvald need to do for the Cubs to win the World Series?"

Sam laughed. "Oh, Joe would have to learn particle physics and jump thirty-six feet in the air." Sam gurgled once more. His head rolled to one side and he was no more.

The Southern general prayed over the dead mimes and arose. He walked over to Joe who was snacking on some oyster crackers.

"My dear sir, would you like to join my friend and me at The Old Town Mexican and Swedish *Café?*"

Joe grinned. "For some of their tacos and Swedish meatballs?"

"Yes sir," said Lee, "those are Heaven's entrees.."

Joe shuddered. "I almost ate mushrooms."

"I know," said Lee, "every family has its moment of weakness over the millennia. That's why my friend and I are here."

A sheepish Erickson nodded and extended his hand to Joe.

CHAPTER 21B-BAD GUYS

Bertie Blackhand walked into the food locker holding his head. "Oh man, I have the mother of all headaches." He saw through his fingers Debbie Devil sitting on a stack of vegan head cheese.

"Did you take minion strength aspirin?" asked Debbie.

Bertie nodded. The effort sent waves of pain crashing up and down his neck. "Do you have an ice pack?"

"Sorry, Bertie, no."

Bertie flew around the room knocking over one stack of wondrous frozen foods after another. "Why can't we have a bloody bag of ice cubes in a frozen locker?"

The evil chef's mad ramblings made him fall onto a 100-pound bag of frozen shrimp. "Blessed bag." He kicked the bag until it tore open.

Even in extreme pain, the cranial synapses of English chefs still function. Bertie plunged his throbbing head deep into the bag of frozen shrimp.

Forty-five minutes later Debbie pulled out Bertie's shrimp encrusted face. She laughed hysterically for another five. "I'm sorry Bertie, but, but, just look at you. Ha, ha, ha."

As we all know, English minions who have been reconstituted after melting down are particularly irritable. "If I could but remove these shrimp frozen to my eye lids, I would see a horny devil who doesn't have a Lutheran hunk between her legs."

Balls of fire flashed from Debbie's eyes. The shrimp on Bertie's head absorbed the heat. In an instant the sauce melted and the shrimp turned a golden-orange. Sauce ran down Bertie's face into his mouth. "Mmm, shrimp scampi sauce. I love shrimp scampi."

Debbie jumped up and clapped her hands. "Me too, me too." For, of course, everyone, evil or bad, loves shrimp scampi. It's the one thing we all have in common. So, remember that when someone cuts you off on the freeway.

Debbie and Bertie spent the next nine minutes in an orgy of scampi eating.

The Supreme Evil looked at her watch. "Oh dear, I have only a minute left before I must be back at my checkout stand." She put a hand on Bertie's right wrist. "Oh Bertie, I am sorry that goody General Lee melted you down with cumin and allspice. It must have been awful."

Bertie nodded. "It was dreadful. And I'm sorry about my comment about the Lutheran hunk. Bless it! We were so close, again."

Debbie nodded.

"Checkers needed, checkers," said the voice on the public address.

"Must run," said Debbie, "Can't keep customers waiting."

CHAPTER 21G-GOOD GUYS

Erickson sat at the long table and hung his head. "I'm sorry General, I froze. I just froze."

"Think nothing of it," said Lee. He went to the energy-efficient mini-refrigerator and returned with two ice-cold bottles of Heavenly Brothers' Root Beer. He put one beside Erickson.

"I brought a root beer for you," said Lee.

"Oh take it away," said Erickson, "God knows I'm not worthy of it."

"I'm not worthy of it either," said Lee. "My internal debate lasted so long Joe almost ate a mushroom. My dear Erickson, our lord God doesn't expect us to be perfect. He just wants us to love everybody, even mimes. For He loves everyone."

"Does God even love mimes who are attorneys for companies that put mushrooms in school lunches?" asked good chef Erickson.

"God loves even them," said Lee.

"*Ja caramba*," said Pedro Erickson, "then God still loves me even after I froze down there."

"Yes, he does," said Lee.

A wrinkled smile spread across Erickson's face. He grasped his cold mug. "I believe I *will* join you in a root beer."

CHAPTER 22-STRIKE

Poway is a beautiful place; the city in the country. People in Poway look out for each other; make sure they eat good food. When they eat mushrooms, Detective Joe Thorvald goes to work.

Joe read the sole headline on Yahoo news. "Bowling Ball Causes Level of Lake Poway to Fall."

Detective Joe Thorvald clicked on the title. The article that came up postulated a man and a bowling ball in a rowboat in the middle of Lake Poway. The article asked the reader what would happen to the level of the lake if the man threw the bowling ball into the water.

Joe guessed the level would stay the same. "Ha, ha," stated the article, "you're wrong." Joe snarled. The article continued, "While in the boat the ball displaces water according to its weight, in the water the ball displaces water according to its volume. Since most bowling balls are denser than water the level of the lake falls."

Joe sighed. He knew he was wasting his time looking for cyber clues about those mushroom terrorists.

That night the level of Lake Poway dropped ten feet.

The next night, it dropped twelve feet.

Joe walked into Dr. Seuss Memorial Building on Monday. The receptionist said, "Good morning, Joe, you'd better hotfoot up to the chief's office. He's mighty concerned."

Joe opened the door to Chief Sedgwick's office. The chief's brow sported an extra line. Joe sighed. What new wave of filth had splashed over Poway?

Sedgwick tossed a manila folder across the desk to Joe. Joe withdrew three 8" by 10" glossies of Lake Poway. "Notice anything, Joe?" said Sedgwick.

"Yes, chief, there's eight topless waitresses on the fishing pier."

Sedgwick waved his hand. "Bah, they show up every weekend. My wife won't let me fish there anymore because of it." He sighed. "No, Thorvald, look again."

Joe scanned the photo for a minute. "That old lady crouching behind the juniper tree appears to be Amelia Earhart."

Sedgwick's fist squished against his avocado-green metallic desk. "No, Thorvald, look at the lake, look at the lake."

Thorvald did so. "It's dropped twenty-two feet in the last two days."

Sedgwick leaned forward. "Yeah, that's what concerns me. Concerns a whole hell of a lot people on the City Council. That lake's our city's only source of water. No Lake Poway, no showers, no drinking."

"But chief, couldn't we import two-gallon containers of water?"

Sedgwick raised his greenish fist. "Danged avocados. I can't see them on this greenish desk." He licked his hand. "Must be a better way to make guacamole. Um, where was I?"

"I was asking if we could import water," said Joe.

"No we can't. For two-hundred miles in every direction, the level of every lake and stream is falling. California's facing a massive shortage of good ol' drinking water."

"What about fizzy-orange water?" asked Joe.

Sedgwick groaned. "There's some left. Not much. They're going to start rationing that today." Sedgwick closed his eyes briefly and sighed again. "Let me tell you, a one-minute shower with fizzy-orange water isn't satisfying." He pointed to his Mr. Coffee machine. "And man, I'm never going to get used to coffee made with that stuff."

Joe Thorvald and Sabado Domingo jumped off the pier into the pedal boat. Joe's partner, Sabado, looked exactly like the stereotypical 6'8" Hispanic detective and operatic tenor he was.

Joe and Sabado exchanged meaningful glances. These professionals knew what to do. They were in a pedal boat; they pedaled. Sabado looked at his Mickey Mouse Rolex and said, "Joe, we have to be back by 10:22; we rented for one hour."

- 203 -

Joe nodded. When they were halfway to the middle of the lake, they let out the mile-long nylon net. Joe said, "It's against international law to use these for fishing, but they're great for trawling bowling balls."

Sabado nodded. A few minutes later, they felt a tug on their boat. Joe said, "I do believe we've caught a bowling ball."

In fact, it was a black Brunswick sixteen pounder. The detectives hauled it aboard.

"Do you think we raised the water level?" said Sabado.

"Only one way to find out." Joe removed a Michelson interferometer from his green duffel bag. He took his measurement and compared it with the reading he'd taken when they got in the boat.

"Yep," said Joe, "we've raised the level of the lake by thirty Angstroms."

"*Ay caramba*, that's not much difference."

"Well," said Joe, "it's a start."

"*Ay*, there must be many, many bowling balls in this lake."

"Yep."

Joe and Sabado hauled in one bowling ball after another until water began to lap over the boat's gunwales. A fly buzzed the open bucket of guacamole and menudo near the bow.

Sabado waved his hand over and over at the fly. "*Ay caramba*, that fly likes my lunch too much."

The fly avoided Sabado's effort and landed in his bucket. The fly provided just enough weight for the overloaded boat to sink. As the lawmen treaded water, Joe said, "Why couldn't you have brought a peanut-butter-and-onion sandwich like me?"

That night the level of Lake Poway dropped another five feet. The governor of California declared San Diego County a disaster area and requisitioned all fizzy-orange water north of Santa Barbara. He applied to FEMA for assistance. FEMA sent eight squadrons of C-143A cargo planes, all of them loaded with the same life saving fizz. Thank goodness, America is still the fizzy-orange-water leader of the world or unknown fiends would have us by the *cojones*.

The next night, the level of Lake Poway dropped another five feet. President Metate flew back from a summit with Swedish Premier Taksamikka to lend his moral support.

Metate stood between Sergeants Thorvald and Domingo. He held in his hands a navy gray, magnetized, NASA-IIIzg, zero-gravity bowling ball, the type used by the astronauts on the space shuttle. He faced the reporter.

"This bowling ball is the enemy," said Metate. "This is making the water level of this lake fall. It's making the level in all other lakes in the county fall as well.

"Soon, there will be no water left in San Diego County. Good people everywhere, Democrats too, will have to leave. And, my friends, it won't stop there. Soon, all America will be without water if we let them. But we won't let them.

"So, as of one o'clock Governor Whistler will sign an order authorizing the California National Guard to gather bowling balls from all affected lakes. And I shall instruct the Navy to bring out of mothballs all of its 346 BBT-133, bowling-ball trawlers." President Metate grimaced. "When the Cold War ended, we thought we'd never have to use these trawlers again." He sighed. "May God bless all involved in this just cause."

Metate raised his right hand to salute the absent National Guardsmen and pilots. Gravity, an ever vigilant force of nature, took the opportunity of the saluting hand to tear the bowling ball away from Metate's left hand. Pulled the bowling ball to the ground, in fact.

The bowling ball gathered speed as it rolled down the ramp to the lake. "Stop that ball," yelled Metate.

Thorvald and Domingo leapt toward the ball. So did two Secret Servicemen. They crashed into each other, letting the bowling ball speed into the lake unmolested.

Domingo and Thorvald got up and dusted themselves off. "Think we lost our jobs, Joe?" said Domingo.

"Probably," said Thorvald. "Hey, wait a minute." Joe pointed to the green measuring device. He looked closely at the output. "Holy cow, it says that Metate's bowling ball made the water level rise 0.25 Angstroms."

"How is that possible?" asked Domingo.

Thorvald slapped his head. Thank goodness, he wasn't holding a bowling ball. "We have all been so stupid."

"How so, *amigo?*" said Domingo.

"Elementary physics, my dear Domingo," said Thorvald. "Throwing a bowling ball into water always raises the water level."

"Not when you throw it from a boat," said Domingo.

"Yes," said Thorvald, "but you had already raised the level of the water when you rowed out onto the lake with the bowling ball."

"So," philosophized Domingo, "when you throw the ball from the boat, you will lower the level of the lake by less than the amount you raised it by getting into the lake with the ball. So, the net affect is to raise the level of the lake."

Joe and Domingo exchanged meaningful glances.

"Is that true?" asked Metate.

"Yes, it is," said Thorvald.

Metate shook Thorvald's hand. "Well done, sir. You've saved America."

Within minutes, Metate authorized the use of a million WWII surplus bowling balls and 300 C-143a transports to fly them.

Soon, Joe watched as clouds of transports darkened the sky over Lake Poway.

"Well, this will make the level of Lake Poway rise," said Domingo.

"Yes," said Thorvald, "but something bothers me."

"What's that, *amigo?*"

"How come the level of the lake went *down* after all those bowling balls were thrown in it?"

"*Ay caramba.*"

"Exactly, something's making our lake drop. The bowling balls were just hiding that."

"We should do something about that," said Domingo.

"Too late," said Thorvald.

A million black, two-holed Brunswick balls splashed into the lake. An incipient tidal wave vanished when a giant sucking sound announced the formation of a whirlpool in the middle of a lake.

Minutes later, all could see the lake had vanished into a massive circular hole in the middle of the lake bed.

A thousand National Guardsmen followed Thorvald and Domingo to the edge of the hole. They heard countless splashes and voices yelling from below.

"What are they saying?" asked Thorvald.

A guardsman with "Fung" on his uniform tapped Thorvald on the shoulder. "I know Chinese. They're yelling something about some damned bowling balls crashing into their tunnel, ruining their plans."

Joe gritted his teeth. "They're up to no good."

Captain Bob the Guardsman stood up and addressed his men, "Soldiers, we've got to stop those Chinese. Can we kill them?"

"Yes, we can!" yelled his men.

The men took out long ropes, standard issue with the California National Guard, and rappelled into the great, flooded cavity. Thorvald and Domingo inched down slowly behind.

"Holy cow, the water is up to our necks," said Thorvald.

"*Ay caramba*, and I already bathed this morning," said Domingo.

From all manner of side tunnels, countless men adorned with hundreds of orange sponges hurtled themselves into the vast lake of the great chamber. Their sponges expanded as the water level dropped and disappeared. Their jobs done, the now immense sponge men squished away into dark recesses.

"Beats a showing of the *Cirque de Soleil* any day," said Joe.

Guardsmen charged forward and fought Chinese soldiers in all directions. That event, unusual even for a subterranean Southern California day, did not fully engage the detectives' attention.

To the west lay an immensely tall, well-lit tunnel stretching to infinity.

"They've dug and built a tunnel all the way from China," said Joe. "They meant to conquer us."

"But *amigo*, where's their army? I only see, maybe, 700 soldiers. Not enough to conquer us. Why didn't they send more?"

Joe peered at the tunnel for a spell. "Well, big as that tunnel is, it's still not enough to send more than 10,000 at once. Hardly enough to conquer the good old USA."

"USA, USA," yelled Domingo.

The advancing guardsmen took up the cry. Joe didn't. Something bothered him. He walked to a far away wall. Domingo followed.

"Look," said Joe.

"*Ay caramba*," said Domingo.

"You said it," said Joe. All along the base of the wall and in its crevasses, as far as the eye could see were large clumps of tungku mushrooms.

"Those bastards," said Thorvald, "those bastards meant to conquer America with mushrooms. They knew they couldn't beat our army fair and square, no one can. So, they decided to poison our meals with tungku mushrooms."

"*Ay caramba*," yelled Domingo.

Thorvald nodded. "Yep, they envied our industrial strength, our military power, our freedoms, our tacos, our Swedish meatballs. They didn't have those, so they weren't going to let us have them either.

"I see it now. They were planning to infiltrate large amounts of tungku mushrooms into our supermarkets and farmers' markets. As you know, widespread eating of mushrooms brought down the Roman Empire and Charlemagne's empire and brought hundreds of years of chaos to Europe. The Chinese meant to do the same here."

"But *amigo*, why didn't they go by double-hulled ocean freighters and hide the mushrooms between the hulls?"

"Because our Customs agents were too efficient. Remember that sting operation we did two years ago against those North Korean mushrooms?"

Domingo nodded.

"Well, they apparently decided this tunnel was the only way to get their mushrooms into our land of freedom. Too bad for them, their tunnel began leaking. That's why the lake began to fall."

"And all those bowling balls in the lake?" asked Domingo.

Joe grinned. "I suspect the Chinese didn't read the same article we did and put all those bowling balls in the lake at night, so we wouldn't notice the lake falling right away."

"It's a lucky thing, *amigo*, that President Metate ordered the bowling-ball bombing of this lake."

"Yes it is," said Thorvald. "Say, Sabado, what do you say we get out of this tunnel and rustle us up some good-ol' Quarter Pounders at McDonalds?"

"Sounds good, *amigo*. No mushrooms there."

"Sure aren't, pal. The biggest burger company in the world, an American company, doesn't serve mushrooms."

"God bless the USA."

CHAPTER 22B-BAD GUYS

"Pull," shouted Debbie Devil.

Bertie Blackhand pulled and the Bushnell Skeetflinger 303 flung a pig ball across Hungry Hank's frozen locker.

Debbie tracked the streaking pig ball with her shot gun. She pulled the trigger. The pig ball exploded fling gory bits all over the stacks of Gut Goner's fish shakes.

"Bertie, you know, that could have easily been you," said Debbie.

Bertie winced. Someone knocked on the locker door. "I heard a shot," said the voice. "Debbie, are you all right?"

"I'm fine, Steve. I'm just skeet-shooting pig balls."

"Having another bad day?" asked Steve the stock boy as he came in.

"Yep. This helps calm my nerves."

"Well," said Steve the stock boy and a credit to Unitarians everywhere, "I wish you'd remembered to use your silencer. It's upsetting the shoppers."

Debbie paled. Attempts to snatch Joe Thorvald's soul and so win supremacy over God would come and go, but an upset customer who left Hungry Hank's would never come back.

"Okay, Steve. I'll be right out. I was done anyway." Debbie gestured to the gore. "Mind cleaning that up?"

Steve the stock boy groaned inside. Of all the Evil things Debbie did: starting wars, damning souls, and breaking up families, he hated her messy streak the most. Better get a hot sponge and right quick too before the pig-ball bits froze to the frozen fish shakes, or no one would buy them.

He'd like to wash off those ketchup stripes, but Debbie had turned him into a pig ball the one time he'd tried. Thank goodness, no one ever hated Unitarians for long.

CHAPTER 22G-GOOD GUYS

"General," said Pedro Erickson, "we won another victory."

"We did indeed," said General Lee.

They clinked frosted mugs of ice-cold root beer. Deep lines appeared on Lee's forehead.

"Is anything wrong?" said Erickson.

Lee put down his mug. "I hope my dear Erickson, it will not spoil our good humor if I inquire why you did not show at those people's last attempt?"

"I was at my mother's birthday party," said Erickson. "I knew you had the situation with the tunnel under control all along. And, I saved you some apple pie."

Lee smiled. "Thank you, sir. Yes, my dear Erickson, Bertie's plan to get the Chinese to bring mushrooms to America's supermarkets, and hence to Joe, via a sub-Pacific tunnel after personally failing to get Joe to eat mushrooms in the Prado Restaurant in San Diego's Balboa Park after watching a mime show and an orange and green mime kill each other was predictable."

Bertie grimaced. "I hate mimes."

Lee nodded. "So do I. So did the whole ante-bellum South."

"I didn't know you felt that way," said Bertie.

"Yes sir, we all did. Abraham Lincoln was known down South as a lover of mimes. We all feared he would spend Federal moneys to oppress our glorious Southland with traveling mime shows. That's the real reason we seceded from the Union."

"*Ja caramba*, General, that was a legend spread by his political opponents during his first political campaign. Lincoln never liked mimes. He hated them. I know. I met the man. You and the South fought America's bloodiest war over a misunderstanding."

"Oops, my dear sir, oops."

CHAPTER 23-WHISTLE WHILE YOU WORK AGAIN

The psyops major stood outside the door of the mud-splattered stone hut. Light flickered through the cracks. His stomach growled. How he hungered for a crispy, shredded-beef taco. Bah! Nothing to eat here but the Army's endless papaya meals-ready-to-eat and the occasional thistlewort berry.

Land of eternal mud. Land of hidden, evil mushroom fields. Louisiana? No, Defghijklorstan. How come he never got to invade the fun Middle-Eastern countries?

Defiant shouts of gibberish blew through the open windows. Damn, another hard case. Well, Joe Thorvald would show them. He patted his leather-clad box. No one, no one stood up to the contents of his Bessie.

Muscles rippled along the arms and legs of his Herculean body as Joe strode to the oaken door. He raised his fist of granite against the thick door. The door didn't even struggle, crashing meekly to the floor. "Knock, knock," said Joe.

Sergeant Perkins got up from his chair, strode toward him and held out his hand. It disappeared into Joe's massive mitt. Tears rolled down Perkins' baby face.

Joe scanned Perkins. "You're not Sergeant Kaida."

"No sir," said Perkins, "Last night, Al Kaida kinda met with a fatal accident at our military checkpoint."

"Oh, that Aloysius." Joe shrugged. "Where's the prisoner?"

Perkins pointed his swelling hand to the dark corner. "He's a real bad ass. Won't say a damned thing."

Joe walked to the dark shape and said, "Shit, Sergeant, he's a puny thing, a real runt." He pointed to the little captive. "You couldn't get that to talk?"

"Nope," said the sergeant, "he's a tough one. I tried everything the Army taught me, tied him up and everything."

Joe harrumphed. Damn the privatization of the army. "Well, I have a few more tricks up my sleeve." He stared at the young man. "How come you couldn't bring that runt over to my building? How come you made me come through all that mud?"

Perkins raised his hands. "He went noodlely on me, sir."

Joe's brow furrowed. "He went noodlely?"

"Yes sir, I tried to pick him up, but instead of cooperating he went limp like a baby, like a wet noodle."

Joe waved his hand. "Enough." He bent over the captive and said, "Talk, dead meat."

Dead meat said, "*Abu haram nabil korasan.*"

Perkins said, "And that's another thing, that's Defghijklorstanian talk, sir. I don't know how to speak Defghijklorstanian. I'm fluent in Khomarian."

Joe sighed. "So?" Damn new army sergeants. Kept babbling.

"We were supposed to invade Khomaria," said Perkins, "but the advance guard kinda got lost. Took the wrong fork in the road. Then, Old Man Salton, our general, didn't want to ask for directions. So we kinda invaded this country instead."

Joe stood up and raised the regulation right eyebrow at Perkins. "Hmph, didn't know. The President said we were going into Defghijklorstan to make the world safe from Defghijklorstanian mushrooms."

Sergeant Perkins allowed himself a small grin. "Well, we are now, but like I said we were sent to wipe out terrorist bases in Khomaria, but we kinda got lost."

"Well, Sergeant, I was sent here to interrogate prisoners, and so I'm going to interrogate prisoners."

Joe's artistic side made a mad bid for supremacy. A thin smile appeared as he contemplated the influence of Van Gogh's paintings on neo-French minimalism. But not for long; he spat at the captive. Damn that vacation in Paris.

"Besides," Joe continued, "I can't think of anything more evil than mushrooms. About time we had a just war."

He looked again at the huddled form on the ground. Looked close. Looked hard.

"Why you miserable scum," said Joe, "I know you. You went to Stanford."

"Don't all Defghijklorstanians?" asked Perkins.

Joe continued staring at the prisoner. "I know you. You're Hassan Amman, the terrorist who put paprika in that huge vat of dough at the Alpha Beta Delta party. For weeks, anyone who ate one of those buttermilk doughnuts got the mother of all bellyaches. I hate you."

Hassan smiled the smile of the damned. "You Americans, it is time you know fear."

"No, you know fear," said Joe.

"No, you know fear," said Hassan.

"No, you know fear," said Joe.

Hassan simulated shaking. "Ooh, look at me. I'm so scared. Oh please don't hit me."

Joe unclenched his fists. "No, Hassan, I'm not going to hit you. Wouldn't do any good with your type. Wouldn't give me enough satisfaction, either."

Joe reached into his bag of tricks and removed a gleaming, platinum dentist's drill.

"No sir, no," said Perkins, "dentists' drills are against the Geneva Convention."

"Calm down, sergeant, I'm just going to fill his cavities. I'll use root beer for anesthesia."

"But sir, root beer isn't an anesthetic, not even Barqs."

Joe looked at Perkins with mock astonishment. "It isn't?" Joe shrugged. "So much the worse for him."

"You're trained to use that?" asked Perkins.

"Nope," said Joe, "but the Defghijkie has lots of teeth. Should get it right by the 32nd tooth, though." He turned the drill on and moved close to Hassan. An almost insignificant movement brought the drill into Hassan's quivering lower lip. A great red gusher drenched Joe's shirt.

Blood drained from Perkins' face. "Excuse me, sir." He grabbed his stomach and ran to a corner to expel great waves of this morning's MRE.

Joe smiled at Perkins. "See why I don't worry about eating spaghetti for lunch? The blood stains blend in." He faced Hassan.

"Oops," said Joe to Hassan, "It seems I missed. I'll get inside your mouth on the next attempt, really I will."

Hassan gurgled and spluttered, his eyes aflame, his body shaking from the loss of blood. His mouth worked spasmodically. His finger beckoned Joe to come close.

Joe put his ear by Hassan's mouth. The prisoner's mouth snapped shut, swallowing an ear lobe. He burped. "Thanks."

Pale-faced Perkins staggered back. "Geez, these Defghijkies aren't human. It's going to be a real tough war."

Joe shrugged and said to Hassan, "Hungry, are we? Well, let's see what we can do about that." He reached into Bessie and rummaged around for something extra, just for show. Hassan raised his left eyebrow to ward off American spirits.

"What are you looking for?" said Perkins.

Joe's fist shot out of the bag clenching the largest, most stomach-churning mushroom this side of Hell. Perkins and Hassan shook. "Major, sir," said Perkins, "that's against the Geneva Convention, big time."

"Ain't no Geneva Convention here," said Joe. He smiled as he rammed the abomination into the prisoner's mouth. "Ain't no Geneva convention on the streets of Peoria, where innocent children now eat those things."

Hassan's eyes grew big as he fought for air.

"As you know, Sergeant, those vermin mushroom pushers wait outside grammar schools, grammar schools, for Chrisake. Well, they got to my boy, just one day before his seventh birthday. His brown eyes used to sparkle with life. Now he just wants to become an economist. So fuck the Geneva Convention."

Perkins gestured to Hassan's flailing head. Joe smiled, reached into Bessie and produced a pair of tongs. "Say Hassan, I could use this to remove that mushroom. Ready to talk?"

Hassan shook his head. He made repeated efforts to chew up the enormous mushroom but couldn't even close his jaw.

Joe stroked his chin. "You know Hassan, even if you could eat that mushroom, it would just end up in your stomach."

The captive glanced at Joe's tongs. Hassan's eyes said pretty please.

"Why Hassan," said Joe, "I believe you want to talk. Ready to tell us the location of those mushroom fields?"

Hassan nodded vigorously. Joe removed the mushroom.

Joe looked at Perkins. "Well Sergeant, we've won this battle."

"Yes sir," said Perkins, "but at what cost? At what cost? Haven't we become as barbaric as that Defghijklorstanian?"

Joe put both his hands on Perkins' shoulders. "No, we haven't, Sergeant. Those scum," he gestured to Hassan, "play the Barney theme song to any of our boys they capture."

Perkins' face turned murder red. "Bastards!"

"For twenty-four straight hours, Sergeant, for twenty-four straight hours."

As Joe watched Perkins pick up his rifle, attach the bayonet, and run screaming into the night, an evil English chef tapped Joe on the shoulder.

CHAPTER 23B-BAD GUYS

Debbie Devil squirted her 22nd stripe of ketchup. Five more to go and then, "Pow." She smacked her hands together

Bertram Blackhand strode into the frozen-foods locker with an enormous, goofy grin. He made a profound bow to Debbie. "M'lady, I am the greatest. I said I would get Joe Thorvald to eat a mushroom and I did. You may now take possession of your Lutheran boy toy."

Debbie snarled. The boy part is correct. Oh, you got a Joe Thorvald alright, Joe Thorvald, JUNIOR."

Bertie stammered. He took off his chef's hat and breathed deeply and slowly into it. He placed the hat back on his head. "M'lady, my mushroom pusher assured me they gave the mushrooms to the right Thorvald."

Debbie stamped her fuchsia slingback and steam shot out her nostrils. "You should have looked for yourself. Those lazy bums don't care if they do the job right."

Bertie thought of several people with strong Protestant work ethics, but of course, they weren't evil enough to sell mushrooms to school kids. There just was no such thing as the ideal mushroom pusher.

Instead he said, "M'lady, a real chef anywhere near a public school would have looked suspicious." Bertie reached into his pocket and produced a mushroom sprinkled with confectionery sugar. "I have some of my school samples left. Care for a snack?"

Debbie's face contorted. "Heavens no, they're revolting! Get me some Twizzlers. Now!"

CHAPTER 23G-GOOD GUYS

General Lee scratched his chin. "My dear Erickson, I'm, of course, most gratified that we prevented those people from getting a mushroom down Thorvald's throat, but I'm puzzled that I didn't see you at all."

Erickson's hat stiffened. "General, I didn't need to be there. I was where it most mattered. I was his neighbor when he brought his economics-spouting seven-year old home from school."

"What did you do?" asked Lee.

"I invited him to a taco barbeque," said Erickson.

"But," said Lee, "you can't cook tacos on a barbeque, the ground beef . . ."

Erickson's hat shuddered. "Shredded beef, if you please. I am a chef of God."

Lee bowed. "My humble apologies, sir. But even so, it is my understanding that shredded beef would still fall through the gaps in the grill."

Erickson grinned. "Not with nano-technology."

"Good heavens," said Lee, "millions of microscopic grills all arrayed microns apart. Ingenious, my dear sir."

"Thank you, General. But our gracious Lord created those grills. On the ninth day, I believe. He does like His barbequed nano-ribs."

"Yes He does. We do have it perfect up here," said Lee, "but I can't help thinking about that how poor boy almost became an economist." He shuddered.

"It's all for the best, General. Before Junior ate that mushroom, Joe Senior was not a fierce soldier defending American values." Erickson paused. "He sold medical insurance—by telephone."

Lee paled. His legs wobbled. He sat down. "My goodness."

"I'll tell you something else," said the man in the white-chef's hat. "I happen to know, God has plans for Joe Junior."

"He does?" said the still-shaking Lee.

"Yes, when Joe Junior grows up the Holy Spirit is going to fill his soul. Junior, the man, will spend his life bringing the word of God to wandering herds of feral economists north of Canada's Arctic Circle."

"Stout soul," said Lee. "I thought we'd draw that duty some day."

Erickson summoned up a heaping platter of nano-ribs. "God is truly merciful."

Lee's nose began to twitch. Erickson paled and started to spin around. But not fast enough. The good general sneezed right onto the platter scattering nano-ribs everywhere.

Erickson's glance darted around the immaculate room. "Oh no, where did they go? How will we find them? They're nano sized."

"My humble apologies, sir."

CHAPTER 24-THE AFTERMATH

Joe Thorvald sat his weary white ass down on the wobbly bar stool. His big ears flopped down like lettuce under an August sun. Sometimes it felt as if his ears would cover his eyes.

The bartender regarded his sole customer with hungry intensity. "Hey pal, what'll you have?"

"Carrot vodka," said Joe.

"Carrot vodka!" said the bartender. "Ain't much call for carrot vodka since those lowlifes moved in." He moved closer to Joe. "Say, ain't you 'The Hare'?"

Joe lowered his head and sighed. "Listen, bird brain, I have a name, Joe Thorvald. Got it?" Joe motioned for his drink.

The bartender flew away. He came back with a bottle of Stoly Carrot and a nearly clean glass. He let them thump in front of Joe. "But everyone calls you 'The Hare,' right? You're 'The Hare,' ain't you?"

Joe sighed, took a swig and belched. "Yep."

"I knew it." The bartender pointed his shiny beak at Joe. "So you're the cocky one that let those lowlifes take over."

"Shut up."

The ruffled bartender knocked Joe's bottle and glass off with one swoop of his wing. "Take a hike, pal. Your money's no good here."

Blood pounded through Joe's foggy brain. "Have a heart, huh?"

"Not to quitters, I don't," screeched the bartender.

Strange feelings of sobriety began to course through Joe's veins. His pink eyes glowed with life. "I didn't quit."

"Bull, everyone in the Sixty Acres saw you lay down and take a nap. Let that damn, slowpoke turtle win the race. And that race, of all races!"

"I didn't quit," said Joe, "and I didn't know what the race meant."

Feathers ruffled along the hawk bartender's back. "Didn't know the race gave the winner the right to establish a military dictatorship for all his friends in the Sixty Acres? Hmph."

"No, I didn't," said Joe.

"Well, you still laid down and quit on us."

"I keep telling you," shouted Joe, "I didn't quit. They poisoned me."

"How?"

Joe closed his eyes and relived the horror. "That was a long, hot race. Really depleted my electrolytes. So you can imagine my gratitude when I saw one of the Hospitality Turtles waiting for me with a big glass of lemonade. 'Here, bunny,' he said.

"Only it wasn't lemonade."

Joe's upper lip curled to reveal a scattering of decaying teeth. "It was yellow-colored mushroom juice. Knocked me out right away. Put me in intensive care. Thank God, that doctor with the tall white hat had enough horse sense to put cumin and allspice in my IV."

"Gee, Mr. Thorvald, I didn't know. Sorry about all those quitting hare cracks."

Joe looked up, perked up his long floppy ears, threw back his furry head and laughed. "Well, of course you didn't know, you ignorant hawk. As Thomas Paine Bunny said, 'Freedom of the press is for those who have one.' And those damn fascist turtles own every newspaper. Every radio station, too."

The bartender mumbled, "I'm sorry."

Joe the rabbit shrugged and motioned for more liquid oblivion.

Tap.

The bartender returned with the Carrot Stoly.

Tap.

Joe took a drink.

Tap.

Joe took another.

Tap.

"Damn, I know that noise," said Joe, "it's . . ."

"Yes, Mr. Thorvald," drawled the approaching jackbooted turtle, "you really ought to know it by now. I've been chasing you for years."

A laser-sighted Bushnell .303 rifle, specially adapted for turtles, perched atop the hard-shelled Gestapo critter. "You're coming with me. You and your seditious hawk friend."

"Never," cried Joe. "Come, hawk, we'll make a break for it. We'll find Colonel Stuffy and join the resistance."

"In the name of our beloved Great Turtle, I order you to stay."

Joe and the hawk bounded out and flew away to Stuffy's lair and freedom. A minute later, the turtle ripped off a series of shots at the vacant room. "Dang, he got away, again!"

But Joe didn't get away from Bertram Blackhand who tapped him on his shoulder. "Not many incarnations left, Joe."

CHAPTER 24B-BAD GUYS

"Yap, yap, yap," said Debbie Devil's massive hound dog, Petunia.

"Get him, Get him, good," said Debbie. "Rip his throat out, Petunia."

Bill, the fox, and the object of Petunia's hunt, said nothing. He just ran and ran around Hungry Hank's meat locker.

Bill panted more and more. Where to hide? Need to distract that dog. What in a meat locker would distract a hound dog? Oh. Everything.

The fox leaped onto a sack of pig balls, ripping it open with its sharp claws. Pig balls, thought Petunia, yippee! Time for lunch! But Petunia had manners. She pointed out a bag of chicken breasts to Bill and bit into a huge pig ball, sending a great gout of pig blood onto Debbie.

Debbie collapsed, sobbing, onto a sack of Little Swiss Girl fish sticks.

Bertie Blackhand knocked on the locker door, entered, and surveyed the munching Petunia. A few moments earlier, he thought, and those bloodied balls could have been his. Bertie waited for his difficult boss to speak.

"We came so close with Joe," said Debbie. We got some mushroom juice down Joe's throat, but it wasn't enough." She pointed in the direction of her checkout stand. "And how am I going to look good out there, with pig blood all over my uniform?" Her mouth quivered.

"And, and, and today's employee evaluation day," she said through her sobs. "In ten minutes. Oh Bertie, I love this job."

"I know, m'lady," said Bertie. "I thought you might be feeling a bit low, so I brought you these."

He took off his chef's hat and removed from it a stunning bouquet of belladonna. "For you, m'lady. They're from France."

"Why thank you."

He rustled around in his hat. "And something more. Where is it? Where is it?"

Debbie leaned forward.

"Ah, here it is." Bertie produced a small bag of candy.

Debbie's eyes lit up. She clapped her hands. "Gummi Lutheran ministers, my favorite."

She threw her arms around Bertie. Bertie's black chef's hat became fully erect. "Oh Bertie, you really know how to treat the Supreme Evil."

She withdrew her arms and gazed at his face. "Too bad you're dead, English, and not Lutheran."

Bertie smiled and held his index finger next to his thumb. "Missed it by this much."

Debbie wiped tears from her face. "Ah well, who knew anthropomorphized rabbits had a partial immunity to mushroom juice?"

"We'll try again, m'lady."

"Yes, we'll do that." She got up. "Time to carry on the best we can."

"Wait, m'lady, I think there's something else in my hat."

"Yes?"

He withdrew a flat box. "Could you use a Christian Dior checkout lady's shirt. I got it at Nordstrom."

Debbie beamed. Nordstrom. What did it really matter if Armageddon were only three stripes away.

CHAPTER 24G-GOOD GUYS

"*Ja caramba*," said Pedro Erickson, "that was close." He looked at General Lee across the long table.

Lee drummed two fingers on the table for a second. "Yes, indeed. Those people stole a march on us." He stared hard at Erickson. "Their actions didn't fit the pattern. After attacking Joe, Jr. in a schoolyard in America, they should have gone after him on a manned mission to Mars."

He drummed his fingers on the table. "But they didn't. Let this be a lesson in tactics to me."

"Thank God, our sensors picked up a heavy concentration of mushrooms in the Sixty-Acres wood," said Erickson. "I got the antidote to Joe just in time."

"Yes, thank God," said Lee. "But why didn't we pick them earlier?"

"The system got inundated with spam telling us how to increase the size of our penises. Believe me, Shorty is sorry he sort of opened one of those e-mails last week."

Lee made a fist and raised it. He lowered it and took a deep breath. "Now we're going to get spam on all our computers, every day to all eternity."

Erickson nodded. "Or until Earth has no more penises."

"I need a root beer," said Lee.

CHAPTER 25-THE DIRECTOR'S CUT

Josef Thorvaldovich's Uncle Ivan always told him, "Never go outside the wall. Never go into the mysterious forest. A wolf lurks there. If it eats you, what then?"

Josef always thought, "Baldheaded fart, I'm not listening to you. One day I'll go outside and catch that wolf. You'll see."

But Josef didn't go outside. He couldn't think of a way past the wall. Indeed, Josef never thought up many ideas at all.

The good peasant uncle walked to the town's marketplace to buy eggs to make a Russian peasant's favorite breakfast, Quiche Kiev.

Sasha, the town blacksmith, wiped sooty mucus from his left nostril and hailed Uncle Ivan. "Yo ho, how fares your nephew, Josef?"

Uncle scratched his head. "Not so good, Sasha, he was once such a bright, lively lad but those mercury-amalgam fillings Dentist Placebovich put in his cavities arrested his mental development."

Sasha moved his right hand up to wipe his sweaty brow. He paused. He lowered his hand and put down the white-hot horseshoe. He raised his hand again and wiped his forehead. "Tsk, tsk, Ivan, how can this keep happening?"

Uncle Ivan pounded his head, bringing indiscriminate death to his herd of head lice. "As you know, village blacksmith, the damn Russian Dental Association says they're safe. But we simple peasants and townsfolk know that mercury vapors leak from the fillings, and enter the brain."

Sasha took a long pull on his corn-cob pipe and said, "Then the mercury binds to the brain cells and never leaves."

Uncle Ivan picked a piece of two-day-old pork out of his long, white beard. "*Da*, that action prevents consistent firing of the synapses in the cerebellum and so, the orderly transmission of thoughts. He'll never learn calculus."

Sasha tsk tsked. "Doesn't Dentist Placebovich eat mushrooms?"

"*Da*, he's evil in many ways."

Sasha puffed on his pipe. "I think so, too. Want to get drunk?"

"*Da*. Vodka?"

"What else?" said Sasha.

"Suits me."

And so the two mercury-aware peasants got stinking drunk and fell asleep with the village pigs.

Josef sat in the rickety chair in front of the small white-washed house. He watched the sun climb to its zenith, but Uncle Ivan did not come home to make lunch. He watched the sun start its descent. But Uncle Ivan did not come.

Rumblings in his stomach inflamed his desire to catch that marauding wolf. Wolf stew, yum, yum!

Furball, the dentist's calico cat, meowed at Josef from atop the vine-covered wall.

"Furball," said Josef, "what do you want?"

The calico purred and pointed with her paw to the tree branch hanging over the wall.

"Aha," said Josef as he climbed the branch with abandon. He fell. He tried again, this time carefully following the cat.

Josef dropped down onto the other side of the fence on his second try. He looked around. What a beautiful, wondrous meadow. He inhaled deeply. Ah! The fragrant aroma of thistlewort berries danced in his lungs. Life was good.

Lovely songs from a Russian bearbird gladdened his ears. "Hello, bearbird," said Josef, the only creature around capable of speech. "Isn't it a beautiful day?"

The bearbird chirped back.

"Well, this won't do," thought Josef. He dug into his pocket and scooped out a rusty key, six inches of string, three white marbles, the top tenth of a Stradivarius, and an inter-species translator. Josef particularly valued the translator. Why, he'd even traded his cousin Pergei sixteen fat earthworms for it.

Josef stuck the translator's earphone into his ear.

"As I was saying," chirped the bearbird, "there's this duck who sasses me every time I fly by the pond. Really ruffles my feathers, it does. Thought maybe you could put some muscle on that pest and make him shut up."

"Lead on," said Josef.

Josef, the cat, and the bearbird made their way to the pond, stopping only to sample the ripest, most succulent thistlewort berries. Then there it was, the biggest, baddest mother of all Russian ducks.

"Out of my territory," quacked the duck.

"Make me," chirped the bearbird.

"I just might," quacked the duck.

"In your dreams," chirped the bearbird, "You're just another flightless duck."

"Sez you," quacked the duck.

Their sub-Aristotlean discourse continued, absorbing all of their attention. Josef, however, being an idiot devoted to the philosophizings of Descartes, grew bored and cast his eyes around the meadow.

There! Behind that tall thistlewort bush a wolf with a black chef's hat crept ever so quietly. Closer. Closer.

"Look out," cried Josef to the bearbird. The bearbird quickly flew away, landing on a limb of the tree that overhung Josef's wall.

The cat, who also wore an inter-species translator, compliments of a wandering sociologist, took heed from Josef's warning and scampered up the tree. The unfortunate duck, friend neither to Josef nor any sociologist, stayed put. The wolf did not. With one mighty leap the wolf pinned the duck and swallowed it in one gulp. Oh crap, thought the ingested duck, "for the want of an inter-species translator, my life will be lost."

Josef's stomach got a bad case of the rumblies. "Wolf stew, wolf stew," it told Josef.

Josef yelled up into the tree. "Hey, bearbird."

The bearbird chirped back, "Yo, biped."

"Think you can distract the wolf while I tie him up with a rope?" asked Josef.

"No prob."

The bearbird dived repeatedly at the wolf, keeping just out of reach of the leaping, snapping beast.

Josef patted his pockets for a rope. Suddenly, a synapse fired. "Aha!" He removed the rope holding up his trousers. The trousers fell to his ankles, turning his stealthy creeping up to the wolf into a Three-Stoogean leap. Good enough, though, to fall atop the wolf.

Josef struggled to tie the legs of the thrashing wolf. "Damn it!" he muttered. "Why didn't Uncle let me join the Kiev 4-F Club?"

To the world he shouted, "Help me! Help me! I'm fighting a wolf. I need help!"

A dark shadow blotted out the sky. Josef looked up, blood flowing from the clawed gashes in his face. "Hmph," he thought, "just another pteranodon chasing a rabbit."

Suddenly, a shot rang out. The pteranodon fell screeching to the ground.

"Yum yum," said a hunter coming out of the woods, "We was hunting rabbits, but got ourselves a pteranodon. Mmm, mmm, I love to eat pteranodon."

"Yep," said his fellow hunter who'd just emerged. "I just love pteranodon ribs with barbecue sauce. Too bad this is the last one."

Meanwhile, back at the tree, the wolf's darting claws became a blizzard. Blood gushed from Josef's face like pus at a buboe-popping contest in 14th century Paris.

"Now, see here," yelled Josef. "I'm terribly sorry but would you mind helping me with this ferocious wolf?"

The hunters noticed Josef for the first time. They stared. And stared.

"Geez, would ya look at the *hotdogya* on Josef," said the lead hunter, Boris Dulldanov.

"Wooeee," said another hunter.

Josef's face turned the color of borscht as he let go of the wolf to cover his exposed *hotdogya*. The wolf, who didn't give two rotting turnips about the *hotdogya*, bounded toward the woods on the other side of the pond.

"Shoot the wolf, shoot the wolf," cried Josef.

Ivan brought down the fleeing wolf with one shot. The hunters devoted the waning hours of the day to patching up Josef, and skinning and butchering the pteranodon and the wolf.

A gust of wind blew away the black chef's hat as the hunters cut open the wolf's belly. Out flew the duck, alive, gloriously alive!

Well, no. Its feeble flight upwards, its hideously disfigured, dissolved face made it abundantly clear to the hunters that Mr. Gastric Juices had been working overtime in the wolf's stomach.

"Looks like a clear-cut case for euthanasia," said Ivan.

"And for duck *à la* orange," said another hunter.

"Yep," said Ivan as he raised his musket.

So, the hunters got themselves some pteranodon, some duck, and being greedy bastards, wolf stew as well.

But Josef made out all right. The hunters talked as long as the Russian winter when they got back to town and for the rest of his life "Tsar" *Hotdogya* could make hot *monkeeluvich* with any beauty he wanted.

Later, in 1917, the Russian peasantry, their brain cells damaged beyond measure from the vapors of their mercury filings, overthrew the Czar and permitted the establishment of a brutal Communist dictatorship. This dictatorship would kill off millions of its own people and point thousands of nuclear weapons at America for decades. But, Josef Thorvaldovich didn't eat a mushroom. That would have been bad.

And oh, many astute readers have seen ducks fly. So how could the bearbird accuse the unfortunate duck of being flightless? Well, in the interests of complete accuracy, at that point ducks couldn't fly. BUT, at the very moment the hunters cut open the wolf's belly ducks all around the world did develop the ability to fly.

Indeed, mass spontaneous evolution happens all the time. So, don't worry. Go with the flow.

CHAPTER 25B-BAD GUYS

"Failed again." Debbie Devil stamped her little foot on a lime-green package of beef hearts. She took a few steps to the far wall. Squish. Squish. She looked down at the gory mess beneath her right foot.

"Oh tidy Heaven, that's the last time I wear my Thom McAn stilettos into a meat locker. Bless it, I'll never get that Lutheran hunk into my bed. Maybe I should give that lesbian Methodist entomologist a call.

"No! There's nothing like the man flesh of a good Lutheran hunk." She sat down on some boxes of Barnacle Bart's Penguin Fillets and removed an impaled beef heart from the stiletto of her shoe. "Good thing," she muttered, "Lady Foot Locker still had pig-ball colors in stock."

Debbie flung the punctured pig ball at the locker door just as Bertie Blackhand opened it. Bertie caught the ball with practiced ease. "Ah m'lady, I see you've developed a taste for English cooking."

Smoke shot out of Debbie's nose and ears. "I have developed a taste for barbequed English chefs. All you do is fail. And you failed miserably this time. I didn't even see the mushroom."

Bertie's chef's hat shook. "Maybe so, m'lady, but I did lay the foundations for the Russian Revolution."

"Lay the foundations for the Revolution," yelled Debbie. "I'm the one who should get laid. So, I'm going to dip you in barbeque sauce and roast you over a hot flame for eternity."

Suddenly, a flock of pteranodons shot out of the south locker wall. The prehistoric birds swooped down on the open package of beef hearts.

Steve the stock boy opened the door and came in. "Hey, Debbie . . ." His alert eyes took in the feeding pteranodons. "Oh man, the boss isn't going to like this. It's against California's health regulations.

Man, they're going to shut us down for a week. They are. That's what happened last month when they found pteranodons at Jumbo Mart in San Diego."

"No, no," said Debbie, "no one need know." She snapped her fingers and the pteranodons vanished. She glanced at her watch. "Look's like break time's over."

Steve the stock boy shrugged and left with Debbie to get back to work.

Bertram Blackhand exhaled slowly. He retrieved his well-worn copy of *How to Deal with Difficult Bosses*. He flipped open the book to the dog-eared page and smiled as he read suggestion 87, "Whenever possible, distract your boss with a flock of pteranodons. Conjure them if need be."

CHAPTER 25G--GOOD GUYS

Pedro Erickson sat across from General Lee at the long table. The message on the big, white board read, "Well done, Lee and Erickson."

Erickson smiled. "Well, General, we licked them again."

Lee sighed. "Yes, but it was too easy."

"Too easy?"

"Yes. Those people didn't even follow basic tactics. I was always told when in doubt march your troops to the sounds of the big guns. They, when in doubt, should have led with their mushrooms. And where were their mushrooms?"

"Our sensors indicated they were on the wolf's head under the chef's hat," said Erickson.

Lee rolled his eyes. "Just where they couldn't get at them."

Erickson coughed into his hands. "They did have a mushroom-eating dentist putting mercury fillings in children's teeth."

"Those people got it backwards," said Lee in what for him passed for shouting. "Their dentist should have put mushrooms in children's teeth. Mercury fillings won't damn your soul to Hell for all eternity, just prevent the orderly firing of synapses in your brain."

"That's still a war crime according to the proceedings of the Nuremberg Trials," said Erickson.

"Yes," said Lee, "those people ARE evil."

Lee closed his heavy eyelids. He already foresaw Debbie and Bertie's next attempt. Would they ever stop being obvious? He drifted into sleep. Images of frolicking with his wife Mary at Disneyland fluttered across his mind. Their roller coaster plunged, but they held their hands in the air to show no fear.

CHAPTER 26-DEL MAR NEEDS WOMEN

"A few safety rules," said Karl the conductor. "This train goes around Old Poway Park two times. Please keep any arms, legs, or any other appendages you're proud of inside the car. All aboard."

Life was good everywhere Joe Thorvald, the once-a-month engineer, looked. Ahead was the Falafel Factory where he had just had the Swedish-meatball-and-taco platter.

Behind in the coach car, a gaggle of cheerleaders from Poway Junior College smiled, chattered, and giggled with their leader and Joe's daughter, Sally. Near the big sycamore trees, Joe's son, Joe Junior, was celebrating with a Thomas-The-Tank Engine birthday party.

Engineer Joe scowled at ten seven-foot tall brown mushrooms by the bridge. These mushrooms hailed from Del Mar. Joe hated everyone from Del Mar. It didn't matter if they were people or animated fungi, they acted just the same--snooty.

But there was nothing he could do about the mushrooms. County codes didn't prevent assemblies of fewer than twenty giant, animated mushrooms. Still, just let one of them interfere with his beloved train on his watch and they'd be mushroom salad at Home Cookin' Buffet faster than you could say, "Tickets, please."

Maybe today he'd get his chance. That eight-foot tall brown mushroom with the black chef's hat was a new addition. And he looked like a particularly bad sort of giant, animated Del Martian mushroom.

Toot, toot. Steam puffed from the smokestack of the 1907 Baldwin 0-4-0. Its big wheels began to turn faster and faster. As the train passed the bridge Sally leaned out the window to wave hello to Joe Junior.

Suddenly, a massive tentacle shot out. Then another from the same mushroom with the chef's hat. Snap, the tentacles recoiled toward that brown mushroom, taking Sally with them. Smaller tentacles ripped off her clothes. Tiny tentacles wiggled all over her quivering, naked body. Then with a giant sucking sound the massive tentacles pushed her into the pulsating brown shape.

The other cheerleaders screamed. "Yippee," belched the smiling, brown shape. The other mushrooms waved their tentacles in triumph. "See," said the Karl the conductor, "I told you to stay inside the coach. Maybe you'll listen now."

"Joe, stop the train," said the cheerleaders. "Stop the train. Stop the yucky train ride."

Tears flowed down Joe's cheeks as the cheerleaders continued their refrain. He told himself, stop the train. Release the long Johnson bar. His hand kept its grip. He had a job to do.

No, let go of the Johnson bar, Joe. Your daughter's been eaten by giant mushrooms. Let go, Joe. Nothing matters anymore. You have no one now. Your wife was eaten by piranhas on that snorkeling trip down the Amazon River and . . . poof! Look, Joe, look, your son, Junior, just spontaneously combusted. But, Joe's hand stayed put.

C'mon Joe, stop the train. Get off and kill those hoity-toity Del Martian mushrooms. Be a man for once, avenge your daughter. Joe unclenched the steel Johnson bar.

"No, Daddy, no," said the image of his daughter that appeared on the boiler. "The rules clearly state that if you stop this train before the end of the ride, you'll lose this position. And then how do you expect to land a job with Burlington Northern?"

Joe put his hand back on the bar, but only with a feeble grip.

"Oh Joe, dearest Joe," said the image of his departed wife, "don't give up. Not like you did with blimp-piloting, sushi cooking, ballet dancing, sidewalk sculpting, bilingual miming or lima-bean inspecting.

"Oh Joe, oh Joe, don't give up, don't quit, not this time. Make me proud. Make me proud, Joe. Whatever it costs you, finish the train ride, for the passengers, for me, for yourself."

Blip.

Joe straightened. Wiped away his tears. "Damn it, I am an engineer on the Old Poway Railroad. I am bound by the rules. And damn it, those rules clearly state I must give the passengers their two laps."

Fireman Roger nodded. "I'm with you. Those mushrooms want us to stop this train. Stop our way of life, too. Well, we're not going to give them that victory. This is Poway."

Joe glanced at the murmuring mushrooms, readying themselves for another attack. "Damn right. This is for God, mom, tacos, and the right to root against the Dodgers." He gripped the big Johnson bar with the strength of Hercules and shoved it forward

The train sped ahead, its big wheels becoming a blur. The unsentimental herd of brown mushrooms rolled in pursuit. Through the parking lot sped the train. The mushrooms rolled after them. Over the bridge chugged the train. The mushrooms rolled behind in single file. Past the train barn flew the train and past the station with the mushrooms in hot pursuit.

"More speed," cried Fireman Roger, "they'll catch us and we won't finish the ride. That can't happen. Not on our watch."

"The boiler will blow," said Engineer Joe.

Fireman Roger shrugged. "I've always been partial to hot tubs."

Joe grinned. "See you in Hell, fireman." Joe increased the pressure on the bar. The needle in the pressure gauge jumped far into the red. The mushrooms rolled wheezing behind in single file. Past the train barn the out-of-shape mushrooms stopped. They could have been in shape, but they never did exercise along with their dozens of Al Gore workout tapes.

Meanwhile, back at the station, the train halted, steam billowing up in great, gray clouds. Engineer Joe pulled the cord once. Toot!

A blonde cheerleader yelled, "O my God, why did you do that? The mushrooms will like catch up."

"Passengers only pay for two laps. We just finished two laps. So, we stop."

"I totally order you to start up the engine," yelled the cheerleader.

"You can't order me, you're a cheerleader. I'm the boss of this train."

"Pig." The cheerleader's hand dropped to a sequined handled Colt .45; successful cheerleading is rather more than pom poms. "Like, I'm really ordering you to start this train right now."

Joe sneered. "You're bluffing. If I'm dead, who will run the train? You? You haven't even taken the written test to be an engineer."

"All right, all right. Start the train. If I have to, I'll buy you cottage cheese and lettuce at Denny's."

Joe shrugged. He'd just lost the last of his family. Damned if he was going to eat rabbit food. "You buy tickets after the ride for your cheerleading friends and I get all I can eat at Taco Erickson."

"Okay, Taco Erickson," said the cheerleader.

"Okay then," said Joe.

But it was not okay. Two massive tentacles already gripped the handrail by the steps to the coach car.

The conductor stood on the platform and held out his upraised hand. "Whoa, whoa, whoa, stop right there, young mushroom. Where are your manners? Let the passengers off first."

But the young mushroom had no manners. Just another smug, horny tentacled mushroom from Del Mar. It grabbed the conductor with a massive tentacle and flung him toward the windmill.

It's always a sad thing to relate the absorption of Earth women by marauding gangs of tentacled mushrooms. So you'll just have to imagine the ripping of tight fitting cheerleader outfits, the . . .

"As if," yelled the pistol-packing cheerleader at the mushrooms. "Like, I'm giving you exactly ten seconds to stop what you're doing or I'll shoot."

The mushrooms didn't glance up. Of course, they couldn't as they didn't have eyes. BUT, if they had had eyes they wouldn't have glanced up, either. Damn spore spawn.

So, the cheerleader pulled out her pistol from its Gucci holster and blazed away. Sure, the mushrooms eliminated much of her competition for next year's cheerleading squad, but their gauche behavior was too much. Like totally.

The mushroom closest to her, Marvin in fact, put an end to this internal soliloquy by choking her with a spare tentacle.

Joe gulped. He knew what he had to do. He put his hand on the valve and turned it slowly. Could he get away with starting the train like this? If the eyeless mushrooms weren't watching.

But was his conscience clear? Yes, all the survivors had annual passes; he didn't need to wait for the conductor to collect tickets. Gentle puffs of steam issued from the smokestack. Soon, larger and larger puffs belched forth.

A tentacle tapped him on the shoulder. Again. And in a pattern. In Morse code!

The tapping said, "Del Mar mushrooms need women."

Joe kept his hand on the valve while he turned around. He saw the biggest, baddest tentacled mushroom ever to wear a black chef's hat.

"And I need a taco," said Joe.

"Come join us," tapped the hatted mushroom. "We'll make you a mushroom. Come on, you know you want to." He pointed a tentacle toward the ravishing mushrooms and their victims.

"No way," said Joe, "You are a mushroom. You are pure evil. What you are doing is pure evil. No way will I join you. Not while I live and breathe."

"As you wish," tapped the mushroom. Suddenly, a tentacle shot out to choke Joe.

But Joe never let go of the valve. The train picked up speed as more and more pressure built up in the boiler. The needle jumped into the red-danger zone. But still, the dying Joe held onto the valve.

Suddenly, the boiler blew, flinging great curtains of scalding steam back toward the coach, toward the strutting, boasting tentacled mushrooms turning them into flaccid strips of shriveled fungi.

Joe died too, horribly, slowly. Everything turned out all right for him, though. The Poway Mushroom Haters Society erected a statue to him in Old Poway Park. And Slim William wrote a song about Joe's legendary last ride called, "Joe Done Died Holding His Big Johnson."

Okay, not everything turned out right. When the mushrooms absorbed the cheerleaders into their brownish bodies, they forever killed Poway Junior College's chances at any head-to-head cheerleading competition with Del Mar.

CHAPTER 26B-BAD GUYS

Bertie Blackhand felt himself being drawn through the meat locker door. Bad sign, he thought, she's usually polite enough to let me knock. How I wish Mr. George weren't working at customer service for the phone company.

Debbie Devil's dainty right foot tapped furiously on the floor. Tiny angry imps danced on her head.

"I beg your pardon, m'lady," said Bertram, "but I really thought the tentacled mushrooms would work."

"Oh, and why is that?"

"Well, m'lady, it worked on the good folks of Del Mar. Got a lot of men there ready to turn themselves into tentacled mushrooms."

"Del Mar, Del Mar," yelled Debbie, "is not a good place to beta-test an evil scheme. There are no Lutheran hunks in Del Mar. Oh, maybe a passable Unitarian here or there, but that's it, you fool."

Bertie held a package of Twizzlers toward Debbie. "I'm sorry, m'lady. Please take this."

"No, that won't work on me this time," said the mistress of Evil. "Not when you tried to convert Joe to evil on the train ride in Old Poway Park."

"What's wrong about that train ride?"

Debbie sneered. "What's wrong about it? What's wrong about it? That train is favored by God. Every year Santa Claus arrives in Poway on that train. Everyone knows that Santa is one of God's right-hand men."

"I didn't know that Santa was even real," said Bertie.

"You didn't?" said Debbie.

"No, m'lady, I didn't."

The imps on Debbie's head vanished. "Oh. Well then, never mind."

"Is he really one of God's right-hand men?" asked Bertie.

"Oh yes," said Debbie. "He really does check to see who's been naughty and nice." She shivered. "You don't even want to think of hatching a major evil scheme in December. And believe me, 'Watch out for Rudolph's Red Nose' really is a byword for terror."

"Gosh," said Bertie.

"And don't even get me started on that Easter Bunny. Before Heaven sent him back, he was one of the Twelve Apostles."

"I didn't know that either," said Bertie.

"Guess I forgot to tell you," said Debbie.

"Let's let bygones be bygones," said Bertie.

"Oh, I could never stay angry with you, Bertie. You're such an English chef."

Bertie bowed. "Thank you, m'lady. I have another plan if it would please you."

Debbie shook her head and pointed to the red stripes on the locker-room wall. "There's time for only one more attempt on Joe before I unleash Armageddon. We've got to succeed. This time, I'm using the ultimate weapon."

Bertie gasped. "No m'lady, not an insurance company."

"Yes, Bertie."

Bertie fainted. He was out cold before he even hit the ground.

CHAPTER 26G-GOOD GUYS

Pedro Erickson strode into the room, smiling and laughing. He spied General Lee sitting at the long table as stiff and somber as ever.

"Hey, General, how's it hanging?"

Lee shivered internally.

Erickson walked over and slapped Lee on the back. "Why the long face, sourpuss? That Joe Thorvald preferred my Taco Erickson food over Taco Bell. Woo hoo! And we beat those mushrooms. Smoked them. You saw what they just tried on us. Tentacled mushrooms on a train! In Old Poway!

"This was their last desperate attempt. I know it, you know it, they know it. They can't beat us, Bobby boy, they can't beat us. We're an unbeatable team.

"Time to break out your complete DVD collection of Patty Duke movies. What do you say we start with *Me, Natalie*? I have some homemade root beer I could bring. And . . ."

What was that noise? Erickson didn't see anything moving.

Tap, tap, tap, came the sounds, softer than the beating of butterfly wings.

Erickson looked at Lee. The general looked like a statue with his hands resting on the table. But Erickson's acute hearing, typical of any reincarnated Swedish-Mexican chef, told him that Lee was drumming his fingers.

Erickson's smile vanished. "What's bothering you, General?"

Lee stood up. "Mr. Erickson, you are indeed correct in saying that those people cannot defeat the two of us. However, they have not given up. They will make their next attack on Joe where we cannot help him. May Mr. Thorvald's Lutheran soul be strong enough to withstand the Last Temptation of Mushrooms."

"Amen. So no Patty Duke then?"

"No, my dear Erickson, no Patty Duke. I feel the need for a good purgative."

Erickson blanched. "General, not gavel-to-gavel coverage of both presidential conventions."

"Just so, my dear Erickson, just so."

"*Ja caramba.*" The good chef edged backward to the door. "Well, if you don't mind General, I think I just might visit the Dead San Diegan Hoofers Club and watch some celebrity rhumba dancing."

Lee nodded abstractly.

CHAPTER 27-EXPLANATION OF BENEFITS

The letter began, "Dear Mr. Thorvald, for nonpayment of your hospital bill, you are being sent directly to Hell."

Shazzam! Lilac-scented clouds swirled about. Sounds of polkas infested the air.

A severe-looking man with a Charlie Chaplin moustache and swastikas on his sleeve walked out of the dissipating cloud. He wiped his brow and said, "*Guten Tag*, quite hot, *ja?*"

"Sure is," said Joe. "Is this really Hell?"

"Oh *ja*," said the uniformed man, "but how did you know?"

Thorvald pointed to the fields of mushrooms stretching to the horizon in all directions with every mushroom the size of Rhode Island.

"*Ja*, you are right. You are in Hell. Wait until you try our English cuisine."

Joe put his right hand over his heart. "Dear God." The German greeter winced and the mushroom fields trembled. "If you get me back home," continued Joe, "I promise to go to church every day."

The man with the designer swastikas said, "But you are in Hell now, *nein?* Let us make the best of it." The man slapped his forehead. "*Ach*, but where are my manners? Let me introduce myself. I am Adolf Hitler, but *bitte*, call me Adolf."

Hitler held out his right hand. Thorvald scowled, ignored the dour dictator's gesture. "Well, I'm Joe Thorvald and I'm glad divine justice finally caught up with you."

The lilac-scented bad guy shrugged. "*Ja*, God didn't take kindly to the millions of dead soldiers in the war. Blamed it all on me. And I do not even want to talk about how picky he was about my campaigns of mass extermination." Hitler shivered like a bikini *über*model on Mount Everest.

"Enough about you," said Joe. "I don't remember dying." Thorvald waved his hands in the Fuehrer's face. "Hell to Mr. Dictator, hello!"

"A thousand pardons, *mein* fiend. You were saying?"

"I don't remember God judging my soul."

"*Mein* goodness," said the Abashed Avatar of Austrian anger, "it *nicht* happened. Sturgeon Bass Hospital sent you to Hell for not paying your bill. Look at the letter you are holding."

"They can do that?" Joe asked.

"Oh *ja*, they're a big business, big corporation, have lots of lawyers."

Joe spat. "That's not fair. The bill was wrong. I went to the emergency room because of a cut on my face. The cut healed hours before anyone came to see me.

"The doctor glanced at me, said my cut was healed, and left. Two months later, the hospital charged me $22,386 for a pregnancy test and hysterectomy."

Hitler shrugged. "Did you pay?"

"No."

Hitler tsk-tsked. A pregnant pause in Hell followed. "Are you going to pay?"

"No," Joe yelled, "all I want is a chance to speak to a damned supervisor from Sturgeon Bass's accounting."

Hitler frowned. "I *nicht* care for them, either. Cheap *schweinhunden*. Just last year I went with their whole department to Chez Bertie for dinner and dancing. Charming show too, a few tasteful disembowelments followed by some spectacular bungee hangings."

"But I digress," said Hitler, "when the time came to pay the bill they all got up to visit the restrooms. I had to pay the bill. Me!" His face contorted. "Men like that give Hell a bad name."

"Not fair," Joe said.

Hitler's lines of rage vanished like autumn on the Steppes. He smiled genially. "I like you, *Herr* Thorvald. Let us be good fiends. We'll face them together, *nein?*"

Hitler held out his hand. There was a happy-face tattoo on the palm. Joe wondered, was this copyright infringement? Would he get in trouble by shaking the hand of a copyright infringer?

Hitler caught Joe's gaze and winked. "You are already in Hell. What more can the happy-face lawyers do to you?" He held out his hand again. "*Mein* fiend, we will have a beer when it is all done."

"German beer?" said Joe.

The Duke of Devastated Denmark hung down his head. "*Ach,* no this is Hell. No German beer in Hell."

"What beer do they have?" said Joe.

Hitler blushed and mumbled, "French beer, they serve French beer."

Hitler's puppy-dog vulnerability caused Joe to think, Maybe he's just a poor, wayward lamb. Quite wayward actually, but he does so want to help me, and, by gosh, I would like a beer. Joe grabbed Hitler's hand and shook it. "Any beer will do."

"*Danke,* you are most accommodating." Hitler clicked his heels. "*Jawohl,* I will help you. You see, I have people skills. And I know they run their accounting department from our seventh level. We go there."

"That's the spirit that conquered France in 1940," said Joe.

The jaunty dictator grinned. "*Danke,* I needed that. One finds so few compliments in Hell."

He held out his arm. Joe took it and they walked arm in arm to the elevator. Hitler pressed the down button. He said, "You know *Herr* Thorvald, it took Hell to teach me patience. This elevator takes forever." He moved a little closer and whispered, "You would think the Devil would have the money to spring for a second elevator. I tell you *mein* fiend, when I ran Germany, you may believe me, the elevators ran on time." Joe nodded in appreciation.

Hitler stared at his reflection in the one remaining patch of metal in the faux-velour elevator doors. Joe thought, Twentieth-century megalomaniacs can be so vain.

The Relentless Regent of Ravaged Russia took out his comb and coaxed an unruly strand of hair back into place and replaced the comb, but the insouciant hair just sprang up again. Hitler recombed the strand. This sequence repeated itself for two hours.

"*Schweinhund.*" Hitler spat at the doors and threw his comb on the floor. "I tell you, *Herr* Thorvald, it is always, always a bad-hair day here in Hell."

The elevator door opened and a horde of gibbering middle-aged, male telemarketers stamped out, all of them wearing plaid tank tops, staggering under a load of wooden crates.

Hitler stared at them. "*Mein* fiends. What are you carrying? Where are you going?"

The lead telemarketer said without breaking step or looking up, "Oh hi, Adolf. We're taking these to Rancho Santa Fe. Every crate is full of George's mushrooms."

Joe paled. Hitler put his hand on Joe's shoulder. "*Herr* Thorvald, you must believe I would have spared you that if I had but known." Joe nodded.

A minute later, they got in the elevator. Graffiti free. Well, score one for Hell. Hitler pressed seven. Instead of Muzak, they heard Nixon's Checkers speech alternate over and over with an advertisement for Flab Blaster. Swarms of imps, trolls, and telemarketers swarmed in at each stop.

Joe gasped as he got out at level seven. "Not one of them used a decent deodorant."

"Not one of them carried a beer keg. Not fair," said the Pouting Punisher of Poland.

Just ahead of them, the sign on the accountants' moss-covered door read, "Abandon hope all ye who enter here. - Sturgeon Bass." Hitler took a deep breath and raised his hand to knock. He didn't. "Accountants have small hearts. We need lots of snipers."

He waved his riding crop and thirty S.S. men armed with machine guns and ice-chip throwers--this was Hell after all-- materialized out of a puff of jasmine-scented smoke.

Joe clapped. "Neat trick, Adolf."

He grinned. Hell certainly agreed with him. "Oh *Ja*, you don't spend sixty years here without picking up a few things."

Hitler waved his arm. The storm troopers stormed in. No subtlety at all, but then they reeked of jasmine. How subtle could they be?

Hitler goose-stepped over to the mumbling, preoccupied receptionist. Her desk bristled with miniature date palms.

"We are here," said the dean of death, "to help correct *Herr* Thorvald's hospital bill and send him back to Earth."

"Oh, drat." The receptionist mumbled as she started recounting a thousand avocado-green and burnt-orange paper clips. After five Hitlerian interruptions and six attempts she said, "Ah!" and looked up.

"How may I delay you?" she asked.

Hectic Hitler clenched his Teutonic teeth. "I said we are here to correct a hospital bill."

She shrugged. "Worse men than you have tried."

"I *haf vays* to make you submit correct forms," said Adolf.

She laughed briefly, closed her eyes, and went into an hour-long trance.

Ten of the troopers disappeared with small pops. Hitler frowned. "Conjured fiends only last so long. We'd better get to the head supervisor before winter sets in."

Winter in Hell? Wow! Would a snowball really melt here?

Hitler thrust his arm toward the gatekeeper. "We must eliminate her. S.S., fire!"

The receptionist yawned and waved her hand without even looking up. A blizzard of form letters appeared. None of the bullets got through.

The Brooding Baron of Bavarian Bloodbaths ground his teeth. "Just like Stalingrad."

"Not so," yelled Joe. "I have weapons your men didn't." He produced his wallet. Joe pulled out an accordion of 672 pictures of his three-week-old niece and thrust it in his foe's puffy face.

"Take this, gatekeeper," said Joe, "If you don't let us through I'm going to tell you in amazing detail the cute things little Sarah does in each and every picture. Twice."

The receptionist turned whiter than an albino accountant in Alaska. "But, but, but, a three-week old can't possibly do 672 different cute things."

Joe brandished his wallet. "Open the gate, or I'll start on picture one."

She shuddered, pressed a button and the door behind her opened. Hitler, twenty S.S., and Joe charged through. They stopped at a desk inscribed with the words "Made from wasteful lumberjacks in the rainforests of Brazil." A single red telephone lay atop the mahogany table. On the far end of the room hung a banner proclaiming "This part of Hell brought to you by your fiends at George's Mushrooms, www.georgesmushrooms.hll." Beneath that, a screen exhibited one of the faces on Mount Rushmore. No, just another empathetic receptionist. Sounds of John Denver singing in 16th-century Russian assaulted their ears.

An S.S. sergeant looked at the grim matron on the screen and tugged at Hitler's sleeve. "Father Adolf, I'm frightened."

Hitler sneered. "Coward, we'll shoot our way through."

"At what, Father Adolf? We have no targets." Five soldiers popped out of existence.

The testy tyrant marched to the desk and picked up the telephone. The phone played "Tie a Yellow Ribbon 'Round the Old Oak Tree." The merry mass murderer even liked that song, but only for two of the three hours. Six more soldiers burst and vanished.

The matron on the screen picked up the phone. "Sturgeon Bass accounting. I can outwait continental drift."

"*Frau* operator, you will let us through."

"One moment," said the matron. "May I put you on hold?" Her finger broke the light barrier in pressing the hold button.

The flash of light from her moving digit blinded them. Hitler and Joe recovered to the tune of "Macarena." For four hours.

No soldiers remained when their vision cleared. The heroic Joe walked to the table and picked up the phone.

The screen's greeter said, "Your persistence makes me puke." And she did.

Thorvald smiled. "Gee, that's swell. It's a wonderful day in your neighborhood. I'm calling because I'd like to pay twice the amount on my bill."

Her jaw dropped. "Pay twice your bill. But why?" She flipped through one manual after another. None satisfied her. Her head exploded spewing gray Gummi brains as she collapsed onto the drawbridge button.

The drawbridge lowered and the peppy pair pranced across. Then they saw, maybe twenty yards away, a colossal red throne. And atop the throne perched Barney the Dinosaur.

Not your ordinary Barney; but one sporting red horns and a long red tail. Dave Devil himself, wielding a mushroom scepter.

"So," said Joe, "Barney and the Devil are one."

"No," said the Devil, "I only appear that way because you loathe Barney so. I'd appear as the Wicked Witch of the West to Dorothy and Toto."

"Dorothy and Toto aren't real," said Joe.

Barney the Devil shrugged. "So you say."

Hitler stamped his feet. His face contorted with the rage of a six-year-old child once backed by a four-million-man army. "Now see here, *Herr* Barney. We are here to fix the medical bill of my fiend *Herr* Thorvald.

"Imagination can be fun," said Barney Devil.

The impatient invader strode toward Barney, his arms outstretched. "My hands across your throat can be real."

"Super dee party pooper." Barney hurled a lightning bolt at Joe's ally. Flames and blood erupted from Hitler's gut.

"Ow." Hitler staggered. Hitler ran. "Run, Hitler, run," said Joe. Barney's next lightning bolt pierced the dictator's chest. Hitler collapsed writhing to the floor.

Joe sprinted to Hitler. The fallen foe of France motioned Thorvald closer. He whispered, "It's too late to save me. I'll be sent to work the mushroom fields." Hitler smiled and laughed weakly. "Good joke, *nein?* 'Too late to save me.' I'm in Hell, not in Heaven. So, my soul wasn't saved. Get it?"

Joe did get it. Hitler had just made a pun. Hitler was in Hell. Punsters go to Hell.

"Go on without me," wheezed Hitler.

Joe sprinted toward Barney waving the offending medical bill.

Barney yawned and drew back his right arm to hurl another lightning bolt. Joe reached into his shirt pocket and retrieved the small wooden cross his wife gave him for their anniversary. He held it toward Barney. Barney's arm froze.

Barney's face convulsed, but the huge grin stayed untouched. "Damn this goofy grin your unspeakable imagination gave me."

Joe laughed. "So, you'll be tearing up this abomination." He thrust his medical bill under Barney's goofy purple nose.

"Oh, no." Barney's voice chilled Joe, as it often did up on Earth when his little son forced him to watch Barney's TV show. "Oh no, Mr. Thorvald, you'll need much more than a cross to correct a medical bill."

Joe knelt.

"Joe Thorvald, what are you doing?"

Joe clasped his hands together.

"Joe, Joe, don't do that."

Joe began to pray.

"Joe, I'm feeling much better. Would you like to sing along with me? Super dee dooper."

These last three words steeled our hero's Lutheran soul. Joe prayed to God. Prayed hard.

A golden cloud formed. The cloud spoke. "Barney, fix the bill. Let my Thorvald go!"

"Check it out," said Barney, "The bill stays as is. Thorvald stays. This is my domain. You can't make me do anything here."

The cloud said, "I can get Hillary Clinton to propose a bill to simplify medical bills, make them accurate, too."

Barney's skin turned lavender. "Don't do that. Incorrect medical bills make people angry. Oh boy, oh boy. Angry people turn away from you, toward me."

The cloud crackled and sparked. "I might have to send your wife down here. Would you like that, Barney boy?"

Barney shivered. His grin vanished. "You win, God, again. The whole point of staying here is to get away from her." He waved his hand. A purple lollipop appeared in Joe's right hand and the huge numbers on Joe's bill became zeroes. "Mr. Thorvald, you're free to go."

Barney waved his big purple hand. A small part of Joe's brain recognized the familiar fog, knew he was back in Rancho Santa Fe, knew he had to face Mrs. Devil, knew there'd be no helpful Hitler to assist him.

Just before he blacked out he heard Barney say, "God, she made me try to overthrow you. But, you know, all I really wanted was to run a soft ice cream-shop."

CHAPTER 27B-BAD GUYS

Debbie Devil tore open a little packet of Heinz ketchup and squirted another red stripe, the twenty sixth. Yes, it was indeed the twenty-sixth stripe of ketchup. She closed her eyes and took a deep breath. Suddenly, a knock rang out.

"Come in," said Debbie.

"Ouch." A moment later, the portal swung back and Bertie entered holding a bleeding nose.

Debbie's faux-Prada eyelashes fluttered apart. "Bertie, most dead English chefs take the time to open the door first."

Bertie sniffed. "Most dead English chefs don't have an impatient horn ball on the other side of the door." Blood ran down his fingers and onto his shirt.

"And Bertie, stop that bleeding. You know I can't stand the sight of blood."

Bertie put his other hand on his nose and mumbled, "Sorry, m'lady, but it just won't stop."

Debbie stamped her foot. "Must I do everything myself?" She looked around the room.

"Aha!" Debbie opened a package of Portugese pig balls and grabbed two particularly big ones. "Here, shove these up your nose. They will stop your bleeding."

Bertie obeyed but, of course, pig balls up his nose altered his speech in the usual way. Do you remember that time in grammar school when the teacher stood up in front of class and warned everyone never to put pig balls up one's nose? And the first thing you did when you got home was to put pig balls up your nose. And then . . .

Debbie shook her head to rid herself of the voices in her head. A tear rolled down. No one ever had any sympathy for her. Just because she was the Supreme Evil, didn't mean she couldn't get migraines like anybody else. And crab legs, how she loved crab legs. She couldn't have them, though. They made her swell up like a blowfish. A tear trickled down from her other eye.

Ah well, she'd always have Paris in 885, 978, 1360, 1725, 1775, 1789-1792, 1830, 1848, 1871, and 1944. Just thinking of that city and its riots, battles, and the guillotining she created there made her smile, as it always did. Yep, Paris alone made being the Supreme Evil all worthwhile.

Time to act the part.

"Bertram, we have run out of stripes. How I have ached for Joe Thorvald's Lutheran manhood. And in VAIN! Bless his sturdy soul! Bless that General Lee and Pedro Erickson. Bless them to Heaven for all eternity for making me lose.

"And if I lose, everybody loses. It's Armageddon time. God says he has Archangels and other helpers. Well poo, I have me, you Bertie, Mr. George the mushroom man, and telemarketers.

She stared at Bertie. "Bertie, Mr. George will be available for Armageddon, won't he?"

Bertram glanced at a little red appointment book. "Sorry, m'lady he is in Chicago making sure people miss their connections."

Debbie glared at the English chef. "Bertram, if you value your chef's hat, I suggest you cancel all his appointments. This is the end of the world after all."

Bertram nodded. "Will do, m'lady. What time would you like to schedule Armageddon?"

Debbie scratched her chin. "Oh, I don't know. How about this Thursday?"

Bertram scribbled in the book. "What time? How about 11 p.m.?"

She shook her head. "No, no, 11 won't do. My shift ends at 10. I'm not spending an extra hour here for anything. Let's say 9:30."

Bertram scribbled again. "9:30 it is." He closed the appointment, looked up at Debbie, and saluted. "See you at Armageddon, m'lady."

CHAPTER 27G-GOOD GUYS

General Lee broke the long silence. "My dear Erickson. Those people have failed with us. They've failed in Hell. Their next step will be to bring on Armageddon."

Pedro Erickson spoke for all good Swedish-Mexican chefs when he said, "*Ja caramba!* Really?"

Lee nodded gravely.

"Then let's roll," said Erickson.

"Your dedication is admirable," said Lee, "but we are not rated to fight an Armageddon level of evil."

"Then General, who will help Thorvald and the world?"

"I expect," said Lee, "our Heavenly Father will send the Archangels to aid Thorvald."

Erickson nodded. "The Archangels would be good. I'd feel even better if somehow Stuffy would be there fighting Mrs. Devil and her minions."

"So would I," said Lee. "Perhaps our Heavenly Father will find a way to make The Scourge Of All Evil available at the final battle."

"I hope so," said Erickson, "Still, I'd hate not to be there at the End."

Lee nodded. "My sentiments exactly."

"General, how about watching a few *Patty Duke* episodes?"

"No my dear Erickson, my worry is too great. I feel the madcap need to watch The Three Stooges. Would you care to watch with me?"

"Why soitenly, General."

"Wee. Dee. Dee. Dee. My dear sir. Wee. Dee. Dee. Dee."

CHAPTER 28-A LITTLE UNPLEASANTNESS

Hungry Hank's would surely give her a negative evaluation if she caused Armageddon; would even dock her pay, if done deliberately. The supermarket's best employee, Debbie Devil, knew this. Still, her body burned for Joe Thorvald's Lutheran manhood. And it was right in front of her, covered only by Joe's tight-fitting pants.

The P.A. system played Gregorian-chants Muzak.

Debbie looked at her Attila-the-Hun wristwatch. Its dagger was after nine, but the long bloody sword pointed only to 27. Three minutes to 9:30, three minutes to Armageddon. Good. Time for one last attempt.

Debbie flashed her sweetest oh-no-lambikins-kissing-me-won't-send-your-soul-to-Hell smile. "Joe, Joe, Joe."

The fog around Joe's head dissipated. He saw Mrs. Devil, looking like Shania Twain on her best hair day, and dressed in Saran Wrap, too.

Wow! Joe wanted to stare, but generations of breeding for Lutheran modesty made him look away. His gaze darted down to the checkout counter. He took a step back in horror and dropped his purple lollipop. His loaf of Roman Meal bread was gone. His selection of pig balls no longer matched, and, and, he saw before him, just waiting to be purchased, a case of George's Mushrooms. He shuddered.

Shania atomized the lollipop with her heel. "So honey, I see you decided to buy mushrooms after all." She arched her right eyebrow and winked. "Does that mean you want to become my love muffin?"

"No, I love my wife."

"Your wife needn't know." She leaned forward and batted her eyelashes.

Joe blushed. "What would your husband, Mr. Devil say?"

Debbie Devil threw back her head and brayed great cascades of laughter. An Albanian by the magazine rack looked furtively up from *The Gay Entomologist*.

"Dave Devil, that wimp, he's nothing, a loser," said Debbie. "Did you know he wanted to run a soft-ice-cream shop?"

Joe nodded.

"Did you also know that he wanted to open it in Gary, Indiana?"

Joe made a face.

Debbie laughed again. "Even a golf-ball retriever like you knows the value of location. Dave never did have much business sense."

Joe shrugged. "I'm sure he meant well."

"Meant well!" Debbie picked up an Andalusian pig ball and hurled it at a debutante in Aisle 8A. "When he married me, that handsome young angel promised me the cosmos. I could have married an up-and-coming archangel, but no, I married a schmoe who wanted to sell soft-ice cream in Gary, Indiana. Blessed impractical! There was no Gary, Indiana back then. There wasn't even a universe."

"Must have been a bit of a disappointment," said Joe.

Debbie Devil wiped away a small tear and sniffled. "The Heavenly Host laughed at us for that. Wouldn't let us play their little angel games."

Joe detected the melting of his heart. Sure, she was the Supreme Fiend, but darn it she had a beguiling soft side, too.

Debbie Devil continued, "Then God held the first-ever job fair. I made my no-account husband go. God offered Dave the position of Fourth Archangel. Dave wanted to take it. Can you believe it? Fourth Archangel, with its ramen noodles and punching of time clocks.

"What an insult. Any husband of mine deserves to be First Archangel with its comfy chair, shrimp cocktails, and turbo-charged angel wings."

The P.A. system played Lithuanian railroading songs. Joe didn't think Rancho Santa Fe supermarkets had any Lithuanian railroaders. Not many supermarkets did.

"So I made Dave go back to God and demand a better job. Differences of opinions arose. Harsh words were said. God and Dave put up their dukes, then, then, . . ." Debbie's upper lip quivered and her horns glowed. ". . . God's three buddies, those blessed, NEW Archangels: Michael, Gabriel, and Rafael came charging in and started waling on my husband.

"Before we knew it, God had cast us down to Hell."

Joe felt his eyes mist. "Gee, that's bad."

Debbie sighed. "It gets worse. The sulfurous fumes down there made my guy impotent. I stood it for a few thousand years, but geez, a gal gets kinda horny after awhile.

"So I packed my bags and headed up to Earth to get me some action. That why I work here at Hungry Hank's, to get me some of those Rancho Santa Fe hunks, like you."

She leaned forward, stroked Joe's wrist and cooed, "But you'd be the best. Say, what do you say we go out for a cup of coffee. An orange-vanilla blend. Just the two of us."

Joe stammered, "Gee, I don't think so."

Debbie beamed. Her fiery red hair splashed atop her beckoning shoulders. "C'mon, it would be great. I get off work in . . ." She looked at her watch. Attila's long blade was on 6. "Oops, sorry. I have an appointment with Armageddon."

She snapped her fingers and dozens of the telemarketers Joe had seen in Hell poured through the door bearing cases of George's Mushrooms. A fashion model gasped. The telemarketers sported white shoes, in March.

Bringing up the rear, cracking his whip, stood the Sorta-Great Evil One himself, Mr. Silas B. George, of George's Mushrooms. And the man looked like a redheaded Captain Kangaroo!

Joe gasped. "What the heck? Captain Kangaroo, no." Joe ran to the man and grabbed his collar. "No, Captain, no. Don't deliver these mushrooms. They're the Devil's tools."

Mr. George sneered. "I'm not Captain Kangaroo. But I did murder him some years ago."

"But why? He was a good man."

"That's why," said Mr. George. "He was too darn active in the Anti-Mushroom League. And he was so close to allying his organizations with all the major churches in America." He shook his head. "Before, you'd get the occasional anti-mushroom sermon in the hills of Arkansas, but with Captain Kangaroo leading the charge. . ." George threw up his hands. "Powerful ministers rousing anti-fungal wrath. Every Sunday. Everywhere." The mushroom magnate ground an Argentine ant beneath his right heel. "Couldn't let that happen."

Joe strode over and jabbed his finger into George's chest. "Well, I'm a Lutheran American and I watched Mister Rogers all the time when I was little, and you're not getting away with murder and you're certainly not going to mushroomize America."

George laughed. "A puny human is not going to stop me. And unlike that wimpy Dave Devil, this demon has balls." George gestured to his crotch.

Debbie Devil finished ringing up a Rancho Santa Fe Young Republican's Twizzlers and George's Mushrooms to yell, "You'd better listen to my brother, Thorvald. It's he and I who really run the Lost Souls concern in Hell."

"Oh, bite me," said Joe.

Debbie bared her Versace fangs. "Oh crudness," thought Joe, "mother always said cussing would come back to haunt me. Mom, couldn't you have been right on something else?"

Debbie advanced toward Joe, intent on sucking the life juice out of the good Lutheran, but George waved her off with his left hand and pointed the ring finger of his right hand. On that finger sat the largest mushroom ring that Joe had ever seen, and he had been to Catalina and Duluth.

The screams of millions of lost souls issued from the mushroom ring. Joe thought this development ominous. He tried to run, couldn't. A white vapor wafted from the ring toward Joe.

"Your stomach is mine," said George. "Your soul, your stomach, and your body is mine," said Debbie Devil. Her leer and everything she had said and done to him confirmed to Joe she was up to no good.

Joe tried to stamp his foot in protest. He couldn't! He said, "I'll still beat you."

George raised his right eyebrow. "How?"

Joe got down on his knees, lifted his eyes to Heaven, and prayed.

Debbie grabbed George's arm. "Where the Heaven is Bertie? It's only Armageddon!"

George shrugged. "Don't know. He said he'd be here."

Joe prayed hard.

"Yes, my Joe," boomed The Voice through the ceiling, "what do . . ."

An overhead speaker interrupted God and the theme song from *The Sound of Music* to blast, "Clean up on aisle seven. Clean up on aisle seven."

God huffed. "As I was saying, 'What do you want?'"

"Dear Lord, do you see what is happening to me?"

"Yes, my Joe, I see . . ."

"CLEAN UP ON AISLE SEVEN. CLEAN UP ON AISLE SEVEN."

"Oh geez," said God. A lighting bolt darted toward aisle seven. Its spill vanished, its floor sported a new layer of shiny, clear wax. "Must I do everything Myself?"

Joe whispered, "Lord, if I may . . ."

"Excuse me, Joe, I do see everything you do."

Joe's face beamed with joy. "Dear Lord, we kind of got a little Armageddon going down here. Could you send the archangels down to help me?"

The Voice in the ceiling coughed. "Well no, Joe. You see, they're on vacation."

George and Debbie howled with laughter and clutched their sides.

"Oh gee, God, I didn't think you would abandon me."

"Did I say that?" boomed God, "I'm sending down four special souls. Favorites of mine. I'm deputizing them and giving them special powers."

Four golden clouds formed in the organic dairy section. From out of them stepped D'Artagnan, Mister Rogers, Richard Nixon, and nothing. D'Artagnan's flintlock pistol put a silver bullet through George's mushroom ring. The evil white vapor from the ring vanished into medium thick air.

Joe lifted his hands to Heaven. "Wow! My heroes." He looked to the worthies. "Do you know why you are here?"

The French musketeer said, "I, D'Artagnan, am the captain of this worthy band. We are here to rid your country once and for all of those evil mushrooms and to pluck a feather from the caps of *Madame* Devil and *Monsieur* George."

Joe raised an eyebrow. "Aren't mushrooms a French specialty? Aren't French chefs responsible for mushrooms being on the menu of every American restaurant?"

D'Artagnan blanched. "*Oui, Monsieur* Thorvald, it pains me deeply to admit that. But you must believe that every Musketeer, every true 16th-century French nobleman never let a single mushroom pass his lips. *Sacré bleu!* Besides, we Frenchmen in Heaven had hoped our vigorous assistance in your war of independence might compensate for our mushroom indiscretion, no?"

"A thousand times over, my French friend," said Joe.

D'Artagnan unsheathed his rapier and performed a low bow.

Mister Rogers stepped forward. "I hear it's not such a beautiful day in your neighborhood."

"No," said Joe, "it isn't."

"Well," said Mister Rogers, "I'm here to teach these two some manners." He pointed to George and Debbie. "Oops, sorry you two. Didn't mean to point." The evil pair laughed. Mister Rogers gritted his teeth. "Let that be a lesson to me, evil manners can be contagious."

Richard Nixon raised his arms and said, "My fellow demon fighters, let me make one thing perfectly clear; if we have the will to fight on, we will defeat our enemies."

Debbie stopped laughing and scowled. "Hey Dick, I thought you were on our side, what with Watergate and all your dirty tricks."

"Those sins don't matter," said Nixon. "I asked Christ for forgiveness just before I died and just like that he accepted me into Heaven."

"Really!" Debbie stomped her foot. "Well, bless it all." Another stomp. "This is what comes of being careless."

D'Artagnan whispered to Joe, "Stuffy should have been in the fourth cloud. He was supposed to be our leader, but he got run over by a Ford Expedition while chasing *Monsieur* Blackhand." The musketeer added bravado to his voice. "But I shall lead in his place."

"Big deal," said Debbie, "George, form your troops."

George snapped his fingers. His troops formed into four battalions. He snapped his fingers again. His telemarketers opened their cases and grabbed cans of mushrooms and held them at port arms.

D'Artagnan told Joe to take a position in reserve and watch George and Debbie. The gallant Frenchman lifted his hat and yelled, "Soldiers of our Blessed Lord, we must attack now." He lowered his sword. "For Captain Kangaroo!"

D'Artagnan plunged into a mass of telemarketers. His rapier darted this way and that, and every time he drew back his blade blood ran down its length. He laughed. "I say, *Monsieur* Thorvald, these soldiers of the Devil are mere popinjays."

"No one ever sees Armageddon coming," boomed the overhead speaker. "And when it does, there's no time to bake that end-of-the-world dessert.

"Thank goodness for Hungry Hank's award-winning bakery. With Armageddon on its way like an unwanted relative, who cares about calories and cavities? So, come on over and have yourself one of our mouth-watering Swedish funnel cakes. Just $4.98 while supplies and the world last."

The funnel-cake-hating Nixon strode, beady eyes ablaze, into his opposing battalion and deleted eighteen-and-a-half inches from the legs and arms of the nearest telemarketers. Nixon puffed out his cheeks and raised his two hands in a double v-for-victory salute. "Minions of Hell, you can't kick Dick Nixon around anymore."

Mister Rogers greeted his group of telemarketers with hearty cheer and pamphlets on courtesy and manners. When the foes bent their heads down to read the tracts, he dispatched them with the Vulcan death grip.

"You can learn a lot in Heaven," said Mister Rogers. "I meet the most interesting beings there."

Joe started toward D'Artagnan to join battle with George and Debbie when hundreds of even more poorly color-coordinated telemarketers poured in through the far entrance carrying cases labeled "WMD, Weapons of Mushroom Destruction."

"*Mon Dieu*," said D'Artagnan, "we have been fighting a diversion. *Regardez.*" He pointed his rapier to the new force. You see how they are unpacking baskets of George's Mushrooms. *Sacré bleu*, I can fight mushrooms when they are in cans, but this is biological warfare."

Joe saw the telemarketers standing at attention, waiting for the order to hurl their evil fungi. Joe also heard the rasping breaths of his friends.

"D'Artagnan," said Joe, "surely we cannot get to those men"--he pointed to the far door--"before being hit with a barrage of deadly mushrooms. Even if we reach their line, George and Debbie will do us in with some evil trick while our backs are turned."

D'Artagnan permitted himself a small smile. "*Monsieur* Thorvald, I see you have a talent for soldiering." He bowed. "*Mon* compliments." He straightened. His smile faded. "*Monsieur*, we can but sell our souls as dearly as possible, no?"

Joe nodded.

"Telemarketers," said Debbie Devil's voice over the intercom, "grab your mushrooms." They did so.

D'Artagnan pointed his rapier to the far force. "Captain Kangaroo!" The heroic three and Joe charged panting to destiny. Joe hoped for a miracle, prayed for one.

"Price check at counter four," said Debbie Devil. No one responded. The first wave of telemarketers lay quiet on the floor. The second wave awaited orders. They were happy to wait. "No one told us we were going up against D'Artagnan AND Nixon," said one of them.

George stood on a ladder taping the last corner of a sign to the store's big window. The sign read, "Hungry Hank's Closed for Armageddon. Please pardon our gore."

Joe and his comrades tore into the second-wave of marketers. Their brilliant combined-arms strategy of cold steel, good manners, dirty tricks, and good ol' Lutheran fists tore great holes in the telemarketers' ranks.

"I said, price check on counter four," screeched Debbie's voice through the store. "I have a customer who's been waiting a long time for a price check on Golden Harvest Organic Milk."

George ran puffing toward Debbie Devil. "Sorry, Debbie, I didn't want more customers coming in, getting in our way."

Debbie's nostrils flared, her cheeks burned red. "Customers getting in the way?! If there's anything I picked up at Hungry Hank's it's that we all come running whenever there's a price check."

George clenched his fists. "Bless it, this fight's for Evil everywhere, for broken homes, for pestilence, for the right to root for the Dodgers. We attack the good ones, now!"

"Hello! Not when I have a customer waiting for a price check."

George shrugged. He conjured a giant mushroom and shoved it into the patient customer's mouth. The customer turned purple and collapsed dead to the floor.

"Oh great," said Debbie, "we'll never get any repeat business from him. Probably going to lose my job, too. Now how am I going to fill my hours between performing deeds of evil?"

Cold steel touched George's neck. "*Monsieur*, you are my prisoner. In the name of the Almighty Lord of Heaven, I banish you, your telemarketers, and your mushrooms to Hell."

D'Artagnan's rapier traced the sign of the cross on George and the evil mushroom man vanished along with the remaining telemarketers. The musketeer waved his plumed hat at Debbie and bowed. "*Madame*, you are beaten. *Monsieur* George is no more. His mushrooms are gone. May I suggest you surrender to *Monsieur* Thorvald gracefully?"

Steam billowed from Debbie's ears, nose, and mouth. "I'll see you in Heaven first."

D'Artagnan shrugged. "Not likely, *chère Madame*." The gallant Frenchman turned to Joe. "Well, *mon ami*, I am most honored to have made your acquaintance, but it is time for us to return to Heaven. *Adieu*."

Nixon said, "Take care. Let me know if that darned liberal media mentions what I did here."

Joe nodded.

Mister Rogers said it was a wonderful day in Rancho Santa Fe after all.

Joe shook hands with all the heroes and said, "I shall never forget you. You shall be in my thoughts always."

D'Artagnan laughed. "Though, I hope not for the next few hours. Your wife and son might claim your attention, no?"

With that, the divine trio headed to the bakery to pick up some Swedish funnel cakes before returning back to Heaven. "Get an extra one for God," said Nixon, "the Big Guy really likes them."

Joe waved goodbye as they stepped into three waiting clouds.

Suddenly, the door to Hungry Hank's east entrance swept open. In strode a scowling Bertram Blackhand toting an Oleg Cassini satchel. "M'lady, I am here."

Debbie yelled at the evil chef. "Big deal! So were D'Artagnan, Mr. Rogers, and Nixon. They eliminated Mr. George and all his mushrooms. You might have turned the battle in our favor if you had been here, but obviously you have no consideration for an evil lady."

Bertie's hat stiffened. "M'lady, I was on my way here when a traffic cop pulled me over for doing a rolling stop at a stop sign."

"Why the Heaven didn't you just shove a mushroom down the cop's throat and zip down here?"

"M'lady, I am not a scofflaw."

Debbie sighed.

Bertie's glance darted around the store. "So, D'Artagnan, Mr. Rogers, and Nixon are really gone?"

"Yes."

"Then there's no one to stop me." Bertie reached into his satchel and produced an enormous mushroom. The size of that evil object froze Joe; his mouth agape.

Debbie's really evil right eye grew big. "Wow. How? D'Artagnan destroyed all of Mr. George's mushrooms."

"M'lady, an evil English chef always has a supply of mushrooms stashed away for emergencies."

"Wonderful, but how will you get that mushroom down Joe's throat? That mushroom's huge."

"With this." Bertie slapped a cherrywood slingshot. "Whittled it myself from a thousand-year-old table."

Suddenly, the door from Hungry Hank's west entrance opened. In hobbled The Scourge Of All Evil, a foot-tall brown stuffed bear dressed in a sheriff's outfit. His flattened right foot dragged behind him.

"Not so fast, Bertie," said the bear.

Bertie's upper lip curled. "Stuffy the Scourge, we meet at last."

"Yep."

Joe unfroze enough to face the bear. "Stuffy, you came to life to save me."

Tears formed below Stuffy's eyes as kept his gaze on Bertie. "Of course I did. You saved me from the trash can every time Frisky sharpened her claws on me." Stuffy pointed to numerous cloth patches up and down his body.

"Fascinating," said Bertie to Stuffy. "Now, I'm going to kill you." His right hand dropped to the slingshot on his belt.

Stuffy's left hand dropped to his holstered dart gun. The P.A. system played the theme from *The Good, the Bad, and the Ugly.*

Bertie glared at Stuffy. Stuffy's oh-so-brown glass eyes glared back. Bertie snarled. Stuffy snarled. Bertie loaded his slingshot with the enormous mushroom. Stuffy grabbed a Swedish meatball and rammed it onto the dart of his gun.

Bertie jerked his slingshot up and let go. But Stuffy drew simulated leather and fired first. His meatball dart exploded up Bertie's nose.

Just as when an anti-matter comet hit matter in Siberia in 1908 producing an explosion annihilating hundreds of square miles of forest, so did the Swedish meatball annihilate Bertie and two neighboring racks of *Penny Savers.* Just two racks. Well, meatballs ARE smaller than meteors.

Bertie's speeding mushroom ripped Stuffy's head clean off, flinging it to Debbie's checkout stand. Horse-hair eyelashes closed over the little brown glass eyes.

Joe ran over to the head and picked it up with his right hand. "Oh Stuffy, oh Stuffy," he cried over and over.

"Good," said Debbie. "I'm glad at least something bad happened to you."

"You went too far with Stuffy," said Joe. He took off the small wooden cross hanging around his neck and thrust it in Debbie's face. Little Debbie began to shrink.

"Tidy Heaven, don't do this to me," said Debbie, "I could not bear an eternity down there with my miserable, weak husband. And Joe, dear Joe, did you know, there are no Twizzlers in Hell?"

"Another reason to follow the Ten Commandments," said Joe. He touched Debbie's forehead with the cross and whispered a quick prayer. Little Debbie melted into nothingness.

"Joe, Joe," squeaked the little bear head.

Joe took the head and pressed it to his cheek. "Stuffy, you're alive! Alive!"

The eyes on the stuffed head opened. "Of course I'm alive. You can't kill a stuffed bear by ripping it apart."

God was good. "I'm taking you home," said Joe. "My wife will sew you back together, good as new."

"Great," said Stuffy.

"And you'll have a new home with my son, Junior. He's five, a good kid, you'll love him.

"Great," said Stuffy as he shut his eyes, "but I need to sleep. I've been through a lot. Don't forget my body by the door."

Joe picked up the bear's body, exited Hungry Hank's and drove home. The lights were out at his house. He opened the door, walked with whispering feet to his sleeping family and kissed each of them on their soft cheeks.

Trumpet fanfare and the theme song from *The Patty Duke Show* blasting from the night sky, told all those who paid attention to such things that Heaven was about to whoop it up for joy. Especially for that genial party animal, the future Saint Captain Kangaroo.

CHAPTER 28B-BAD GUY

"Woo hoo, I'm single." Dave Devil repeatedly pumped his fist in the air. His Hellhound 303 BLT speakers blared "Sympathy for the Devil."

"Woo hoo. Hell's going to rock tonight." Dave looked at himself in the mirror. Just how long had he been sporting that shit-eating grin? Since Joe Thorvald had melted Debbie. Blessed fine folks, those Norwegian-Americans.

Dave checked the mirror again. Bless it, he looked good in his Brooks Brothers tux. Maybe with his bitter half gone he could run for President. Who knew more than he about dirty tricks? He'd win for sure. Think of all the mischief he could do once elected. Why, he could start a nuclear war or two.

Aching down below interrupted his thoughts. His balls ached! His balls ached! He wanted sex again. Woo hoo! Oh sure, Debbie had been hot before they got hitched. Then she let herself go, growing two ugly little horns atop her head, that long bony nose, and that arrow-tipped tail. Yuck!

Dave pawed his pecker. Nothing. No matter, the come-to-Hell-as-you-are Devil would just score himself some Viagra up on Earth.

Earth! He could go to Earth, now that Debbie wasn't chaining him to his dead-end job. "Work hard, you bum. We need to maintain our place in Hell," she'd always said.

Well, the ball and chain was gone. He was once again the Supreme Evil, just like in his bachelor days. Dave looked at the map of the world in his office. Blue lights flashed all over the world. Blue lights--cold spots where peace and decency were breaking out.

Well, those cold spots would have to wait. Dave riffled through the Yellow Pages for San Diego County, then picked up his lime-green phone. "Is this the pharmacy? I'd like to place a rather large order for Viagra."

He flipped the switch. The blue lights went out. He adjusted his bow tie. Dave Devil was stepping out.

CHAPTER 28G-GOOD GUYS

"Now, Raphael," shouted Pedro Erickson as he pulled down his blindfold, "it's my turn to pin the tail on the donkey."

The eternal archangel nodded. The good chef didn't like to yell, but he had to be heard over the sounds of Gabriel and the Heavenly Host. Raphael smiled. He looked at the dancers and smiled. He loved to see young folks having fun. The God-fearing young punkers slam dancing to "When the Saints" gladdened his heart the most. And those moves from Captain Kangaroo!

"Ow!"

Erickson lifted his blindfold. His face reddened instantly. "Oh sorry, Saint Thérèse, sorry. Not a donkey's ass at all." He removed the tail with its thumb tack from the young beauty's butt. He giggled nervously and apologized more.

"*De rien, Monsieur,*" said Thérèse of Lisieux. "My apologies for not getting out of your way."

"Gosh," said the good Swedish-Mexican, "you're awfully kind, and so beautiful too."

Thérèse flashed a small saintly-plus smile and curtsied. "*Merci, monsieur.* But you are very sweet. And congratulations on your glorious victory over *Madame* Devil."

Erickson blushed as red as a ripe Albanian tomato. "Oh gosh, that was nothing. Say, would you like to dance?"

"*Mais oui,* but if you would not mind, could we perhaps wait for a slower song?"

"Oh sure, sure." Erickson tapped and tapped his foot until the song and the slam dancing stopped. He smiled at Thérèse. She smiled back. He took her hand. She didn't withdraw it.

Wow! He was in Heaven. Okay, he REALLY was in Heaven. He took one step forward.

The lights by the row of seats dimmed. "Ladies and Gentlemen," said General Lee, "my gracious wife, Mary, and I will be starting *The Patty Duke Show* marathon in one minute."

"Appomattox to you, Lee," muttered Erickson as he took his hand away. "Gee, ma'amzelle, I wanted to dance with you."

Thérèse put her hand in his. "*Monsieur*, I believe my hand is still yours. Will you please lead us to our seats? I have come to like *The Patty Duke Show* very much in the last few years and with you I shall be seeing it in the company of a handsome gentleman."

The happy couple sat down, her hand still in his. He smiled and smiled. What a beauty. Nice girl, too. No worries about her character. He relaxed as much as his racing heart would let him. Debbie Devil and her mushrooms were gone. Dave Devil would be too busy chasing beautiful women to cause any evil.

Sure, eventually his true nature would reassert himself. Dave would up and marry a bad type, lose arguments, get riled, start a few world wars, and go trawling for souls. Then General Lee and he would go back to work for the Lord.

But that wouldn't happen for a while. Meanwhile, a real angel held his hand. *Ja caramba*, afterlife didn't get any better than this.

About the Author:

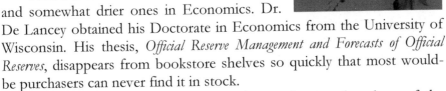

Paul De Lancey writes in multiple genres: adventure, westerns, morality, time travel, thriller, and culinary, all spiced with zaniness. His cookbook, *Eat Me, 169 Fun Recipes From All Over the World* and his novels *Beneficial Murders*, *We're French and You're Not* and *The Fur West* have won acclaim from award-winning novelists.

Paul is also the writer of hilarious articles and somewhat drier ones in Economics. Dr. De Lancey obtained his Doctorate in Economics from the University of Wisconsin. His thesis, *Official Reserve Management and Forecasts of Official Reserves*, disappears from bookstore shelves so quickly that most would-be purchasers can never find it in stock.

Paul, known to his friends as Paul, was the proud co-host of the online literary events *Bump Off Your Enemies*, *The Darwin Murders*, and *Tasteful Murders*. He also co-collected, co-edited, and co-published the e-book anthologies resulting from these events. Perhaps Mr. De Lancey will someday become a literary giant without having to die for the title.

The humorist is a direct descendant of the great French Emperor Napoleon. Actually, that explains a lot of things. Paul ran for President of the United States in 2012! Woo hoo! On the Bacon & Chocolate ticket. Estimates of Bacon & Chocolate's share of the votes range from 3 to 1.5% of the total. *El Candidato* also lost a contentious campaign to be *El Presidente* of Venezuela. In late 2013, Chef Paul participated in the International Bento Competition.

Mr. De Lancey makes his home, with his wonderful family, in Poway, California. He divides his time between being awake and asleep.

His books are available at: www.lordsoffun.com and amazon.com.

Made in the USA
Middletown, DE
18 November 2015